THE DOGWOOD PLANTATION

PART ONE: FEAR

By Clare Dundas

Cover Design by Denise Baker

Copyright © 2019
By Clare Dundas

All Rights Reserved

ISBN 9781099742064

.

For my husband and three children, who have supported me, encouraged, and urged me on throughout this ten-year project.

"I will not detain you long for I stand here a slave—a slave at least in the eyes of the Constitution. It is a slave by the laws of the South who now addresses you. My back is scarred by the lash—that I could show you—I would I could make visible the wounds of this system upon my soul."

Frederick Douglass, *Speech* at Faneuil Hall, Boston, Feb 4, 1842

<u>Main Characters in Part One</u>

Soola
Slave woman, leader of the slaves, in charge of turpentine trees

Archie McLachlan
Owner of the Inveraray/Dogwood Plantation

Judith
Slave woman, cook for the farm

Tabitha
Slave woman, cares for children on the farm

Adam
Slave man, Soola's boyfriend

Jake
Slave man, Tabitha's boyfriend

Mittie
Slave man, Judith's boyfriend who disappears

Gertrude Munro
Archie's wife

Bruce Munro
Gertrude's brother

Paddy and Mary Ann
Soola's daughters

John
Son of Soola and Adam

Robert
Son of Gertrude and Archie

Bejida
Plantation medicine woman, born in Africa

Pete
New antagonistic slave boy

Sally
New slave girl, arrives with her baby Joanie

Tim Blakesley
Local slave trader

Alfonso
Young slave boy from the islands

George
Slave boy, takes care of animals on the farm

1783

Chapter 1

    The wind blew high along the Carolina coast in November of 1783, as if to celebrate the good news that had recently arrived in the city of Wilmington. The British and American diplomats had signed the peace treaty in Paris ending the long and bitter Revolutionary War. A few days after that arrival, a Charleston packet approached along the coast from the south, scudding fast over the whitecaps, so fast that sailors were rushing up the two masts to furl in the sails. The vessel was drawing near the beaches of Bald Head Island and soon rounded the headlands into the Cape Fear River. It was a stirring sight; some fishermen on the beach waved and hollered at the throng of finely dressed travelers gathered on the starboard bow. Freedom was in the air, on the land, and on that pretty schooner. The great word *Liberty*, a word that would found a nation, was bandied about, in poetry, in song, and in political discourse.

    But then, on the port side of this vessel, sprawled on a pile of junk—old cordage too worn for safe use and other rubbish chucked onto the pile by the sailors—lay a group of African people, their wrists and ankles chained and locked. They had been hauled up from the hold below in preparation for landing at Wilmington and were wriggling around striving to find positions that would grant them comfort. These people were poorly dressed, the women and children in flimsy rags, the men in torn trousers and threadbare shirts. None of the clothing protected them against the chill wind coming off the sea, nor shielded the boney protuberances visible through the worn patches in their garments. Some of the men, more numerous than the women, muttered and laughed with each other. Most were young.

    Rising from among the few women and children, whose arms were free of chains, one woman, black as ebony, stood up tall, stretched, yawned, and looked around with curiosity at their surroundings. She seemed near six feet tall, well made and strong, despite her emaciated condition. Her wide mouth and dark eyes could not conceal a sense of absurdity, mixed with outrage, at their predicament. Thoughts rushed through her mind. How can those fancy folks over there look perfect and happy, how can they not show pity for our plight, what is wrong with them? She wondered what they would say and do if their roles were reversed.

On a box nearby, sat a man in a broad brimmed hat smoking a pipe, chewing on a thick chunk of bread, all the while holding ready a vicious whip with a long and snake-like tail. The slaves on the pile stared longingly at that piece of bread as it entered his mouth. This man with the whip called out, "Hey, you there, sit down, I told you not to stand, not to kneel, in fact to shut up and keep still." He stood up and approached the woman.

Another woman pulled on her friend's ragged skirt, "Please sit down, Kanky, we'll all suffer if you don't." The tall one sat. She knew what would happen if she remained standing, didn't care about herself but did care for Missy and Fred, the baby and the boy. She looked through the ship's railing at the banks of the river, the broad marshes and inlets running among islands and sandbars, and then again at the white people clustered on the other side of the boat. She had never, before being tied up on this boat, seen the ocean, nor the wide-open spaces of salt marsh, nor had she ever seen this many seagulls or heard their screeching as they circled the ship. She thought about the forest plantation in South Carolina where she had spent every moment of her life until last week. Here the world seemed to open up and show her the whole sky unhindered by the giant pine trees of the forest. Eventually, several miles upriver, as the channel narrowed and the ship, propelled by rowers now, approached the town of Wilmington, she caught whiffs of the rich odor of harbor and marsh—dank vegetation, shells of sea creatures, dead fish, tar and timber, all mixed together. If only she could jump off the boat with the passengers, free as the birds, but here were the chains and locks and the cruelty of the white trader beside them. This tall, stunning woman, looking at the other travelers, realized what a joyful thing life might be, while the lives of Africans were enclosed in a prison located in a special corner of hell. The walls of this prison were made up of stern pale faces and whips that kept the slaves like her inside.

She wondered why she had not completely understood this before, during her first twenty-one years of life on the turpentine plantation, through the good and bad times, then the journey here. It seemed she had not then truly seen the life of white people, in fact had seen few of them, well Massa Jimmie, yes, but he was usually her friend. Oh, and yes, there had been that Red Devil, Mr. Anders, but he had been an aberration of the human race. And there, cruelties from him to herself had been the result of her big mouth, which she had difficulty controlling. But on this journey, cruelties had popped up all around when no one was misbehaving—the chains, neck collars, locks, whips, pens were a matter of course, used, she supposed, to prevent rebellion and escape. The other fearful sorrows during recent years at Pine Forest—the pain of the punishment shed, the long hours of working up and down the trees, the lack of adequate food and clothing, and the worst, the sale of their children—all this had stemmed solely from that Red Devil and his outsized helpers, so she thought. Thus, in the days since their departure from Pine Forest, her thinking had broadened out to match a new vision of a world in which the people chosen to suffer would be the slaves from Africa, her mother's birthplace, and their children forever, yes, and to suffer without having done wrong.

She saw an elegant lady dressed in silk and lace holding tight to the left arm of a gentleman clad in silvery gray, from three-cornered hat down to elegant buckled shoes. The lady held a fan in her left hand, waving it frantically in front of her face as they stepped over ropes and boxes towards the gangplank. "Oh, Mr. Hill," she clearly heard the woman say, despite the raucous crying of the gulls, "next time we travel north, please let it be by land; to endure the frightful odors of this ship is a torture to my soul."

The tall woman looked at her chained friends with sparks in her black eyes and proclaimed in a loud voice, "Folks, we're just a dark smudge and a bad odor to them eyes and noses," then, turning to the pipe-smoking trader, " so, Mister, when can we get off this ship to relieve the sensibilities of these white folks?"

The man turned to her in a rage, "I said shut your mouth, woman. You wait until we get you inside, you'll regret this rude and foolish behavior." Fred and Missy both whispered at her to hush. They held her down.

For the next few days they would experience a real prison in the form of Wilmington's slave pen and auction block at the bottom of Market Street, but the prison in the woman's imagination, the prison in the corner of hell, would remain with her always as one of the deepest truths of their lives.

The African slaves were the last to descend the gangplank. Since the auction yard and slave pen were only half a block away, the trader was able to move the bedraggled group straight there, forcing them to huddle together and limp along as fast as possible to that destination, encouraging them with quiet, almost whispered, threats, the long tail of the whip wrapped around his hand. The building stood quite innocent in its red brick clothing, posing as a schoolhouse or perhaps a theater. But inside the massive green front door, all pretense vanished. The tall woman watched the men pushed into small cells, three to a cell, surrounding a large room on the ground floor. Then she and the women and children were hurried upstairs to another large room, led by an expressionless, rough servant woman whose face matched the gray of her dress. As they entered, a powerful latrine smell hit their noses. The boy cried out in disgust, but the guard woman made no comment, only told them all to sit on the floor in a row against the back wall. "And sonny boy, sit by your mother and don't you dare to move. And you," pointing at Missy, "keep that baby quiet, put it to the breast, do whatever you have to do." The tall one wanted to say that Missy was not the boy's mother, but neither she nor anyone else uttered a word.

Until the boy said, "But ma'am, I need to pee real bad." He clutched himself between the legs.

"Go over there. You'll see a hole in the floor going into a pipe."

"Oh, so that's the source of the stink," came a voice from the group. The guard woman's face bore the look of thunder as she noticed that the tall dark woman was staring at her without fear. "And you, woman, what is your name?"

"I have a lot of names," came the answer, "and forgot them all. Seems like you white people can't make up your minds who I be."

The guard woman reached over and slapped her across the face. "All right then, we'll call you Soot to match the black of your face and your uppity temper."

"I accept that, until the next person to change it," replied the ever defiant and fearless woman. She held the side of her face in her hand, laughed and looked at Missy who was endeavoring to create a wide space between them. After the woman left and locked the door, Missy turned to her friend and hissed angrily, "You need to stop this silliness about your name. What you should do now, when anyone asks for your name, you should say 'my name is Soola.' It's a little bit like what the woman called you so no one'll notice the difference. It has no insult or meaning inside it; it bears an African lilt, and it's easy to say and remember, so keep it and shut up about it." The newly named Soola nodded silently. She asked her friend what was an African lilt, but Missy couldn't answer that. Few were familiar with the stories, or with words from Africa. Soola's own mother had spoken only a small number of words of any kind, had rarely talked about the land of her birth or the journey across the ocean. Some songs and rhythms were all that remained into the ensuing generations.

The women now looked around to assess the degree of their discomfort. The room was empty of furniture except for a rough round table in the center. One small window high up in the wall allowed a sliver of late-in-the-day sunlight to fall into the room, enabling them to notice through the dim light a few other women and children against the wall in the far corner. Finally, enveloped in darkness, they laid themselves down on the jagged wooden floor, midst the hazard of splinters, slept, and waited for the morrow. They huddled together against the chill. The only sounds were dogs barking on the city streets and small whimpers from the baby who couldn't seem to draw much milk from her mother's breast.

With morning came a surprise. Big pewter platters of beans, pieces of pork, and bread were carried in. As the platters were set down on the round table, great joy erupted in the slave pen, especially among the children. Then the slave trader from the ship wandered in, accompanied by three massive men. They unlocked the chains while the leader spoke to the slaves. "You folks are here to be sold, and the auction will take place at the end of the week. When you go out on the auction block, it will be important that you show your best behavior—both for yourselves and for your future masters. The best masters will be looking for quiet and hardworking servants to help them on their farms."

Soola interrupted him, speaking ever so quiet and polite, "Sir my name is Soola, and here is my friend Missy. She is always quiet, hardworking, and obedient. But I am not like that. I have a big mouth and like to speak out. So, what will become of me?" Her eyes met his as if to penetrate his thoughts.

"You and others like you will be left until the end unsold, finally to be purchased cheap or perhaps even given away at a loss to me, your trader, and your new master will be a poor and ruthless man with a scrappy, poorly kept farm." He shouted these last words close to her nose, trying to scare her, no doubt, but this undaunted person felt no fear. She considered spitting in his vicious face but for Missy's sake decided against such recklessness. She turned away and sat down beside her friend, whose fear was palpable. She put her arm around Missy's shoulders.

The trader continued his instructions: "You will eat as much as possible in the next few days, and the woman will bring in tubs of water and soap so you can clean yourselves up. She'll also bring new clothes so you can look pretty on the block." He gave a great laugh at that word *pretty*, then "Remember it is up to you how well you do here. Bad behavior will result in bad treatment, good behavior will result in rewards." He stomped out with his retinue, slammed and locked the door.

For the next three days the slave women, with some anticipation, awaited the auction. They washed and dressed, primped and laughed, and began speaking to the women and children in the far corner of the room. They discovered that the others had arrived in the last couple of days, from far and near. Most had endured difficult journeys. All hoped for a kind master and mistress to miraculously appear at the auction and save them from their misery. One short, thickset woman named Tabitha assured them all that she would perform any kind of work for a new "Massa" if he only, please, wouldn't beat her.

But it was Tabitha's friend Judith who attracted the immediate attention of all. She was burdened with a large white birthmark all over one side of her face. The children stared at her in fear. When Missy's boy started giggling, she tried to apologize to Judith, who then assured the child that she had a special gift from the gods. They had covered the black skin on half her face with a thin sheet of white and she considered herself lucky to have it. "It keeps unwanted men away from me, they run when they see me." Judith laughed. Soola laughed too, suspecting that such a white covering was beyond the realm of possibility.

When evening came Soola spoke quietly, "Missy, I wonder what happened to Taylor. Taylor of the forked tongue and two faces."

"We'll never know what happened to anyone, Soola." Missy's face grew sad. She stroked her baby's face and held her tight. "Remember the men with red coats who came through? In the end, they were defeated and were kicked out, forced back to their ships, that's all we heard. Except we did hear too, remember, from Mr. Rawlins, that the mistress died down in Charleston, and the son fought with the Red Coats, so he probably got kicked out with them, and who knows, maybe Taylor went too. Wasn't he with the Red Coats, Kanky, I mean Soola?"

"Yes, he was. When they came to Pine Forest, he was with them. He crept up behind me and put his hand over my eyes; I knew it was him because I could feel those long fingers." Soola reached over and touched Missy's arm. "But Missy, thank you for my name. I like it and will keep it; it's a name for this new life, good or bad. I'll do what you say. But you can always call me Kanky, just between you and me."

"No, you will be Soola to me now, and anyway, after the auction, we may be going our separate ways." Soola watched as her friend picked up the hem of her skirt and wiped her eyes. She had known Missy and her sister Prissy as far back as she could remember. In those old days, as she had approached maturity, the sisters had explained to her about being a woman, about the monthly bleeding, about how to avoid violent treatment from men, about not walking out on the forest paths alone with them, about what men always wanted to do to you, but that sometimes you would want to do it too. And on that subject, she remembered Prissy's words: "Well, if you want to do it with one of them men, you'll want to be real careful he's not violent—you gotta stay in control of that love." And Prissy had added, "Kanky, the men will be attracted to your beauty, and to the way your body moves.

They'll be like pigs gathering around their troughs." Prissy had laughed; she had always shown a rougher edge than her sister.

That is, until the terrible day when the Red Devil and his wicked helpers bound up Prissy and all the little girls, chained them in the cart and sent them all down the muddy road along the river to Georgetown with the traders. Prissy was weeping and praying; the hard edge gone, all the people in an uproar, the turpentine business in chaos, a third of the workers hauled away. Those were Missy's girls, and there was Soola's own beloved child, little Kayla, crying and waving for her mama to come too. They didn't take the boys, boys were of no interest to the Britishers downriver, so Prissy's boys stayed with Missy, but the younger one died in the cold that winter. It was on that terrible day when the girls were sold that Soola glared at the sky and declared her secret promise to all the gods on high that she would get even. Every minute of that memory had remained clear and sharp in her mind. From that day til now she hadn't cared much what happened to her.

"Soola," said Missy, "why do you say Taylor had the forked tongue?"

"I heard him one evening, as I was cleaning up in the dining room. He was out on the front porch with Massa Jimmie, and they was talking deep stuff, and Taylor said he thought that freedom might not be best for the slaves right then 'cause they showed neither good sense nor control of themselves, or it was something like that, when all the time he was himself a slave. Then he would come back with all us and pretend to be our friend and looking out for us with Massa Jimmie." Soola smiled as she remembered Taylor and his wily ways. Missy smiled too and said yes, she remembered him being like that.

Soola looked at Missy with affection, "Still, Missy, those were our good times, our happy times, before Massa Jimmie died." She couldn't remember exactly the sequence of events; in her mind it was only the good times and the bad times—before Massa Jimmie's death and after Massa Jimmie's death.

Upstairs in the Wilmington slave pen, on the Friday morning of the auction, the woman guard appeared early, examined the slaves for cleanliness, looked behind their ears, at their feet and hands, sniffed around their bodies too. She took out a damp rag and with a rough gesture wiped their faces, muttering all the while it wasn't possible to detect dirt on these people, no different from trying to keep a dog clean. The woman then threw a woolen shawl around each slave's shoulders, lined them up and escorted them downstairs to the large room, where they were reunited with the menfolk. Fred ran to them and hugged Missy and the baby, then the boy. Soola expected no hug. She and Fred had never been friends, not since they were tree partners at Pine Forest. He and the other men working on their tree had been resentful of her skill in scampering fast up and down the ladders, cutting the V-shapes through the bark, channeling the sap down into the box. But mostly she remembered Fred's anger that she repeatedly sassed the drivers who brought Red Devil over to yell and curse at them, then Fred's mocking laughter when she was hauled off to the punishment shed.

Still, now, her happiness overflowed that Missy had found the gentler side of Fred. Certainly, his ass-kissing ways had eased their pain on the journey. After the wagon had pulled away from the Pine Forest Plantation, Mr. Rawlins had granted Fred's plea to unchain the people. Fred had assured Massa Jimmie's old friend that, because of the years of starvation and cold, his arrival with the slave trader and the wagon was more of a rescue than an imprisonment. Of course, Rawlins was no longer with them on the sea journey and so did not witness the tight confinement, the seasickness, the stink, the torture of the hold on that ship.

"Pay attention, woman," whispered Fred to Soola, whose mind was brought back to their present surroundings. They were being herded and hurried into a holding area between the slave pen building and the auction block. This area was tacked onto the northern wall of the brick building, the other three walls being made of chain metal fencing twenty feet high. Thus, when Soola and her friends walked out into it and the door clanged shut behind them, she sensed they were transformed into animals in a cage. Even quiet Missy whispered that this was ugly treatment. Soola said she knew that was right, they were like caged monkeys. "Y'all hush," said Fred, holding tight to the boy's hand. Soola looked through the fencing at the auction block. A block of wood about twelve feet across sat on a larger block, both of which appeared to be scrubbed clean. In front of that, a crowd of men and a few women were gathered; behind them, along the street were parked many carts with horses shaking their heads and stamping against the flies. Pooping too, making a big mess, thought Soola. The men were moving around, checking each other's slips of paper, scratching their heads. Oh my, anyone of those could be our new master. Growing anxious as she watched clouds creeping across the sky and shadows of clouds on the ground. She turned to Missy, "Looks like rain coming, damn, we'll get a soaking and our shawls will be a mess." Fred told them again to hush, and that anyway the shawls would be taken back when they got in the new Massa's wagon. A fella back in the building had warned the men that any garment or object handed to them for the auction would only be on loan, or that the new masters would be charged with the price of clothing.

"Do you think these fiends would give away twelve shawls?" said Fred. "Bad enough they had to give us clothes …hey, but maybe they'll charge for them too."

Soola watched carefully what was going on near the auction block. She saw their trader with the same big hat and pipe, talking to a rough, powerful man who soon turned out to be the auctioneer. The trader had a piece of paper. He pointed to something written on it, while speaking to the auctioneer and tapping on the paper emphatically, apparently berating the man, who eventually nodded and lifted his megaphone. The auctioneer's face, ugly, large and fleshy, gave Soola a bad feeling. What sort of man would take on this line of work—an ugly man like the Red Devil no doubt, ugly in face, deeds, and soul. On the other hand, she reflected, their trader possessed a thin, handsome appearance, and yet he was mean as them little yellow wasps that look so pretty but then shock you with their sting. So, in her mind, she called him Yellow Wasp.

"Hay, Kanky, I mean Soola, wake up from that daydream, where is your mind?" said Fred.

"My mind is in my imagination, which is as wide as the sky and blessed with more stars than you will ever see," replied Soola, ever quick, ever quarrelsome.

At that moment came a loud voice from the auction yard. The auctioneer was calling through his megaphone, "We want the family of Fred, Missy, their boy and their baby. Get out here onto the block and let us take a look at you. Fred, get your family here fast. We gotta get this show going." All the slaves froze. They looked at each other. Then there arrived in the cage their trader, the one who had delivered them here and who was now shouting at Soola's friends to get the hell out there and stand on the block. He grabbed Missy's arm, dragged her off. She clutched at the baby and turned to Soola, who darted forward to kiss her good-bye, but the trader put his hand on her chest, and pushed her hard, hard enough to send her flying. Fred rushed to follow Missy pulling the boy. When Soola scrambled to her feet, her friends were lined up on top of the auction blocks like a lineup of cattle for sale at a fair. As a child on the Pine Forest Plantation, she had seen a picture of such a fair in a book at Selma's house.

The auction of Missy and her family began immediately. For Soola, watching in loss and grief, the horror was not so much the fear of falling into the grasp of a malicious master; rather, it was witnessing for the first time the humiliation in the details of the sale. Some of the men stepped forward onto the lower block, squeezed the muscles on Fred's arms and legs, made him bend over and jump back up, then poked Missy's breasts amid some jokes and laughter. Missy tried to slap a man's hand away, but the auctioneer called out for her to stand still. She saw one prospective buyer take a small stick from his pocket, poke it into Fred's mouth and pry open his teeth. The man shouted, loud enough for Soola to hear, "This one's lost a couple of back teeth." Missy and Fred stood there with heads hanging down until the auctioneer spat out for them to lift up their heads. The boy kept looking up anxiously at these two people he loved and admired, and the baby in Missy's arms. The baby they had named Welcome, began crying lustily. Soola clutched and shook the chain link fence until it rattled, her body taut against the links, her face distorted with worry. With a smile, Missy handed little Welcome to the boy, who knew how to entertain her.

Finally, the bidding started with the auctioneer crying out that on order of their original owner, this family would be sold together. "The young man is worth £75, the woman £50, and we'll hear offers starting at £130 for the package. In the prime of life, this young couple and their two children, four servants for the price of two, you won't find a better bargain anywhere in the Carolinas."

Suddenly from the crowd a thin piping voice arose, "I'll give you £90 for the man and woman; I don't want the children." A small wiry man stepped forward. Soola watched in terror, praying the auctioneer would stick to his assurance that the family would stay together. She stared at this odd-looking bidder; thin mouse-colored hairs flew out from his head in the breeze like strands of corn silk, and his meager body was attempting to swagger like a big man. She suspected his eyes were blue but couldn't determine much about his face from that distance. But she could see that his rumpled clothes must have been stitched for a larger man.

The auctioneer replied to this potential buyer, "No sir, the seller will not split the family, next bidder please. Soola's body relaxed against the fence. Thank you, Mr. Rawlins, she sighed. The bidding went on, each bidder creeping higher, while men stepped forward again to open the shirts of these two, feel their flesh, check out the shapeliness of the woman and the condition of her torso. Multiple scars would indicate a troublemaker. The auctioneer called out through the megaphone, "No scars, no scars on these, they're a good bargain." After a quarter of an hour, a man and woman stepped forward, and the man called out loud and clear that he would pay £135 for the whole family. The auctioneer slammed his hammer down and cried sold. Missy and Fred with the children were led to a wagon on the street, while the man stepped over to the accounting table. Soola desperately pushed her arm through the chain links, waving at her friend. "Fare thee well, Missy, fare thee well," she cried out as loud as she could. Missy turned quickly and waved, bent her head to her shoulder to wipe an eye, at which point one of the auctioneer's helpers ran forward and grabbed her shawl. Fred had been right about that.

Soola was then cheered to see the young man, after paying his money to the accountant, walk briskly over and gently lift the boy into the cart. He took little Welcome and handed her to his wife, while he gave support to Missy as she climbed over the rim. No chains were evident in that cart.

Soula sat down on the dirt floor and wept, partly from relief that her friends had found a kind master and mistress, but also from grief that she would never see them again, nor have knowledge of their whereabouts. Her tears, too, were for herself. She was aware that the itchy fingers of buyers would discover the scars on her back, those scars which would reveal her bold and ornery nature.

Chapter 2

The next morning, the tall slave named Soola awoke to find herself on the cold damp ground, chained with other women to a tree beside the king's highway some distance north of Wilmington, she guessed. This main road wasn't much more than a deeply rutted mud path, making a journey for two small horses pulling a heavily loaded cart very slow indeed. Thus, this cavalcade had made only slow progress from the slave market the afternoon before. Since the war had reached the Carolinas three and a half years back, most landowners along the highways had repeatedly ignored the colonial governor's requirements for road repair. Many were engaged in partisan skirmishing in eastern North Carolina. Some even followed General Cornwallis in his back and forth wanderings, while others headed west to help the patriot leaders Morgan and Greene. Chaos reigned over some stretches of the farmlands and roadways of this colony, now an independent state.

Soola had witnessed guerrilla bands of British, then patriot soldiers passing through the Pine Forest Plantation in South Carolina, but she had no knowledge of the larger story, nor did it interest her. She concentrated on her own story and that of the people who now shared her fate. They were among the slaves who, at the end of the auction, for one reason or another, had remained unsold in the slave pen.

The scrappy looking man who had tried unsuccessfully to split Missy and Fred from the children, had stepped forward and scooped up these "dregs" for bottom prices. Among them were Tabitha and Judith, plus two other women and sixteen men. None of them had arrived with Soola on the packet from South Carolina the week before.Their new master had, with the aid of auction helpers, pushed and pulled them into his wagon and chained them to rings in the wagon's sides, while threatening with whip and pistol. He told them his name was Archie McLachlan. To his new slaves, he became Massa Archie.

Thus, in the morning, here they were, having bedded down for the night as darkness fell. Massa Archie had told them to sleep, dammit. Soola was the first to awaken and check out the landscape—nothing much to see to the southwest, mostly swamp visible through tall pine trees. Through hardwood trees with remnants of leaves to the east she caught glimpses of a red sunrise—red sky in the morning, sailor's warning. Oh my, more rain. She wondered why she felt a gripping dread in her heart, but then her dream came wafting back to her. In her miserable discomfort, she had dreamed she was back at Pine Forest, wandering down the path towards the river, holding Kayla's hand. Delving deep into her dream, she was able to pull together the pieces: she and her little daughter were laughing and singing together when suddenly a specter jumped out of the trees. Kayla screamed. It was a decaying body, dripping with water and with wet strands of red hair trickling down its face. The screeching specter snatched Kayla, and they vanished into the trees. Soola had awakened and sat up. She cried out, "Oh no, please, dream gods, leave me be!"

"Massa Archie, please, nature calls. Please come, unlock these chains. We won't try to escape." Soola had already spied their new master sitting up inside the wagon.

Archie climbed out and shouted to all the slaves. "Yes, it's time to git goin'. I'll untie you from the tree, but you women will have to stay chained together, go off together into the trees and do your business and same for the men. But make it fast, we have a long day ahead." When Massa Archie came close, Soola saw him clearly in the morning light for the first time and judged him to be definitely a "scraggly man." Massa Jimmie would not have had him at his dinner table. His eyes were, as she had suspected, blue and sunken, his whispy hair a light brown. The face was not unsightly but not handsome either. It had an uneven look, the right side being a bit more prominent than the left, the jaw slightly pushed to one side. Soola pondered whether perhaps he had taken a blow to the left side in early childhood when the bones were soft and growing. The nose had not been damaged, however; it was prominent and strong. The whole aspect of the man struck her as wiry and somewhat crooked. Where is his greatest weakness? she wondered.

Soola noticed that he carried a small bag with pieces of moldy bread. These he handed out after getting them all back into the cart and chained to the rings. He had chosen one of the men the day before to be the driver of the two heavy-hooved but underfed horses. He was the only one of this load of human chattel who remained unchained, while the master rode a chestnut, thin-necked, mangy nag behind the cart. He carried his whip ready to strike and kept a pistol carefully visible sticking out of his trouser pocket. Soola watched him, thinking he probably imagined himself to be a fancy plantation owner, now he had bought all these slaves. Next, she checked out the huddled mass of humanity. As well as huddled, they were squashed, the women pushed up against her, right behind the driver's seat. The men were bound tight in packs of three or four at the rear of the wagon. They had it worse than the women because each wrist was tied to that of a neighbor and the same for the ankles. The worst troubles for all emerged from the splinters that stuck out uncovered from the sides and floor of the cart.

The sky in the west, light-colored with strands of long thin clouds above the trees, promised a fine day for their journey—in contrast to the discomfort and the mood of this cartload. In fact, the sailors' warning seemed not to hold. The weather dried up, the road improved, the cart made better headway; although the horses from time to time had to stop, then struggle their way around patches where the road had degenerated and backslid into bog. Soola noticed that the journey was more and more stressful for Archie. He began shouting and yelling at his defenseless chattel, sending out a few lashes over the cartload, spitting out instructions for what they would be doing on his lands: digging canals, felling trees, creating open fields, caring for livestock, planting crops, especially rice, above all performing immediately any tasks assigned by him and him alone. Soola suspected what he had in mind for the five women: constant childbearing, field work too. For the men: she added constant toil in the fields, without reward, and plenty of whippings. She looked around at them, noticed their scars, same as her own, the "whupped" expressions in some, sarcasm and anger in others. She understood these were the ornery ones, or inept, or were on the lookout for an opportunity to flee. Massa would have his hands full with this lot. One man gave a rough guffaw, then with a curse, "This little Massa's full of spite, ain't he? Who's bettin' he ain't got the guts to deal with us devils?"

"What's that, what's that you say, boy? What's your name, boy?" cried this edgy master.

"Mittie, Massa, the name's Mittie. And I said the weather's lookin' fine."

Mittie's reward was a sharp whiplash across his face. "Y'all just shut up, all of you, not one more utterance," replied Archie, perhaps braver than they thought.

Soola noticed a smug tightening of the mouth and a subtle glimmer of pride in the eyes that exposed the ugliness in the master's soul. She surveyed him all over again and noticed this time the musket in its case tied to the saddle bag on his left side. He's lefthanded. Two guns. The small hope of mutiny faded from her mind. Her gaze traveled across the endless forest swamps to the west of the track they were following, swamps that would defy any attempt to escape, even if they were able to free themselves from the chains. Further north, as they moved along, frequent patches of pine and cypress forest emitted their rich odors, reminding her again of home. Warmed with these memories, she slept.

When Soola awoke, she called out, "Massa, we need to stop somewhere along here. It's gonna be dark soon, and nature is callin' again. And our legs is all stove up and stiff. We won't even be fit to walk if you don't stop." The other women looked nervous as they told this bold Soola to hush—she was enraging the master.

"Shut up, I told you to stay silent," was his quick reply.

But soon, while the autumn shadows lengthened, they approached a town and readied the horses to pull the wagon onto a ferry for a river crossing. The river was full, spilling over its banks from the recent rains. Trees still laden with leaves of red and gold leaned over the flood. The light was fading. Archie looked around with impatience until the ferry man, heavily bearded, big and burly, and with eyes full of sleep, appeared out of his house, obviously dismayed at the sight of this heavy load so late in the day. He scratched his head and shouted in a booming voice that to carry a passel of angry slaves was sometimes like carrying a pack of wolves, but these folks looked quiet, and the river's not far across, he added. The driver descended to lead the horses onto this long, flat bottomed raft. The ferry man made sure that the pulley spanning the waterway was securely fastened to its wheels and to the ferry, then began pulling the heavy boat across. Archie, intent on watching the ferry man, did not notice that his driver had failed to climb back onto his seat.

Out in mid-current, as Archie turned his head to survey the town, the driver suddenly jumped over the railing, and into the river. Perhaps he was hoping it was shallow water, perhaps he thought he could swim. Neither was true. The man sank below the water. Archie, with a cry of rage, threw the reins of his horse to the ferry man and rushed to the rail. The driver came up gasping for air. Archie hesitated, then drew the pistol. The ferry man grabbed an extra rope and threw it out to the drowning man, but when he came up for a second gulp of air, a shot rang out, and the slave's head became a bloody mess. The body sank again, while in the water around it spread a circle of red. Soola had a sudden and terrifying memory from her childhood on the Pine Forest Plantation, where she had witnessed, through a crack in the door of the Punishment Shed, the Red Devil beating a slave to death while a screaming woman hung from the thumb screws. The man's head had been a bloody mess like this one. Massa Jimmie had come running down to stop him, shouting that the foreman should not be smashing up his workers, but it was too late.

Now, as all witnesses cried out in horror, it was also too late. She felt the same horror at the power of white people, while Archie looked around, somewhat bewildered, and shouted out, "See, that's what happens to you devils when you try to put anything over on Archie McLachlan."

"You damn vicious fool, we don't shoot our people dead like that around here; I could have saved him for you," bellowed the ferry man.

No one uttered another word until Archie pulled the horses out onto dry land, at which time, the ferry man, while tying up the boat, turned and stared at him. "Sir, I know who you are, and the sheriff will pay you a visit tomorrow. In the meantime, you better come back here in the morning and be searching for the body because it's soon gonna be too dark to see it now. That's your responsibility."

"Mind your own damn business. I'll do what I wish with these people. They are my property, not yourn." He pointed to

Soola, "You, git up here and drive these animals so we can git back home tonight."

"Massa, I can't move with these chains,"Soola said bluntly. Her shock, at witnessing such a brutal and careless murder, tied her tongue against sassing the master on the remainder of that journey. She drove the horses as she had learned back at Pine Forest and kept her mouth firmly shut. Soola now realized that the slaves on this man's farm could expect vicious treatment, not only because they were powerless, but also because Archie McLachlan appeared to be ignorant of both common practice among most slave owners and his own best interests.

It was dark when the exhausted team pulled their burden into a long driveway beneath the forest trees. Since crossing on the ferry, they had sloshed through creeks and toiled along a muddy track until the master had shouted at Soola to turn left. The horses seemed to perk up, to resurrect their energy, and to feel they were home. She dropped the reins. They came to a stop beside a ramshackle two story-house, faintly lit by the almost full moon peeking its face out from behind a cloud. Nothing else was visible, except a dark structure that emerged into their vision to the left and a couple of whining dogs that timidly approached the master.

Archie dismounted. "Now, I know you are a sad bunch because I got all of you on the cheap, but if you don't work hard for me, you'll be a lot sadder. I got this piece of paper here, see…" He rooted in his pocket and found the bill of sale. "and it says you all belong to Archie McLachlan, and that's me, your new master. You'll do what I say or there'll be hell to pay. There's a barn over there with straw, and that is where you will sleep. In the morning, two of you women will build the cooking fire, cook up some beans and corn for our meal, then I'll divide you into work teams. Two of you men will tend the animals." He began to walk away. It was unclear when this tending to the animals would take place.

"Massa, if you don't unchain these folks, they ain't gonna neither sleep in the barn nor cook nor work on the morrow." Soola became conscious that she was to be the spokesperson for this bunch. And their new master appeared senseless to understand what to tell them.

"Damn you, woman, if you're such a cocky bitch, I'll put you out on the trees for the turpentine tomorrow along with the men." He unchained them. "And if any one of you run away, I'll set the blood hounds on you, you'll have nuthin' but swamp and jungle around you, and out on the highway you'll find the patty rollers. When you get back, you'll likely get the same as that fella floatin' in the river back there." Soola glanced down at the pathetic mongrels and smiled to herself—bloodhounds? She couldn't stop herself from saying quietly that it was too far down in the fall for the sap to run on the trees but then hoped he hadn't heard her. Just in case, she stepped nimbly towards the barn.

"The man's crazy, stupid too," she whispered, as they all staggered in silence, groping in the dark, stumbling over the roots of trees and stumps of former ones.

"Hey, Soola, quit that sassin' him, you won't be the only one he beats the shit out of," whispered Mittie who had quite lost his sense of humor in the past few hours.

"Well, Mr. Mittie, if we don't git food in us soon, there won't be no shit to beat out of us, so you tell him that in the morning." She felt around. There was straw, but she wondered how they could survive in such a place with the weather getting colder. Would there be blankets? And what about warm clothing? She saw Archie come back, carrying a flaming torch, to shout and berate them again.

"The beans and corn are in sacks up that ladder, so in the morning, like I said, I want you women to light the fire, git that pot out and cook it up so's we can all eat. You the white face one, you will be in charge of food for this place, and I'll let you keep the fire lighter." He handed her a flint from his pocket. "Now, git some sleep." Soola noticed a faint touch of kindness, a softening of the voice, in that last comment. Perhaps he was relieved that at least he had succeeded in getting his slaves home, except for one.

She took advantage of that moment, "Massa Archie, can you help us with blankets and clothing, too?" She spoke quietly and politely, but Archie stomped away without answering.

In the morning, Judith and Tabitha found the beans and corn and cooking pot and after accomplishing some cooking, found pieces of wood for utensils. The ravenous people began to eat, but there was a problem. One of the men told them quietly that the beans were too crisp, they needed to soak 'em before cookin'. Judith said Oh my. At that point, the desperation to eat was stronger than worry over unsoaked beans, but this man became Judith's advisor and so acquired the name Cook among the slaves. Soon, Archie arrived to divide the men into three teams for turpentine workers, canal workers, and field workers. He pointed out to them what to do and where to find two shovels and a rake. He provided them no tools to work the trees for turpentine. Still he expected them to get to work. It soon would become clear to the workers that they knew more than the master, but the death of the driver had quieted their tongues. They all looked to Soola to speak for them, which she did in asking Archie if he knew all their names and if not, would it help him to know them.

"Yeah, well, I know you're Soola, and those are Tabitha and Judith. Who're the other two women?" Suzannah and Phyllis timidly raised their hands and told him. He looked over the fifteen men, and a few called out their names—Adam, Mittie, Ibo, Jake, and Killease, and the newly named Cook. Then three more found the courage to tell him—Frog, Lucas, and Sam. The others said not a word, so Archie declared those would all bear the name No Name. As he turned to walk away, smiling at his little joke, Phyllis smiled shyly and whispered to the other women that the dead man deserved a name and they should refer to him as The Driver. She looked at Soola for approval, which she did receive.

Outside, Soola's eyes swept the surroundings, to find a wretched group of buildings—the large wooden barn with loft reached by a ladder, and a two-story shabby house which faced down the long, treacherous and rutted driveway where they had made their way the night before. Deep mud appeared dominant on the ground, except where the autumn leaves and pine needles had fallen. A smaller building ready for farm equipment completed Archie's plantation. Behind the house, a path through woods of ancient pines, live oak, cedar, tulip poplar, black gum and sweet gum, creeper vines, sourwood, and dogwood wound along a creek to the river. In some large areas of standing water stood the elegant bald cypress trees creating a wide canopy overhead for much of the year. Lining the driveway, they could see very young oaks and dogwoods. Someone had planted those saplings quite recently, she thought, maybe right before this childlike master had bought the property. A fresh, watery smell came from the wide river, blown their way by a soft breeze. Soola considered this to be a possibly hopeful sign, and when she heard the *purty, purty, purty,* song of the red bird, her hopes grew stronger. She remembered the birds at Pine Forest, and at the same time saw through the shadows of time a vision of her brother's face, little Amos, also sold away. Where were they now, these long-lost loved ones?

Soola bent over to stoke the fire and noticed Archie's legs in her peripheral vision. He had returned to spit out another short speech. "All right you people, you need to listen to me." He seemed nervous. They all stopped where they were but failed to look directly at him. "Damn it, look at me and listen." They looked, never sure whether he might shoot them dead. A very thin brown and white dog ventured out from behind the barn, wandered slowly over to sit beside Archie, and whined quietly. It seemed the dog already knew never to touch his master without an invitation. Soola would soon confirm that the herd of bloodhounds on this place consisted only of these two or three sad nomadic mongrels more interested in begging for food than chasing runaway slaves.

"When nature calls," a slight crooked smile crept onto Archie's face, "git as far from the buildings as you can, we don't need bad smells. And you men are gonna help build up Inveraray Plantation, that's what I've named this place, do you hear me? And you women, you're gonna have babies so there'll be workers for the future." Soola noticed the embarrassed flush on his cheeks, suspecting that short sentence had been well rehearsed.

"And how is that gonna happen, Massa?" she asked, casting her eyes slyly towards Tabitha.

Archie stopped short in mortified rage. He picked up a stick and went for her, beating her over the shoulders. She laughed, "I'm makin' a joke, Massa, do you not know how to laugh?" Archie's face grew redder as he pushed her to the ground. Leaning over, he threatened to kill her before night if she didn't keep her mouth shut. She had landed in a muddy puddle, which splashed up and clung to Archie's face, adding to his ridiculous appearance. She discovered to her surprise that his blows with the stick were limited to the shoulders and were neither heavy nor painful. She considered standing up and laughing at him like a child but thought better of it.

"Who's gonna show you how to git the turpentine out of the trees if I'm dead? I don't know nuthin about canals, but I do know about the turpentine trees and could show you, that is if you've got the equipment," she answered, endeavoring to stand.

All the women had their hands over their mouths, their eyes popping open, the smell of terror hovering around the men. Archie's face struggled to remain calm, while it was apparent to all that their master needed help in working with slaves and running a farm. He turned and marched away. "I'll kill you yet, you be assured of that," he shouted back at Soola. But no one yet had specifically told them where to go or the location of materials necessary to complete some of the tasks. The master left them there gawking at each other.

Later, on that first miserable day, the slaves saw the sheriff ride up the driveway with his assistant. The two went into the house with Archie and came out an hour later. They mounted their horses and rode away. Nothing more was said about the death of The Driver, except when Massa Archie wished to threaten his slaves. Archie did not leave Inveraray to help find the body in the river. Soola reflected on this lack of punishment for a murderer. It hit her finally that killing an escaping slave was not considered murder by the white people. In fact, Soola remembered Selma, the "all-wise," back at Pine Forest Plantation, who had told her about that after the Red Devil had beaten the recalcitrant slave to death. The master held all the power, and if a slave died while "under correction," or running away, killing him was not murder. Furthermore, Selma had assured her, no slave could ever bring a legal protest against a master, and that master wouldn't get much punishment even if it was murder without cause. Selma had been the source of much guidance and knowledge during her childhood. But now, Soola wondered, what about The Driver's body? —no marking on his lonely watery grave, no family, no mourners, no name for an anonymous man, carried by the deep river's current and swept out to sea. She wiped one tear from her eye.

That evening, as the twenty enslaved people, only three days known to each other, and fearful of what was in store for them the next day, huddled together for warmth in the big barn. As they tried to keep the fearless rats at bay, Soola, already their leader, spoke: "This man is angry, crazy as a bee-stung bull, stupid and ignorant too. And that's a dangerous combination. I'll quit angering him more."

"You promise us that?" whispered Judith.

"Yes, but he needs advice, and if we help him with that, maybe our lives'll be better." Standing up, Soola placed a hand on her hip, always looking for a solution to an intractable problem, sometimes ready with an answer. This time she could only wonder about the difference in the law for them as opposed to white people, especially when it came to murder.

"Girl, how come you don't already know about that?" asked Mittie, to which she replied with a touch of sarcasm that she had experienced a sheltered childhood.

"So where did you git them scars," asked another man. She didn't answer that but cast her great dark eyes upon this man whose face revealed itself through the dappled firelight. She asked his name, and he said Adam. At the same time, the song of a thrush floated in like a stream to sooth her heart.

The next day three white men arrived on horseback, and it wasn't long before the workers learned of their purpose. The men were advisors, hired to show Massa Archie how to start a farm and deal with slave labor. Because she had been vocal about her knowledge of the turpentine business, Soola was the first one to be assigned to the trees, even though it was, as she had said, too late in the year to get the sap to run. She explained that to her boss, but he didn't believe her until one of the hired men assured him she knew of which she spoke. These men immediately told Archie to listen to this tall one, then gave the slaves some rudimentary instructions, and more shovels, rakes, and hoes, which enabled them finally to begin their labors. Soola was surprised by the tingle of pleasure in her body, her feeling of power when they recognized her skills. But the other slaves knew neither pleasure nor power. That evening after their first day of real labor, Tabitha said quietly to any who listened, "Will no one help us? Where's the orishas of my grandmother? Where's the new god and his son

Jesus?" She heaved a great sigh and laid her thin body down on the straw.

Soola's answer was bolstered by her new feeling of power, "None of them invisible folks will help us, Tabitha. We will help ourselves and trust to our friend Mr. Luck; although I agree, he ain't our friend neither right now because Mr. Luck has handed us all over to the scrappy kind of master our trader down there spoke of. So mostly, we will trust in ourselves."

Mr. Luck, however, did hand them a small boon the next week in the person of a fast rider who brought Massa Archie a note. They saw their master read it then jump up and down in glee. It took a few days for the news to reach his workers' understanding, when Soola's clever ears picked up that the master's father and uncle had both died over at Cross Creek of the typhoid, and that Archie was now a somewhat richer man. Enough richer perhaps to repair the barn and house, and order more food, clothing, and blankets for the winter? He did. Soola acknowledged this small shred of kindness. "But nay," muttered Mittie, "Perhaps not kindness in the man, perhaps only what he had been told to do by his three advisors."

Indeed, as they learned over the next few years at Inveraray, Mittie's pessimism was more accurate than Soola's suggestion of kindness from Massa Archie. Purchases to aid or comfort his "damned lazy bastards," as he called them, would be meager; while punishments for slow performance, sulky behavior, or outright defiance would fall heavily on their shoulders and backs. Most of the latter rained down on Soola's already scarred frame. However, she learned to control her tongue so that the others might not suffer. The little band of twenty struggled through those early years at Inveraray, grappling with childbearing, long hours of toil in weather either too hot or too cold, crop failures, snakebites, illness, more thoughtless beatings, and often, heavy spells of despair. Only the indomitable spirit of humanity saved them, the spirit that encouraged jokes and laughter, love in its many forms, and even their own small daily successes.

The slaves at Inveraray sometimes allowed themselves pride in their spring plantings. Naming the songs of the birds became a contest, and occasionally they awoke in the morning with hope in their hearts. Soola rarely omitted to tell the master, on a Saturday, the amount of sap she had collected that week. It became a contest between them as to whether he would ever congratulate her. Likewise, for sleeping quarters—would he ever provide them with more comfort, more clothing, more protection from the cold. "It looks like never," said Soola to Tabitha.

It was extraordinary that most, not all but most, survived that wretched time. And they survived to experience a gift that came suddenly one afternoon, several years later, surely from the hand of Mr. Luck, or even from Mr. God. It was a boon that would finally, and forever, alter their lives.

1720-1788

Chapter 3

Maps of the Carolinas drawn in the earliest days of European settlement show amazing accuracy in depicting the ragged coastline and the wide, slow-moving rivers that have for hundreds of thousands of years carried water from the mountains to the sea. The colors of the waters have reflected the colors of the soils picked up along the way, ranging from black to reddish brown. The result of the long river journeys has been a flat and gentle landscape.

The sounds, beaches, lakes, marshes, and ever-changing strings of sandbars have beckoned to migrating birds, especially the gracefully beautiful swans and geese that like to spend the winter along this coastline. Human creatures too have cherished the far-reaching skies and waters, as Soola did when she filled up with wonder as her schooner approached the Cape Fear River in 1783. In those early days, too, the dry land supported dense forests—massive hardwood trees, overshadowed year-round by the evergreen longleaf pine. In more recent times, as European farmers became more and more numerous, the rivers came to be avenues for travel and trade with the Indians further inland. Towns grew up along the waterways, often situated on sites of old Indian settlements. Such was the case with the little town glimpsed by Soola as they crossed on the ferry that murderous evening on their trip to Inveraray.

In earlier years of the 18th century, soon after the Tuscarora Indians surrendered and moved up north to join their cousins, and after the division of Carolina into North and South, a Scottish farmer named Hamish Munro acquired a large tract of heavily forested land blessed with several open meadows long ago cleared by native people. He, his wife, and little son James settled there, across the Middle River, just north of the town where Archie McLachlan would, later in the century, sell his farm products. These Munros were early migrants, among the first in the massive migration of Highland Scots to the shores of the New

World. They were just in time to pick up some rudimentary clues from the few remaining natives, as to how to live and farm the rich black soil midst all those trees—how to fell them too. Of course, Europeans also had the advantage of metal tools. Nevertheless, it is almost unimaginable to have predicted success for this small family traveling with only a few other Highlanders from the Cape Fear north, following Indian paths, even though unencumbered by hefty possessions. The group had joined together to buy one horse and wagon to carry their scanty goods and children. The adults and older children walked. For these families it was the hunt for land that propelled them, and they had been told, down on the Cape Fear, that land was going cheaper further north, rather than west up the river where many other Scots were headed. It was always land, land that would replace the vast stretches snatched from them by sheep back in their homeland of Scotland.

Hamish Munro and his family worked hard, lived in a lean-to that first winter while they cleared fields, built a small house and barns, all the while fighting the endless battles against weather and the hungry jaws of death. Mr. Munro's wife died after giving birth to their fourth son. This was followed within the next two years by the deaths of the new baby, and then two of the other boys, both of these from scarlet fever. These family tragedies notwithstanding, Hamish and the oldest son James benefited from the British subsidies paid to naval stores producers and succeeded in developing the farm with a good turpentine business as well as varied crops. Although they disapproved of owning human chattel, they succumbed to this practice out of what they assured themselves was necessity.

When James reached seventeen, he married a local farm girl. Fiona was her name, which meant "fair" in Gaelic. They raised four children on the farm, first a daughter, then three sons. The daughter Gertrude was like her mother—strong and tall, not a beauty, but kind and energetic, with little time for, nor interest in, women's society life. Gertrude's face bore a chiseled look, with a long chin. Her hair was as brown and straight as the longleaf pine needles she learned to bundle into rough baskets and brooms. Her face also bore a barely perceptible defect—the upper lip on one side receded slightly upwards towards the nose revealing a hint of white tooth when her lips were closed. The midwife who had helped at Gertrude's birth had whispered right away that this was a harelip baby and some in the neighborhood added it was a mark of the devil. So, the child grew up somewhat set apart, despite the fact that the hare lip grew less and less noticeable. Her parents ignored all comments about their daughter's lip and considered her a true gift from God.

Gertrude, indeed, the whole family, suffered a terrible heartache in the year 1771. Her mother died from the swamp fever, and thirteen-year-old Gertrude took over much of the work, both inside the house and outside on the farm. She grew close to her father and grandfather and became mother to the three boys.

Then, at the age of twenty-five, after much indecision on her part, and several months of persuasion from an elderly admirer, Gertrude agreed to marry him. On the day Hermann Spencer rode up to the Munro farmhouse and knocked firmly on the door, she was ready for a change, ready to accept. "Miss Munro, I am here today to address your father regarding my wish for you to be my wife. Have you for sure agreed, inside yourself, my dear, to finally accept my proposal?" He smiled, took her hand as she closed the door, and gave a slight bow.

Gertrude bent her head as he bowed and noticed the thinning of his hair, as well as the increasing gray shade to the thick black curls she had admired during the years of their acquaintance. "Mr. Spencer, although my father and brothers need me here, yes, they have plenty of help now, and I will go with you, if Father agrees." She led him into her father's office, where James sat worrying over the increasing cost of clearing new fields. He looked up when Gertrude and Hermann entered, smiled broadly, and stretched out his hand. "Mr. Spencer, come in, please, take a seat." Gertrude slipped out closing the door behind her.

When Gertrude walked Hermann to his horse, she looked up at his face with questioning eyes. He answered, "Yes, my dear, he says he is loath to lose you but still is willing to give you up if it be the best for your future."

Gertrude began laughing. "My, my, Mr. Spencer, and did he give his consent in exchange for a good deal in business arrangements?"

"Oh no, Miss Munro, of course our conversation didn't follow in that direction. It was much more centered on my admiration for you." He smiled broadly and said he was a lucky man.

She ran back in the house and opened her father's door, "Oh Father, so how much did he pay for me? Are the coins rattling around in your pocket?"

"You'd better not tease me too much, my daughter. You might not like the answer," James replied. He took a few steps round his desk, took her in his arms, "He is a good man, my darling; and he is the one benefiting in this bargain. It is all loss for us here on the farm."

Gertrude certainly knew that as far as beauty was concerned, she wouldn't count for much. Up until now, no young man had shown the smallest interest in her. At local socials, the boys had always chosen other girls to dance with. Her brothers teased her about being a "wall flower" then whirled her around the floor and into the highland reels themselves. So now, finally, she was pleased that this older man, Hermann Spencer, a businessman and bachelor, insisted she was the only one for him. Nonetheless, she knew that his mother had recently died of extreme old age, and poor Hermann had been quite bereft without a caretaker.

Thus, in the spring of 1783, Gertrude and Hermann were married at the Munro farm. She moved into his house that overlooked the river, in the growing residential section along the south bank. It was a lovely little wooden house, painted white, with two dormer windows poking out of a steep roof. It had a basic floor plan of parlor and dining room downstairs, bedroom and "necessary" room on the back and two bedrooms upstairs. The kitchen was out through the back door. Gertrude loved the house and kept it scrubbed clean with the help of a slave woman, whose husband worked outside on the grounds and with the horse and cart. As for decorating Hermann's house with fine furniture, pictures and the like, Gertrude wasn't interested in any of that. What she relished was the river setting—the sound of the water lapping against the banks and its dark color that changed as the water roiled and swirled in the currents and in the wind. A habit grew on her to stand at an upstairs open window, with the wind blowing in, watching these changes, enjoying the fresh smell of the water. She felt as if the river were a person, revealing to her its several personalities.

Hermann was involved in the marketing of farm products, helping the larger farmers get their crops to town for the markets, then dealing on their behalf with the buyers and shippers. Gertrude became active in her husband's business, bargaining like a man, people said. Gertrude loved that too. She had been schooled by her mother, learning to do everything just right, which fit in well with her as businesswoman. Since she remained childless, she persuaded her youngest brother Bruce to move in with her and her husband. Revealing to her father that the house needed a son, she explained with a smile that Bruce might fill that longing, adding that she could help him get some education. "And, dear Father, I miss all the jokes and laughter we had at home. Hermann is such a nice and kind man, but he's very serious. Bruce will liven us up—and my husband will enjoy that. Although Bruce is not to call me Gertie—Gertrude it must be."

There was something else that she felt was missing in her life with Hermann. Her mother had urged her sternly to never set her heart on comforts and beauty, but rather, to trust in the teachings of Jesus and set her heart on the humanity around her. Gertrude retained her mother's deep religious faith, a faith that included all mankind as the creation of God. She believed deeply in that trust and tried to match it in every action of daily life. Therefore, as partner in marriage, she was determined to see that the young slave family belonging to Hermann was well treated and comfortable in their enslaved life, like the slaves under her father's care. She had noticed that her husband sometimes spoke too sharply to Aurelia and Hubert and was easily irritated by their children. "Father, I believe Bruce can help me in honoring the teachings of Jesus which our mother taught us. These teachings could soften Hermann in his treatment of our slave family. You see, he is not a church man. He does not even say his prayers at eventide."

James was thoughtful on the matter. "Gertrude, I would urge you to take care. Not all folks feel the same in their hearts as your mother did. She used to get after me sometimes, and I felt that all of us, when we reach adulthood, make our own promises to God, and as adults, we make individual decisions. I have heard that our leaders in the fight against the King and Parliament would agree. They are not all pious men. And, take special care in discussing slavery and treatment of slaves. It is a sensitive subject."

"Yes, Father, thank you for that guidance. All the men I have encountered thus far in my life have been kind. Hermann is no different, always tolerant of my wishes. But he may have a point where he puts up his flat hand and says no. A horse is like that. If you try to make him jump a fence too high, he will toss you off quick. Oh dear, I don't mean that Hermann is like a horse, I only mean that I'll listen to your advice, on all topics." They both laughed.

The next morning, Gertrude, while cooking breakfast, very gently asked her husband if he would attend church with her next Sunday. He looked up at her with a quiet smile. "My most considerate wife, that is one thing, I hope the only thing, with which I cannot oblige you. Please forgive me, but there will be no discussion on that subject. I am not a church man, nor will I ever be." Gertrude never brought it up again. Furthermore, she made no attempt on the topic of slavery. She had no argument against that bedrock of Southern life. Didn't even search for one.

By 1788, when Gertrude and Hermann had been married for almost five years, Hermann was slowing down, showing signs of illness, and lately he had been leaving more and more of the business to her. She in turn began to depend on her brother for help. So it was, on a bright sunny morning in early summer that, yet again, she had to rouse him. "Bruce, it is time for you to arise, eat some breakfast, then take this cartload of corn to the market and get a good price for Father, you must stop being a lazy boy." Gertrude called out to him as if he were still a child; although he had turned seventeen years the past week. Bruce appeared, a tousle-haired boy, tall and lanky, hurrying into his clothes. He ran out to hitch up the horse to the cart, promising "Gertie" he would come back with money for his father in his pocket.

Gertrude grew stern. Is he never going to stop that? All three brothers had clung to the bad habit of the nickname for their sister since they were little. However, she thought, today I won't quibble about my name, it's more important that he concentrate on business, get a good price, and do that all on his own. She had decided the night before that Bruce must do this for her today because she was fearful about Hermann's health and needed to stay home with him. In the past month, as the summer heat came on in earnest, he had taken to his bed, weak and without appetite for food, or even for business.

Gertrude walked upstairs slowly, dreading to witness again her husband's decline. He had been a truly gentle husband, always expressing gratitude to her for taking him on in his old age. Although there was no flame inside her for this man, she dwelt in her mind on the word *fond* to locate her exact feelings for him. Dear Hermann. As she entered the bedroom, a bare undecorated chamber with only minimal furniture, she noticed the little smile that appeared on his face but was alarmed by his pallor and labored breathing. The sick room odors were becoming unbearable, so she called downstairs for Aurelia to come up to empty the chamber pot hidden in its own little bedside cubby hole. Aurelia was a servant of many talents, Gertrude often said, bragging to her husband, hoping in that roundabout way to discourage his sharp words.

It wasn't only the odor; the room seemed stuffy, almost suffocating, so Gertrude went to each of the three windows, opening them as wide as possible. The problem with that, however, was that flies and mosquitoes would crowd into the house unhindered. Poor Hermann wouldn't care if she left the windows closed. He complained of the cold now in the midst of heat.

Two glass medicine bottles, one dark green, the other brown, and a spoon sat on a little tray on top of this bedside cabinet. She transferred the tray to a table on the other side of the bed. But it wasn't time for another dose, so she picked up her knitting bag and commenced knitting fast on the bright green sweater for Aurelia's boy. Gertrude remained there for the rest of the morning, only placing the knitting in her lap sometimes in order to hold Hermann's hand. She reflected on her life from time to time, realizing, as she had lately, that she had not yet reached her potential, the crowning actions of the life that she believed awaited her. She had been contented here with her husband but did not feel lifted into the glories of the Christian message. No, not lifted up. Would she perhaps one day become a missionary to the heathens in Africa or South America? But maybe a woman would not be welcome in that Christian army. But wait, were there not Africans all around her and many still heathen on farms out in the country? Do they need a missionary? She would look into that. After all, Jesus had told his disciples, go ye into all the world. Jesus did not exclude women. Jesus did not exclude Africans. Writing out a message, she sent Aurelia's boy to the doctor to see if he could come by on the morrow.

Gertrude looked carefully at her husband, and her searching seemed to reach his fading mind. He opened his eyes, "My dearest Gertrude," he mumbled slowly, "have you been happy here with me? Is it not too dull for a young, charming woman to be stuck in this house without attention from a young, vigorous man who loves her? A man more vigorous in his love?" He reached out for her hand and clutched it weakly.

"Hermann, there are so many things you have done for me. You have loved me in a way I never expected. You have introduced me to your business and taught me the subtle ways of men in the business world; you have shown me the way women live in town and made me a more sophisticated person. And, therefore, you have forgotten, dearest Hermann, that I am rarely alone in this house—either helping you with business, cleaning my church, knitting with my group of ladies, and add to all that, I have had Bruce to teach and chase after. I have had no time for being bored." She smiled and held tight to his hand, while he fell into slumber again.

Gertrude dozed off in the late afternoon after reassuring her husband every hour that yes, she was still right there beside him. Most of the time, he slept. Then suddenly she heard the front door open and slam shut, followed by Bruce's voice shouting out that he had had a good day with the market and where was she, he needed to tell her something. Gertrude roused herself, tucked the knitting into its bag, and went downstairs. There was Bruce with a big grin on his face, kicking off his boots beside the door.

"Gertie, I sold Father's corn to the cattle farmer upriver for a good price," he said, "and then bought potatoes from that peculiar man downriver. I can't remember his name, but we've seen him before when me and you were there together. In fact, he asked after you and wondered where was my mother." Bruce almost fell on the floor laughing. "I didn't correct him, so he still right now believes you're my mother." Bruce continued to think that was the greatest joke he had ever heard and started calling out, "Mama, Mama."

"Bruce, stop all that caterwauling. The only reason he thinks I'm your mother is that you act like a child still. When on this earth are you going to grow up? When our father was your age he was married to our mother." But it did occur to her that maybe Mama was better than Gertie. She grabbed a towel that was hanging over the banister and began flicking it at his legs, chasing him into the parlor. She had never told Bruce that she needed a son in the house; that subject had popped up all by itself.

"Anyway, Mama, he said that next time I went to the market, I should bring you, he wants to ask you something. I said you were home taking care of my father who's real sick. And I do believe that disappointed him because he kept on and said oh, so she has a husband? And I said, yes of course, although she might not have him for long because he's real bad off."

"Bruce, that's not even funny. You can't make jokes about a sick man, and now, what am I going to say to this man next time I see him?"

"You're going to say that your son was joking and that the man you live with is not your husband but your paramour, so you are free for courting." Bruce was still laughing.

"Get out of here, go out and put the horse away and feed her. Stack the bags of potatoes in the barn, and, you can be planning which vegetable vendors you will persuade to buy them tomorrow. Anyway, you have done a good job, and thank you, Baby Brother." Gertrude began stretching her memory back to identify this potato grower from downriver. It wasn't every day that a man expressed interest in her, no matter what the reason. She was neither pretty nor flirtatious. So, what did he want to ask her? Hmmm. She reckoned something to do with business.

For the next few weeks Gertrude became distracted by her husband's illness. and forgot about the farmer from downriver.

Hermann died quietly one night during the last of the hot weather. Remembering the death of her beloved mother, she found the sadness to be especially poignant and the burial painful to watch. She had held up through preparing the body and sitting there all night, but it was the visualizing Hermann himself in the box with the lid shut tight and lowered into the ground that brought the lump to her throat and tear to her eye. Hermann had been known to many in the county and had few enemies, so she was required to put on a good face and produce a reception back at the house. They all came; she and Aurelia, both clad in black from head to feet, scrambled to feed and entertain the crowd with the huge number of dishes brought to the house by the women of the town. Many expressed praise and gratitude for Hermann's honesty and fairness in business, complimenting her on her good sense and ability in helping him during his declining years.

At the end, her father took her aside, "Gertrude, you might like to come home now, spend some time with me and help us around the house. And, with all three boys now moved into town, I would enjoy your company. Did you hear that Benjamin is off to Campbelltown next week, looking for work, and Edward's opening his law office here?"

"Thank you, Papa, but it suits me best to stay right here and continue with the business and keep up the house. And yes, I know of the boys' plans. But, did you not know that Campbelltown is now called Fayetteville? And, Bruce says he will stay on as my partner here. You see, I understand from Hermann's lawyer that he has willed everything to me, especially since he has no other family." She waved the little fan she'd been holding and wiped the sweat off her brow. August was nobody's favorite month in North Carolina. "And, Father, I shall not change my mind, this is my home now, isn't that right, Bruce? And if Baby Brother be conscientious as he has been of late, I'll make him a full partner next year."

"Yes, Father, you know Gertie. She'll never give up once she's settled on something," added Bruce.

That evening with all the visitors gone, Bruce told her that the little farmer from downriver had come to the house after the funeral, just to express his sympathy, he said, but he couldn't stay, had to get home. He asked to give his regards to "your mother."

Bruce said that this time he assured the man that he was Bruce Munro, that she was not his mother but his sister and now his business partner, and that she would appreciate his concern. The man told him he was Archie McLachlan from the Inveraray Plantation and he looked forward to doing business with them in the future. Gertrude smiled and kept that in mind.

1788-1790

Chapter 4

During the year following her husband's death, Gertrude Munro Spencer stayed quiet, businesslike, remaining draped in black from head to toe. She felt she owed that to Hermann's memory. And it seemed to her during that year that brother Bruce was developing into a sensible and helpful young man. There was not so pressing a need for her in the business anymore. In fact, Bruce was conducting most of the business while Gertrude became more and more involved with charitable pursuits—aiding the poor with food and clothing, teaching poor children in her house, and always teaching the words of Jesus.

However, the Africans she could not help much because most were slaves and that would be interfering between a slave and his owner. She, indeed, did not know whether it was strictly unlawful to teach a slave child to read and write, or whether it was just the custom. She had never seen such a law in writing, only heard it in her knitting group. Anyway, that didn't matter because a slave owner would raise almighty cane with her if such behavior were discovered, and she certainly did not wish for punishment on a slave family, nor upon herself. She definitely would not disturb any deeply held belief among her neighbors with these lofty plans of hers. However, Gertrude did sometimes accept a free Negro child into her small home classroom. She thought again of her beloved mother, trusting that she would approve.

Bruce helped her move furniture around in the parlor and buy some small desks to accommodate her pupils. Gertrude was excited and pleased with these efforts on behalf of the poor. Yes, there were other schools available, but the cost rendered them unreachable for families on the edge—white farmers scraping out a living, and Negro families, free, but living in the depths of poverty. She put a sign at her front door—The Munro Free School—and provided lunch for the children.

As for the farmer downriver, Archie McLachlan, she occasionally saw him when she went to the wharf or the market with Bruce. He seemed somewhat bashful in her presence, always doffed his hat with exaggerated politeness, but preferred to conduct business discussions with Bruce. By the time the hot weather arrived, she found herself occasionally wishing that Archie would look at her, talk to her, recognize her presence as a businesswoman. There seemed to be something false about his politeness. One day at the market, Gertrude looked curiously at him. He certainly wasn't a handsome man; he would never enjoy the attentions of a beautiful woman. But his slightly crooked face and smile interested her. He was a half inch shorter than she and most likely his age was less too.

The next week, Gertrude, without Bruce, watched this man from a hidden spot at the edge of the marketplace while he was negotiating to sell his corn to the cattle farmers. It was odd; he appeared to be a different person, more aggressive, becoming angry, but she couldn't hear his words exactly, only a few— "damn rascal," and "fooling me." Eventually, Archie put money in his pocket and walked away whistling and smiling to himself. Hmmm. Who was this fellow? Perhaps he had already seen her but had decided not to approach without Bruce in attendance. There weren't that many people at the marketplace yet, so it was likely he had seen her. Now the crowd was growing, dogs were prowling, and the doves waddling, clucking, and cooing all over. "My toe hurts Betty"—she remembered her grandfather quoting the old pigeon rhyme from Scotland; although these American birds never completed it properly, cutting off the Betty part. Just "My toe hurts." It was a hot day with a storm threatening from the west. The breeze grew stronger lifting up the cloth covers over the farmers' stalls and scattering some papers across the grassy meadow. Soon, this area in the middle of town, surrounded by shops and houses, would have to be extended, and the only way to do that would be to remove some large trees at the western end.

Gertrude then, somehow encouraged by the confusion, the loud voices, and fiddle playing of the market, decided on a bold move. She spied Archie in the far distance approaching his horse and cart midst those big trees and immediately began moving fast in pursuit. "Mr. McLachlan, Mr. McLachlan."

Archie turned around, saw her approaching, and his face took on the look of a frightened doe. He backed up to the side of his cart and lifted his hat.

Gertrude stopped in great embarrassment too, and they stood there, neither knowing what to say. She blurted out, "Mr. McLachlan, last year while my husband was ill, you told my brother Bruce that you wanted to ask me something, but you never did say what it was. I thought it must be something to do with our business." Her black long-sleeved dress suddenly felt too warm for a day like this. She noticed that he was flushing fiercely.

"No ma'am, it was a personal matter," he mumbled, looking at his feet.

"Well?"

He took off his hat allowing those strands of hair to fly. "Well, ma'am, it can wait, I gotta git home now." He jumped up on his cart, jiggled the reins, then realized he hadn't untied the beast from the hitching post and so had to get down, then back up again, his face filled with humiliation.

But there was embarrassment in Gertrude's mind too as she walked slowly home, blaming herself for such foolish and aggressive behavior. I should never have chased after him like that, he'll think I'm a forward woman. She went upstairs, opened the window, and listened to the river.

The next week, Gertrude's mourning came to an end. She went to the dry goods shop and bought two new dresses, one blue, the other a deep wine red. Thence to the office of her middle brother Edward who had recently opened a law practice in town. She asked him to arrange the paperwork to change her name back to Munro. She wanted to be herself again and had persuaded her conscience that Hermann wouldn't mind.

September arrived; summer was moving to its end. Two weeks after that strange encounter with Archie McLachlan, Gertrude noticed from the parlor window that weeds, especially that pernicious crabgrass, were enveloping her garden. When she went out to pick beans, she found the pods to be nearing the too-tough-to-eat phase of their existence. She snapped off all that were left so that Aurelia could pick out the beans and toss the pods. Even the tomatoes were looking somewhat scrawny, begging for rain. Bruce had not mentioned Archie lately; the man was fading from her mind.

Gertrude reached for her basket and, straightening up, was immediately surprised to see that same farmer standing by her little front gate. Well, speak of the devil, she thought. "Good morning to you, Mr. McLachlan, this is a surprise, quite startling in fact. What can I do for you?"

"Well, Ma'am, I didn't mean to scare you, but since I did not see you at the market, your brother neither, I sold my stuff, then stopped by here to pass the time." He appeared to be less frightened of her than at their last meeting.

"Well, come on in and have a cup of tea," she ventured, hoping he wouldn't stay long. He raised his hat slightly in response and followed her into the house. "Please have a seat, sir, I'll be right back." He sat on a chair near the window in the small corner of the room set apart from the school desks. Gertrude knew that her parlor lacked a warm and welcoming atmosphere. Adorned by two or three small landscape paintings on the wall, three straight back chairs, a table in the near corner, and years-old curtains that badly needed replacing, this front room lacked even a hint of the flowery décor popular at the time. So, it was only the floor that created in Gertrude a touch of pride. A month before, she had replaced the old boards with new, fine, wide boards from recently felled long leaf pine trees. She had hired a young free Negro man, new to the town, to sand and polish the new floor and stain it a dark brown. It almost worried her that the children's feet, so fast moving and unnoticing, might mar its beauty. Indeed, she had already discovered some faint scratches.

As she left the room, she noticed out of the corner of her eye that Archie remembered just in time to snatch off his hat. In the kitchen, Gertrude asked Aurelia if she wouldn't mind making a pot of tea with cups for two. Aurelia gave her a knowing look and smiled. Gertrude laughed, "Noooo," and waved the thought away with her hand.

When she returned to the parlor, Gertrude noticed for the first time that her guest carried with him a little cloud of odor, the smell of a hardworking man she thought. Well, that's putting it politely; in plainer language, she would say simply that he stinks. But it wouldn't look good for her to walk around the room and open all the windows wide, wider than normal. So, she just sat down and asked him if his morning at the market had gone well.

"Well, Mistress Spencer, ma'am, yes, I always try to walk away with extra money in the pocket. It's me Scotch blood that does it. Me faither and uncle taught me that too. But the folks here are tough to deal with sometimes, thinking that I should be raising corn to give away, that's what they've got in their minds."

"Same for all of us, Mr. McLachlan, I have the Scotch blood too, my grandfather came here more than fifty years ago, from the Highlands of the far Northeast, he was, the town of Cromarty, and he had the name of a true Scot—Hamish. But, sir, I have taken back my own name. I'm not Mistress Spencer anymore, I'm back to Gertrude Munro, and don't know if it's Miss or Mizriz."

Archie didn't seem to approve of that, "Well, why'd you do that? Did you not like your husband?"

That surprised Gertrude. She was about to answer when Aurelia came in with the tea tray, behind Archie's back so he couldn't see the look on her face. Was it a look of questioning or perhaps of disgust at the smell? Was Aurelia disapproving of this man altogether? Gertrude, who was facing him, could not respond but stored it in her mind to talk about with Aurelia later. Then, as she poured the tea, she explained about her name, "Of course I liked my husband, Mr. McLachlan, he was the best man in the world, but I wanted my own name back, I want to be a Munro. He would understand."

"Well, I wouldn't approve; a wife should always keep her husband's name, but that's your business, not mine," replied Archie.

All Gertrude could think of in reply was "Yes, indeed." Her comment referred to "your business," not to "keeping her husband's name," which was purposely unclear. She certainly didn't want to get into an argument so futile with this man. She wanted to say that, anyway, he would be dead if that same thing was done by his widow. But she refrained. Instead she asked him about his father and uncle, very polite, "what part of Scotland were they from?"

"From around Loch Fyne, the city of Inveraray to be exact." He looked at the floor, didn't appear to wish any more conversation on that subject.

Gertrude wondered what they could talk about next. Her mother had told her many years ago that conversation was not merely to convey information; it was also to knit together friendships and partnerships. If that be true, she thought, then I must conjure up something that might interest him. Oh dear, this might turn out to be difficult. But Archie surprised her with more information, unprompted, about his origins. "Me faither was a hard man, bitter and hard, aye." He lapsed into the Scottish voice of his childhood. "He liked, seemed eager to give me the taws every day on any part of the body he could put that leather strap to."

"The taws?" asked Gertrude.

"Aye, that's the thick leather strap with the fringe on the end that they use to beat the wee ones in Scotland, usually on the palm of the hand. But my uncle, he was a softer man and used to slip me money when I got older. I used to wonder where my father found that strap in America. Perhaps he got it from another Scot who came over the ocean with a pack of bairns."

"So, were you born in Scotland and came over here with your parents and uncle?" She was truly finding this interesting now and was picking up on the hint of sarcasm, of mimicry, in his use of the Scottish words and pronunciation.

"No ma'am, I was born at Crosscreek and Campbelltown, which just recently have been joined and named Fayetteville. Me mither came along the year after the two brothers; she had already married Douglas, me faither, back home before he left. She was a slippery one, she was, said that the boiling, baking sun got to her brain. And she never liked the sighing of the pine trees neither. Right after I made my appearance, she handed me, the wee baby, to my father, then caught a boat down the river and back home to Scotland. My father hated her memory, never forgave her that wicked desertion; although him and Uncle Duncan built up a fine lumber business, managed to escape fighting in the war, even made money off it. They're both dead now." He stopped. "But this looks like a real nice place you got here Mistress Munro. I always did hear that your husband did real well for an Englishman." He smiled and gave a little cackling laugh. Gertrude recognized that it was common practice for the Highlanders to make jokes about the English. Oh well, that had not been true of her family. Her grandfather's beef had always been with some of the clan chieftains, who, in order to graze sheep, had thrown the crofters off the land. The wool business triumphed.

When he got up to leave, Gertrude felt that maybe they had enjoyed some conversation which would create the beginnings of a friendship; notwithstanding it was a somewhat one-sided exchange. She watched from the window as he mounted his horse and rode away. He looked better on a horse than on his own two feet. But why did she care? Gertrude pondered that question for the next couple of weeks, kept dwelling in her mind on this man, remembering now and then that he had suffered a bitter, motherless childhood. That surely explained his lack of physical cleanliness and grooming. This man seemed different from the men of her life; in her innocence, she reflected that she had known only kind and gentle men, especially in their treatment of women. Archie was rougher.

A slow loneliness began to creep into Gertrude Munro's mind as months went by, her thoughts turning more and more on a life purpose, a goal that she believed would elevate her into the light of God. Teaching became the center of her ambition, but eventually she knew this little school would not be enough—too easy, too normal. She wanted something that required sacrifice, a challenge, difficulty, something for which she must build the strength that she knew was in her. Bruce was spending more and more time on the business nowadays, even looking into a rudimentary shipping enterprise to help farmers and craftsmen move their products downriver to wider markets. He made friends easily; his open and humorous approach to life would take him a long way, she knew. Hermann's business was in good hands. The men liked Bruce, women too. He was already courting a young girl of the town and would soon turn nineteen.

Through that winter, Archie McLachlan made a habit of stopping by Gertrude Munro's house to chat. At first it was about once a month, then twice a month, and, by the time the wild cherry trees bloomed with their blossomed branches almost sweeping the ground, this bristly farmer was knocking on her door every week.

Whether it be rain or shine, she thought, wondering what his final purpose would be. Bruce teased her unmercifully. He knew about the consequences of courting because he and his young lady had been married at Christmas. Gertrude gave them the two upstairs bedrooms, and young Mrs. Munro went into a frenzy of decorating and furnishing the whole upstairs of the house. Gertrude smiled to herself, she's a real woman. I wonder what's wrong with me that I'm not like that. But she enjoyed having this bossy little thing around the house. Her name was Priscilla, and she and her young husband spent much of their time laughing and teasing, then quite early in the evening, chasing each other upstairs into their private, now elegantly adorned, suite, and closing the door with a bang.

Gertrude had her own bossiness inside her which she became determined to finally unveil to Archie. It was the problem of the body odor. In May, the produce business was booming. She couldn't say the same of her school. Two of the white mothers had threatened to remove their children if she didn't get rid of the two black boys who had begun their studies two months before. Her reply was polite but curt, "They are your children, so you must make that decision. My decision concerns all my pupils, and I would never turn any one of them away for any reason at all, whether it be their color or the texture of their hair, or even for their behavior, because my teaching involves helping them to behave well." Gertrude had never deeply considered the existence of the enslavement of African people in the southern states, or in fact of free people of color. If anyone had asked her opinion of slavery, she would have firmly answered that she believed in the law. What she had always dwelt on was the treatment of slaves, or servants, as she and many other white owners termed them. All those of the "lower orders," both slave and free, should always be treated with charity in mind, but not lawlessness.

However, the two women removed their children midst threats to talk to the sheriff and even to have her school closed down. That night, Gertrude wept, both in sorrow and in anger; so, when Archie arrived, late the next afternoon, she determined that it would be a good time to talk to him about cleanliness. She needed to lash out at someone, about anything. She knew him well enough by now, so she thought. As she opened the door, he seemed to be in a cheerful mood, and, if that mood continued during his visit, he might be more cooperative upon hearing her advice. However, here was a surprise: as he entered the parlor, her olfactory glands searched the air and told her that the little cloud of odor had vanished, well not completely gone, but much less apparent. Oh dear, how could she approach him on this subject now?

"Mr. McLachlan, I am certainly pleased to see you looking so happy and bright this morning." That was all she could manage to say. It was disappointing to find that her introductory topic and the words she had arranged in her mind were no longer appropriate. She couldn't say, oh by the way, you usually have a bad smell and it is lovely that you don't have that today. He took off his hat and laid it on the window seat, then turned to face her. He was smiling, and his hair was brushed carefully down, looking more manageable.

"Mistress Munro, please sit down, because I have something important to say, and if I delay, I may not have the courage to say it." Archie spoke in a rush of nervousness, his eyes scanning around the room, his hands smoothing his shirt. They both sat down. "Mistress Munro, you know that I have a successful plantation down the river and a small turpentine production as well. I feed and provide shelter for about twenty-five slaves who help me with the field and forest work and keep my house clean and cook for me. But there is one thing that I lack and would like to have."

It was dawning on Gertrude exactly what was on his mind. "Yes, Mr. McLachlan, and what is that?" she uttered in her most innocent tones. In fact, in recent months, bombarded with much teasing from Bruce, she had already allowed suspicions to enter her thinking.

"I lack a wife, a woman to help me to soften up the place, to complete my ambition of creating a well-run plantation with a family. And I do believe you are just the person to make my life complete. So, if you be willing to take me on, you will find me a positive and generous man. We have had good conversations together at the market and here at your house, and lately I have come to the knowledge that you would make me a fine wife."

Gertrude was not startled by the nature of this proposal; it was similar to that which Hermann Spencer had tendered to her and her father six years back. No mention of wild love or happiness for her had been part of that offer either. However, she suspected that this man was quite a different being from Hermann; in fact, he seemed to even have more passion in him. Well...she wasn't sure of that. She thought of Bruce and Priscilla and their great love and happiness together. She sat with her hands in her lap, head down, thinking. Finally, she looked up; Archie's face indicated anxiety. He sat forward on the chair and reached for her hand, the very first physical contact the two had experienced during the past year. His hand was dry and rough, but also warm. She smiled. He smiled. She began to soften.

"Mr. McLachlan, I am deeply honored by your proposal and am quite surprised by your asking me to be your wife..."

Archie's face changed, his mouth turned down, registering a slight annoyance, "Why surprised? Why did you think I kept knocking on your door all these months? Just to eat biscuits and drink tea? No, I've been planning this a long time, but always fearful you'd turn me down, and is that what you're going to say to me now?" He turned his head and looked out the window. "I'd have said it on that first day if I hadn't had the fear, so is it yes or no?"

Gertrude was not pleased by his cross words and impatient look. "Mr. McLachlan, you do not need to send cross words my way. And do you not want to say that you have enjoyed my company while consuming that uninteresting tea and biscuits?"

"Well, yes, ma'am, isn't that what I just said? I have enjoyed your company and our conversations." He took his hand back.

"I would prefer not to say yay or nay today," she said, folding her hands in her lap again. "Today I will say thank you and I am honored that you are putting your trust in me to be mistress of your plantation. I would like a period of two weeks to consider whether Bruce is now mature enough to run our business and will also investigate the workings of my own heart with regard to our marriage. Also, whether enough time of my widowhood has elapsed before I embark on a second conjugal contract. I shall speak with my pastor and my maker and will give you your answer in exactly two weeks. So, will you please to return here on the first day of June?" She spoke with strict formality while looking straight and seriously in his eye.

Archie stood up and gave her a mocking bow. "Well, madam, I shall await your answer, with much anticipation and hopes. And I regret if I have offended you. Your tea and biscuits are excellent." He gave her a small smile, turned, donned his hat and walked out. She stood there shaking her head in bewilderment. She would talk to her father. She would indeed talk to her minister at St. Michaels. She would search her soul. She would search for clues that God was guiding her. Gertrude had two weeks in which to hear God's mission for her. If she didn't hear it, she would not marry Archie McLachlan; if she did, she would go.

Chapter 5

That evening, she told Bruce about the marriage proposal, and he immediately laughed. "No, Bruce, this is not a laughing matter; this is considering a matter for the rest of my life. My question for you is: can you now manage the business without me, and can Priscilla run the house? Would you both like to stay in the house and take care of it for me, and take care of Aurelia and her family?"

Bruce became unusually serious, "Why, Gertie," he said, "When you marry, remember, everything you own will become Archie McLachlan's property, including Hermann's slave family. For instance, money given to Priscilla by her father before our marriage became mine. So now, I must hand it back to her whenever she asks, and that was the agreement sworn to between the two of us because she thought the law to be so unfair. But Archie mayn't do that for you—he may keep it and not let you have any, ever."

"Oh dear, so that is definitely a reason to turn him down. I might say no to his offer, knowing that. On the other hand, Brucie," she put her hand on his arm and with a sweet smile, "you could do something wonderful for me. I could sign over to you the house and all my business assets and the rents that father gave me as my dower."

"Wait," cried Bruce, "Gertie, am I to be trusted with all this?"

Gertrude laughed, "Yes, of course you are to be trusted. You both can continue living in this house. You're here anyway, and you already run the business and you will take good care of Aurelia and Hubert and their children. I know in my heart and soul that you will. You can make out a will saying that when you die, these properties and my share of the business will go to my children, if I have any, then to your children, with a dower, of course, to Priscilla. Would that work? We'll talk to our brother Edward and see what the law says. In the meantime, if I have need of money, you will give me from time to time as much as I need from my agreed-upon share of the business proceeds. We shall still be equal business partners in our minds, if not on paper."

"All right, sister," he answered, "we'll see. But now, before any of this is done, and definitely before you make your decision, I shall ride down to the Inveraray Plantation, have a visit with Archie, take a look around, and see if it's suitable for my sister. I shall go tomorrow."

"Bruce, you are my dearest brother, and we can work together like this far into the future. But, by the way, you must talk to Priscilla about her treatment of Aurelia. She is not always polite and considerate to that hard working and very dear woman. It's 'Aurelia, do this, do that' even for little things that she should do for herself. I'm fearful that this could get worse as she grows older. It might could be better for me to retain ownership of that family. We'll see."

Bruce looked at the floor and muttered, "Gertie, she gets that from her mother, she thinks it's normal, and I apologize for her. I'll remind her from time to time that in our family we have been taught to treat our slaves right; despite slaves in other families being kicked around like dogs. We all tend to use the word *servant*" instead of *slave,* even though we own them head to toe, maybe somewhat hypocritical, don't you think?"

Gertrude looked at her brother quizzically. "Well yes, I reckon so. The custom of slavery is part of our way of life. It's difficult to imagine how we'd manage without it, but we can certainly recognize their humanity and treat them accordingly. I remember our beloved mother saying that."

The next morning, Bruce took off with cheerful demeanor, riding his new black mare towards the Inveraray Plantation. But, when he returned in the late afternoon, Gertrude noticed a change in mood. She looked upon her brother's solemn face, and furrowed brow as he dismounted and handed the reins to Hubert. The weather had turned to rain and wind; and it was obvious that Bruce had experienced neither a pleasant visit with Archie McLachlan nor comfortable ride home, with rain from the sky and mud underfoot.

"Gertrude, my dear and honored sister," said he in strangely highfalutin' tones, taking a seat on one of the window chairs. "I bring you mixed tidings of the Inveraray Plantation. In fact, I am puzzled as to what kind of report to give you on Archie McLachlan's farm. I want to think it'll be a happy place for you to start a new life, but from my observations, I'm not so sure about that"

Gertrude scrutinized him carefully, somewhat alarmed by this serious expression on a face that was usually wrinkled up with smiles. "How so, Brucie?"

"Where do I begin?" he replied. "The place is a mess. And forgive me, but the overweening smell of the place will remind you of the cess pool over near the little river in town. I am a little bit concerned about Archie's slaves. I didn't see any rows of cabins, the kind you see on most country plantations, so I am assuming that the women probably have quarters in the house or around the back. I was not able to conjure up in my imagination where the men might sleep. And I saw no water pump; thus, I suppose the slave women carry buckets from the creek which runs down behind the house, thence into the river. When I arrived, a child of about six came out to take my horse, but my bright and frisky Flora was too much for her. I had to help her lead the horse over to a mangy looking barn and paddock. She told me her name was Paddy, and upon my query about the whereabouts of the master, she said they were all in the fields working this morning, including George who she explained oversees horses and dogs. The main house appeared unkempt and in poor repair, but a few carpentry jobs would cure the broken steps and window frames.

"Of course, it was the owner himself that I wished to talk to, and I think you'll be better pleased to hear what I have to say about that. I walked out to the field that lay near the river, a scenic vista of trees along the water striking my vision as I walked. Far up the field, I saw a line of people—men and woman—bent over, then standing up, again bent, then standing, planting I presumed, or perhaps hoeing, and there was your Mr. McLachlan working alongside his slaves, and it seemed shouting at these slaves all the while. I opened the gate, stepped inside, and closed it behind me. I shouted and waved at Archie. He looked up, waved back, spoke a few words to one of the slaves, then turned to a very tall woman, who said something back to him. I could not hear the nature of these words but assumed they were not gentle or friendly because he pointed his finger at her and yelled something, I couldn't hear what. He came running down the field and acted very polite and glad to see me. Curiously, he seemed apologetic about having to work in the field himself. I assured him that was a sign of a good master, a good farmer, but he disagreed, explaining that if he didn't oversee the workers, they wouldn't work. 'Morose and lazy, most of the time, you gotta watch them every minute, and they'll not do a speck of work without punishment. But, what can I do for you, young fella?' I thought that label to be somewhat pompous, because he's still young himself. I didn't like to ask what the punishments might be, but I could guess. And, about his insults against the slaves, I couldn't truly be too critical. It sounded much like the complaints of most of the farmers we work with. I wanted to make the same comment I often lay upon them: why don't you give them rewards for their hard work? But I wished not to become engaged in an argument.

"Mr. McLachlan then showed me around the place, while I pretended that I was seeking land to buy, and did he have any acreage to spare. He said no but led me around, anyway, seeming proud of his 'plantation.' The yard behind the house seemed well cared for, as well as the much-trodden path to the creek. I saw only the close-in couple of fields, and they were well cultivated. But surprisingly, it was the turpentine trees that stood out as the best organized and the cleanest project that I witnessed. 'I have a woman who manages the turpentine business. She apparently had experience in her past life with these pine trees, but she's working in the field today. The sap runs down the tree by itself all right I suppose,' said Archie, giving me the impression that he leaves all that in her competent hands.

I met and greeted a slave with a white birthmark on half her face. She was bent over a large cooking pot set over a fire near the barn, while at the same time watching over a small group of children; although little Paddy, for all appearances, was taking care of the young'uns herself. I greeted with cheerful voice this cooking lady and complimented her on the wonderful smell of her cooking, but no raised eyes acknowledged my greeting, only a faint smile. An offer to me of a taste of beans on a half shell, handed over with a sideways outstretched arm, head still hanging down, was the only greeting. I thanked her profusely, which thanks were ignored. She wore a ragged and dirty scarf around her head and a gray cotton dress of similar kind. I finally peeked into the hay barn and knew by the rubble of straw beds and cast away dirty utensils that my initial glance was true—this was the living quarter for the men and perhaps a few women too. I didn't like to further question the master about sleeping locations because he laughingly snatched me away from that muddled place, punched my arm softly, and tried to make light of it. 'Well, Mr. Munro, you can see this is a bachelor's lair, and I admit that I am in great need of your sister's female touch, please tell her that I am greatly looking forward to her presence here, both for a thorough cleanup, and for help with the female slaves. There's one who's been trouble from the first day, but she's also our expert with the turpentine trees so I'm loath to sell her.'

"Gertie, my beloved and much respected sister, if you say yes to Archie McLachlan, you will have a job to do, a very big job—scrubbing, painting, digging for underground water, and pondering on appropriate quarters for the slaves, just to name a few of the most obvious needs, needs that cry out, nay, that roar like a lion to any who might wander up that entrance road. Add to that, you might want to study on the spiritual needs of these people and Archie himself. He seems a nice enough fellow but lacks the instinct for simple kindness to others of lower position. He undoubtedly never had a teacher on the words of Jesus that were taught to us by our parents. So, your loving heart would be welcome, and my conclusion is: he knows that.

"I was happy indeed to say my good-byes and mount Flora for the ride home. Archie had one more comment as I was on the point of leaving. He told me that he understood I was not looking for land to buy, but that I had been sent by you to check out his place. I replied that he was right as to my purpose, but wrong about the source. I had decided to do this on my own."

Gertrude listened to her brother without a word, and at the end, only a "Thank you, brother, you have helped me immeasurably with this report." In fact, instead of discouraging her, this information had emboldened, even inspired, her. The missionary spirit, which had ever been part of her thinking, now strengthened and encouraged her towards saying yes to Archie McLachlan. Yes, these people will be the humanity around me, the humanity spoken of by Mother on her deathbed. Thus, the ideal would triumph over the practical for Gertrude, her mind being easily caught up with her own interpretation of situations with which she had no day-to-day experience. Bruce's story had created in her veins a rush of excitement and in her mind a conviction that this would be the life's work she had been seeking.

As she had guessed, missionary work in Africa would be far beyond her reach, but right here in Culbreth County, there was much work to be done, both regarding Archie himself and the slaves.

Bruce had one more question that evening. "Sister, have you ever heard that Archie once killed a slave, in the river south of town?"

"No," she answered, looking up, concerned.

"Well, I did hear it briefly, in secret, from a man known for his lies and hyperboles. He's from that lousy Buck family. He said it to me in the process of trying to get out of a debt he owed me. I asked around, but no one else had ever known of it. So, I thought of it no more."

The next day Gertrude crossed the river to talk to her father. James looked at her closely, "My dearest Gertrude, am I to understand that Bruce has determined this man may not be the best husband for you? Whereas, I have always observed you to be a person of the highest moral and practical habits."

"Yes, that is true, Father, well partly true. Bruce didn't say I should not marry him. He just believes his farm is not the best of places, but I could possibly help him make it better, cleaner. I could work with him in bringing the farm to greater success." Her father raised his left eyebrow and cocked his head a little to the side. "And have you thought carefully of the fact that beyond all your ideals and wishes for the good of mankind, you must share a bed with this man?" He did flush a bit and concentrated on his shoes as he said these words, Scots not being given to discussion of private matters.

Gertrude also blushed and felt uncomfortable but answered clearly, "Yes, of course, Father, I have spent many an hour pondering that question, and I believe I can manage it. I even find him attractive in an odd way, but that's hard to explain."

"Yes, my dear, of course you can manage it because you are a queen. I would like to know, though, that a small ragamuffin man like him will acknowledge you as queen of the soul and will bow to your superiority. I would like to know that he will not spend his waking moments trying to bring you down to his lowly level nor try to convince you that women are inferior."

Gertrude looked into her father's rugged sun-darkened face, saw the little smile that she loved, and knew that the deal was done. She teased him about his acceptance of society's hierarchies. "All right, daughter, you've got me on that one," he replied. "The hierarchies here are different from those in Scotland, but they do exist."

"One more question, Father. Have you heard a rumor that Archie once killed a man?
In the side river over there?"

"No, child, never heard of that one."

"All right then. Thank you, dear Father." Then, thinking of beds, Gertrude wanted to ask him who the pretty light brown girl was who had answered the door and who obviously was keeping the house so spic and span of late, but decided to save that question for her brothers. She embraced her father, peeked into the bedroom to say a few words and kiss her grandfather Hamish, who no longer had the strength to leave his bed, then hurried home to prepare for Archie's visit. He was due in a few days.

The day came and no Archie. Hmmm, said Gertrude to herself. I've spent time and thought on this matter, and he can't even arrive on the appointed day. Perhaps he's miffed that Bruce came snooping around at his place. So, until the doorbell rang the next morning, she became quite anxious. Sleep evaded her that night. The expression on Archie's face when she opened the door was difficult to read. Apprehensive? Yes. Suspicious? Yes. Happy? No. And his first words did not reassure her. "Well, Miz Munro, so have you at long last made up your mind?"

"Mr. McLachlan, why did you not appear yesterday? That was the appointed day."

"Well, Madam, I thought I'd give you an extra night to consider our future. You seemed to be uncertain as to the answer, and if it's no, then I'll be swiftly on my way. And, by the way, did your brother tell you not to marry me?"

She looked at him, saw the false pride on his face and heard the sarcasm in his voice, but all she could say was "Oh I see, please come in." Over his shoulder, she saw the rain begin to fall and the dogwood branches to bend. A little voice in her mind told her yet again that this was a difficult, self-protective man indeed. She was on the brink at that moment of telling him no. But she thought again of the glum and gross discomfort of the Inveraray slaves reported by Bruce and their apparently immoral living conditions. "Come and sit here, Mr. McLachlan."

He sat in his usual place with the movements of his body and his sighs telling Gertrude that he was in high suspense and irritation. "Mr. McLachlan, I have decided to say yes to your proposal."

Archie jumped up, grabbed her hand, and kissed it. All the hesitancy and sarcasm vanished. "I am overjoyed that you will join me at Inveraray Plantation. You will be welcomed by me and by the animals and by the slaves. You will bring happiness to our home." Her heart was touched, and she laughed too. Now he became full of plans, but she bade him sit down and listen.

"I do have a few demands," she said quietly, taking a seat opposite him. "I will want to be in charge of the female slaves and to make some changes to their living conditions. It has been difficult for you, a man alone for six years, to understand how to arrange things for your servants, and I can help you to do that. I grew up helping the slaves on my father's farm. And it will be necessary to have regular and ample meals for all concerned. I would like to oversee all that. And one more thing, I would like to wait four months before our wedding—for me to make the plans, to post the banns at church, and to arrange for the minister to be here." She stopped and looked at him. His face had fallen, but there was no evidence of anger.

Archie replied slowly and carefully, "I like to oversee my own place, it has always been thus. However, it will be all right, yes, all right."

There was indeed much to do, and Gertrude went into a whirl of activity—clothing for the slaves, stores of food, cooking pots, blankets, wedding plans, and very important—sessions with her brother Edward, the lawyer, regarding her assets. She also had to close down her school and apologize to the parents for this desertion. However, one of her knitting friends said she would take it over and try her hand at teaching. Four months was barely enough time to complete everything on her list. Archie stopped by the house once a week; they chatted, talking about his plantation; he courted her, putting on his best manners, said he wanted her to be happy at Inveraray, and kissed her both in greeting and in parting each time. For the kisses he had to reach up an inch. Gertrude did not divulge anything to him about her conversations with her lawyer brother; neither did she mention his body odor.

Early in the morning of her wedding day, Gertrude had a nightmare that turned into a dream of great blessing and affirmation. She was sinking in a muddy bog, struggling to get out, crying out for help, her clothes and skin covered in mud. Archie stood on the bank of this shallow pond surrounded by cypress trees, laughing and dancing around, clapping his hands. Why wouldn't he throw a rope to pull her out, but no, he seemed joyful in her desperation. Unexpectedly, there appeared a shaft of light from the sky. It encased a bright angel clothed all in white, and this vision extended its long arm all the way to her hand and pulled her out of the quicksand, out onto dry land, whereupon the shaft and the angel disappeared. Gertrude awoke in great confusion. She knelt beside the bed and thanked God for this message of encouragement for her new mission; although she did wonder why Archie seemed to wish her to be buried in the marsh. Was this a prophecy as well as an encouragement? Or was it a warning?

The wedding was small and simple with only her family members present. Gertrude had many friends and acquaintances in Culbreth County, but the difficulty of attempting to choose among them while not hurting feelings was too great, so she let the word out this would be a ceremony and celebration for family only. Still, there was a crowd. Her mother's family from across the river—aunts and uncles and cousins, plus her father, her brothers and their wives and children. Only Grandfather had to be left behind because of his frail health. One of the cousins came all the way from Fayetteville, a city lately raised to prominence, not only by hosting the state convention which ratified the new

Federal Constitution, but also by putting in a bid to be the new North Carolina capital city. This cousin Jeffrey, at Gertrude's house after the wedding ceremony, was full of news telling that the bid had been denied and a site in the forests of Wake County chosen—near the upper reaches of the Neuse River. He had heard it would be named Raleigh and assured all assembled that plans for building the brand-new city were being drawn. Most of the men jumped into the conversation, boasting they had read all about this in their own city's newspaper and expressing their disappointment that the state's capital would no longer be near the coast.

Gertrude heard these snippets of male conversation as she moved around the parlor, helping Priscilla and Aurelia with the food. She noticed that Priscilla and Aurelia were working together with greater harmony than previously. She had forgotten to talk to Priscilla, so Bruce must have had that talk with his wife, which eased her mind considerably. After all, Bruce would now be the official owner of that slave family. She looked around to find Archie and saw him standing not far from Bruce, but apart, listening to the conversation but not participating. She saw her father approach her new husband and attempt to make conversation. Archie became uncomfortable, gave some fake guffaws, and wouldn't look at James, who eventually moved on. She had already seen that Archie had a difficult time forming friendships with men, perhaps fueled by his attitude of rivalry and fear of being beaten in competition. But he had resentment against women too, because of his mother. Oh well, she didn't want to think about that right now.

"Mr. McLachlan, I do believe it to be time to start our journey, before it becomes too dark." The cart was already loaded and the horse hitched up. Hubert had been busy while the white folks were celebrating. So, Gertrude said her good-byes. With tears and with expressions of gratitude and regret, she circled the room midst her many kinfolks, while receiving from them their comments of how much she would be missed. She had many times been told that the family relied on her good sense and kindness, and these words were used again by the company assembled. She glanced at Archie, saw he was becoming impatient, resentful even, so she took his arm and descended the steps beside him. Beside the cart, Hubert and Aurelia were waiting to say good-bye along with their children. She hugged the children and Aurelia and shook Hubert's hand. "Yes ma'am, we're gonna miss you," he said. Aurelia began to weep quietly.

"But you will be in good hands, and I will see you from time to time," Gertrude assured them, as she rushed to get up in the cart. Archie was about to pull away without her, muttering that he had never seen such carryings on and chatterings in his life. Settling beside him, she admonished him, "Why Mr. McLachlan, I can't believe you're such an impatient man" and glanced one more time at her friend, the great dark river. But, looking forward, she remembered her mission—hard work to be done, slaves to be fed and comforted, a difficult man to persuade. She reminded herself that the river would yet be with her, in larger form, at the Inveraray Plantation.

The journey was slow. She studied the profile view of her new husband's face and smiled as he placed his weather-beaten hand on her knee and caressed it. She liked that; although she wondered if perhaps it was an unnatural or feigned gesture, neither spontaneous nor loving. She looked at him again trying to find an answer, but none was to be had. Then, sitting up straight and watching the surrounding woods, Gertrude took her mind back to the fields and forest of her childhood, the animals and birds that had been the subject of study by herself and her brothers. This would be a big part of her new life.

Archie's voice broke into her thoughts, "You are very quiet, wife, you should not be thinking so much. You should be talking and wondering about your life as my wife at Inveraray." He turned his head and gave her his odd crooked smile.

Gertrude laughed, "Well, I am indeed thinking about my new life, and before that truly starts, I must say something to you that is important, but I don't want to hurt your feelings." She looked carefully at his face, which turned to her again.

"Yes?"

"Mr. McLachlan, do you have a shower bath set up behind your house?"

"No, indeed I do not."

"Well, I will help you to set one up. We will put up some boards around it." She knew now that she must work carefully around this subject.

"The slaves are too lazy to work on such a project, but you can try if you like." He gave the horse a lash with the whip and the cart jerked forward.

"Yes, I do like because it will always be necessary to keep our bodies clean," Gertrude spoke quietly with her head bent slightly to one side, her hands folded primly in her lap.

"Who are you talking about, woman, you, or myself?" Archie was definitely getting irritated, but she hadn't even mentioned the real problem yet.

"Mr. McLachlan," she began weakly, "First, I don't like to be called *woman*, and second I must tell you that sometimes it is you who gives off an offensive smell. However, I will say no more about it since you are offended, and I'll leave it to you to think about it." She was hoping that would end the conversation for a few minutes, but she could see a cloud pass over Archie's face, which he turned towards her with an angry demeanor.

"I suppose your previous husband, that old Hermann Spencer, smelled like a rose every morning. He had money coming to him, I'm sure of that, not from his own toil, but from the work of others. No sir, he was never out in the fields working alongside the darkies, sweating to get them to put their shoulders to the plough, bending over to do the work himself. No sir, he could afford to be a soft man covered in sweet perfume."

Gertrude's lip trembled. With a tight, hard gaze, she turned and confronted her new husband. Any witness to this ugly scene, unfamiliar with the woman, might have expected an immediate blow to his face. "No, Mr. McLachlan, my husband arrived here a poor man and spent his life in service to his neighbors." Her eyes looked back at the road ahead, and she spoke no more. Archie let out a sneering laugh and slapped the reins on the horse's rear.

In a few minutes, in spite of her continued silence, Archie began talking about something else relating to Gertrude's former husband and his supposed fortune, "Now, Miz McLachlan, there is another matter about your first husband which I wish to ask: I am supposing that he left all his money to you? And where will we find that fortune?"

Gertrude's heart did go pitta-patta for a few seconds as she answered, "He didn't leave much cash of his own, he had his business, his house and the slave family, and I just handed it all straight to Bruce and Priscilla. I didn't want to be worrying about the business when I left town, and Aurelia and Hubert favored strongly to stay with the house. I also wanted Bruce to come into his own in the business; he knows it and will do well with it. I couldn't see how any of Hermann's belongings would be useful to me in my new life."

With a cry of anger, Archie turned to look at his new wife, "You mean you did not think of your husband as rightful owner of your properties? You didn't consult with me about this? Did you not think I would have an opinion on your belongings? On your properties? And now it all belongs to your brother? And you would consult those slaves before me?"

Gertrude did not want to continue this conversation with Archie. She only chuckled to herself and drew a sigh of relief. She knew at that moment that she had done the right thing. She confirmed also at that moment the major reason Archie had sought her for his wife. There was an element of surprise in her eyes as she looked at him. It struck her mind again that she had never before encountered a man so openly selfish and grasping—like a weasel? Well, like most animals; although humans, under the tutelage of God, felt shame. Perhaps, not this one.

So, she quietly assured him that she had thought solely of Bruce, Priscilla, and Aurelia when she signed those papers; it had never occurred to her that he would have his eye on Hermann's properties, nor that he might be marrying her in order to claim these properties. Believing that Hermann's material goods had never really been hers, she continued, in severe tones, "Those goods certainly never belonged to you either, and I never want to discuss this matter again. It is my business and mine alone; it should never be a source of friction between us." As she spoke these words, she silently apologized to God for telling blatant lies, and yes, she understood they were not white lies because their purpose was to protect herself.

The newly married couple continued down the road in silence, and as they turned into the Inveraray drive and approached the house and other buildings, Gertrude began to smell the powerful odor and to sense that glum, unhappy mood described by Bruce. The new mistress of Inveraray surveyed the barns, the house, and the ragged, dejected slaves standing around a cooking pot. She saw the broken steps and porch rail on the house and the poor condition of the hay barn. She remarked to herself upon the lack of cabins for the slaves and the lack of water pumps. Dear God, this will be the test of my life; I now fully understand the reason you sent me to this mission. She felt she was entering an underground lair, a burrow fit only for animals.

Chapter 6

The Inveraray farmstead had been built, then abandoned, by settlers during the Revolutionary War. It was not known where that family had gone. Perhaps, as someone had heard, they had headed west, even into Kentucky with Daniel Boone along the Wilderness Road. That early family by the river had built the house and three barns: the large hay barn where the slaves still lived, a smaller tool shed on the other side of the house, and a third up the slope on the edge of the main field that bordered the river. That third shed would eventually be used for drying tobacco.

When Archie McLachlan brought his wife to Inveraray in the late summer season, the place looked much as it had when he first arrived six or seven years before. The only difference consisted of two new fields stretching out behind the house, which had been cleared by the muscle and sweat of his slaves, fueled by his whip and by their suppressed rage. These fields were dotted with decaying stumps and little forest startups encouraged to sprout by this sudden gift of sun on the soil, presumably not seen for hundreds of years. Autumn was not yet appearing in the woods when the horse and cart entered Inveraray's long driveway. Green leaves still hung drooping on the hardwood trees, and the browned pine needles were still awaiting the autumn push by the new green shoots.

Soola sat with Adam, leaning against a tree outside the barn, while he tickled her neck with a pine needle. She laughed and pushed him away. Judith was leaning over the great iron pot, stirring occasionally, while Tabitha ran around playing with the band of children. Three other women, two of whom held babies, formed a second group at the other side of the barn. Soola was pleased they remained separate because these were more recent arrivals, not part of the original group of Massa Archie's slaves. She certainly did not want any newcomer challenging her position as leader of the slaves. In fact, these three newer women, who had survived their first four years at Inveraray, had apparently soon learned the respective positions of each woman slave —Soola chief turpentine worker, and spokesperson for them all, Judith chief cook, and Tabitha chief caretaker of the children. These jobs protected them from full-time canal and field work; although Massa Archie frequently used both as threats, especially with Soola. The work of the three was mostly in the fields. They all understood the nature of their other job, in fact the main job of women—childbearing. They had been only moderately successful at that.

Suddenly, Adam sat up straight, "Whoa, who's acomin'? Must be our lovin' Massa."

Soola jumped to her feet and walked through the trees to the driveway, came back and assured him he was right, but he could leave off the loving. However, he could add something—a white woman was with the Massa. When they heard Soola's pronouncement, all the slaves looked up and watched intently as the horse and cart pulled up in front of the house. Little George ran out to grab the reins and talk to the horse, while Archie jumped down and started up the steps, seeming to have forgotten to help his wife, which didn't surprise those watching. Soola stepped forward and offered to help her descend from the cart, for which the new mistress expressed gratitude and smiled. She then called out to her husband, "Mr. McLachlan, will you not show me to my room, please?" Soola had been taking mental notes that the new mistress had large, rough hands with a purplish tint and that her lip drew up on one side when she smiled.

Archie stopped, turned, appeared to be embarrassed, came back and said, "Yes, I shall show you to our room, which we'll share." He turned and told the men standing around to carry her bags inside.

The white woman looked at him with irritation and replied, "No, I would like my own bedroom, please, that is what I have been accustomed to for many years."

"Well in that case, Soola, take the mistress upstairs and show her the back room behind mine." The Massa's voice immediately revealed his disappointment and resentment.

Soola was pleased to lead her up the stairs with Archie following. Looking back, she noticed the mistress surveying with curiosity the bare and paint-chipped walls, the broken bannister, while sniffing the musty smell of this house. She heard, too, Massa Archie say in an undertone that he hoped he would be permitted to visit her. To which the mistress replied in a clear voice that he would be admitted if he cleaned himself up and got rid of the bad odor.

Soola could hardly suppress a giggle as she opened the door to this back bedroom. The smell of mildew overpowered them, and as Gertrude touched the bed covers, a cloud of dust flew into the air. "Oh My," said the new mistress, "I'll be sneezing and coughing all night, Mr. McLachlan."

To which he replied with heavy sarcasm, "Well, ma'am, then you'll have to come into my room, I'm right next door."

She didn't answer but turned to Soola who stood at the door, "Soola, I am your new mistress, my name is Gertrude, and tomorrow, will you help me clean up this mess?"

Soola noted immediately the soft tone, the polite words, and the kindness in her eye. At the same time, she knew that Massa Archie would seek revenge for the insult about his lack of cleanliness and about the rooms.. Indeed, he replied before Soola could open her mouth, "Soola is our chief turpentine worker, and she will be busy all day tomorrow with the turpentine men, who won't know what to do without her. In another month they'll be preparing to close the trees for the winter. She will have no time for housework. And the other women all have their assignments decided on by me, so you'll have to clean up the room yourself." He turned and clomped off down the stairs.

Oh Lord, thought Soola, what kind of marriage is this gonna be? Not happy, I'm sure. Nothing this man does or says brings happiness. She looked at Miz Gertrude as if the woman needed guidance, but the new mistress just smiled, thanked her, and assured her she could manage. Yes, there was that lip drawing up again. Soola couldn't wait to get back to the barn and tell her friends about this not-so-meek woman.

So, she returned to her friends full of information. And with the three new women and the children and some of the men gathered round, she told what she had seen and heard about Miz Gertrude, while assuring them that they could not plan on her friendship yet, only watch and wait. There was no guarantee that she could continue to stand up to her husband, he would probably start beating her, the same as he did the slaves. As for right now, they must carry the tray with two dinners up to the big house and hope to get acquainted with the mistress on the morrow. Soola told Judith to be sure to give them a generous portion of the pulled pork, something that the slaves were only allowed every other Sunday. Soola remembered the beatings and hullabaloo raised by Massa Archie when a few years back he had discovered they were sneaking pieces of his hog meat. I think that was right before Mittie and Ibo ran away, she recalled to herself. She and Judith had suffered the heftiest share of the punishments. And the memory of that scene arose in her mind—the master beating Judith with a stick until she, Soola, had rushed at him, grabbing the stick out of his hand, then he, lifting another stick against her, beating her shoulders until Adam charged in to her rescue. Her true love for Adam had started at that moment; although she remembered there had been something about his eyes on her from the start that had stirred her heart. The morning after that horror, Mittie and Ibo were gone, run away to the swamp camps most likely.

The next morning, Sunday, after the arrival of Miz Gertrude, Soola told Tabitha that she would stay around the barn for the day to help her with the children, "There's not much more for me to do with the turpentine til next month, and us three must show the mistress around the place, and she must know that me and you are with child. Because, girl, there ain't much time left for me, and yours will be comin' along soon after, and maybe she can help us with the births. Massa's out in the field with the men, so he won't care."

Tabitha, always fearful, timid, looked nervously around and adjusted her dirty head scarf. She said she hoped so, didn't want the same thing to happen to her what happened to Suzannah. Soola said she didn't feel fear, that life was hell and she wouldn't care if she had to meet Mr. Death. Tabitha said she bet the new mistress was just as mean as Massa Archie, because who but a mean or simple-minded woman would be with him. At that very moment, Gertrude appeared through the trees and greeted them with a cheery "Good morning, ladies." It seemed she hadn't heard that last comment. The crows had set up such a chatter and raucous warning on the approach of a stranger that the women could hardly hear each other. The birds flapped their wings and withdrew in alarm high up into the tree tops. There they sat in a row looking down at the people.

The women peeped up in surprise, then all eyes except Soola's were quickly cast down. Soola and Tabitha gave sullen replies, Judith said nothing. So as not to be looking at the mistress, Judith worked hard at washing the wooden spoons and shells that they used for eating. But Soola stared straight at her and saw that Gertrude was wearing a blue, buttoned up dress today, that her back was straight, and her brown hair pulled tight back into a bun at the nape of her neck. Only the rubbing together of her rough hands betrayed a slight nervousness; her face showed an open, friendly demeanor. Soola wondered whether she had spent the night in her husband's room. Damn, what would it be like to have that man touch you? They waited.

But not for long for Gertrude spoke up, "I am your new mistress, and you can call me Miss Gertrude if that suits you well." Soola considered this asking any opinion from them to be a good sign. Gertrude continued, "I would like to know your names and who all these children belong to so that I can become acquainted with all the families here on the farm."

The slaves of Inveraray had not once, since the first day here, heard a white person talk to them in tones of respect, so they remained silent, expectant, but still mistrusting. Then Judith mumbled, "Ma'am, Soola is our leader, and she will tell you."

Soola laughed out loud, "All right, Miz Gertrude, I'll tell you what I know, but not what I don't know and there be plenty of that." Gertrude smiled. The people began to relax.

Soola launched into a bold speech, bold, she knew, because it was from a slave's outlook, "Well, Mistress, it's like this. Among the women here, we have two groups. There's us three right here—me, Tabitha, and Judith. We were the first ones here near seven years ago. We have counted the years as time has gone by; we count them by the number of hot weather seasons and keep the count with twigs in a small pot. We're not sure of the months, but we have always watched the moon and tried to figure that out too and put hickory nuts in the pot for them but then we don't always see the moon. Now, this year Massa Archie has been sticking a sign on a post behind his house that tells us what month and year it is, but I'm the only one that can read, so for most, those signs don't mean nothin' unless I tell them. Now we have three other new women, and they stay to themselves, and we call them One, Two and Three. Massa Archie brought them up from Wilmington last year so the men wouldn't be fighting so much over female partners. And the children, we have five of them in our group, two boys and three girls have survived, though we had some die in their first year. Now, those two girls are mine, Patty and Mary Alice," she pointed with her long arm to her daughters sitting under a dogwood tree, "Tabitha has Lil Jake, and Judith has Ida, that's her over there. Now we also have George, who spends his time with the animals. He's Massa's favorite, the one you saw yesterday with the horses. It was Phyllis had him, but then she died having another baby who died too, so Tabitha took Lil George in. And now me and Tabitha is both expectin'. And the three women over there, they have two babies, but one is real puny. And, about the men, you'll need to ask them about themselves. They all roam around and act like men if you know what I mean. A lot of the original men who came with us died of fevers, one got snakebit in his heel, and Massa Archie gave one of them such a beating that he never recovered. It took him about three months to die, though we nursed him with care. Then there was Mittie and Ibo, they up and disappeared in the night, and we saw them no more. Miz Gertrude, you have seen Massa Archie's blood hounds and so you know that they didn't go sniffing out for the runaways, and we never saw a paddy- roller bring them back. Not one of us, that I know wanted to follow Ibo and Mittie into them vines and swamps, nor let paddy-rollers get their hands on us, so no one since has tried escaping. We know the miseries here and don't want to go seeking miseries that's unknown." All three women giggled a bit when Soola mentioned the blood hounds; she looked at Gertrude, who appeared to understand the joke. "Oh, and two more folks—The Driver, the one who drove the horses from Wilmington, got shot dead in the river, and our friend Suzannah, she had three babies to die, then she died too sloshing around in the canals that will never be finished. That's why we don't grow rice here. So, you see, Miz Gertrude, Mr. Death has been our everyday companion." Soola threw out all this information fast, with barely enough interruption to take a breath, bringing it to an end with, "So, Mistress, I've told you about our people, the slaves of Invary, and I invite you now to sit down and join us. Judith go in the barn and get that rickety stool."

Judith did what she was told without complaint, and Gertrude sat down, indicating that she would like to hear more about the slain driver. Since Soola said no more and none of the other women ventured to add to her account, Gertrude used this lull to take out Hermann Spencer's gold pocket watch, wind it, apparently note the time, and place it back in her pocket. The slaves watched in fascination; in fact, as soon as her glance moved away from them, they stared at this woman as if at an apparition, perhaps waiting in intense excitement and anxiety for her to divulge what was in her mind. Soola wondered if it would be possible for a white woman to be their friend. She waited, also in silence for once in her life. Mistrust and suspicion of white people was deeply ingrained in her and in the others. But there was a difference—while Soola knew that in most of the slaves the mistrust caused fear, for herself there was no fear.

Gertrude's hand moved up to straighten her hair back, but finding it already straightened, the hand returned to her lap. Her face formed itself into a smile, one that to all present appeared genuine and affectionate, and at last she spoke. "Dear people," she said, "I have looked around this immediate vicinity, the house, the barns, the driveway, the paths. I have seen your meager clothing and your inadequate sleeping quarters, and, I believe, your insufficient food. Also, I am smelling the unpleasant smells of this place every minute. I know we need many changes, and I would like to make a promise to you—all these changes will happen. I see dejection amongst you, and as I sit here making you this promise, I am thinking that in the future, there might be smiles on your faces and hope in your hearts. I will be speaking to my husband about the things we need." The women looked at each other with wide open eyes. Soola told them the meaning of the word *dejection*.

Gertrude removed from her pocket a small piece of paper and a remnant of charcoal stick, but before she had a chance to ask them of their needs, they all heard the heavy footsteps of the master approaching and soon his voice shouting and barging in. "Woman, what are you doing sitting down here with my slaves without my permission. You need not bother yourself with these. They are my business. You need to learn today how things are done around here. I need to tell you what your responsibilities will be."

Most of the women fled, quickly finding some insignificant work to make them look busy, all except Soola, who remained seated, staring at the master. Gertrude stood up straight, "Mr. McLachlan, do not ever again call me 'woman.' I will only answer to 'Mistress. McLachlan,' and yes, I will talk to the servants exactly as I please. How dare you enter like this shouting at me. It is you who need to learn some lessons this very day, and the first one is how I will be treated by you, my husband, how you will speak to me in future." Archie stopped in his tracks, his face flushing pink.

"And furthermore, Mr. McLachlan, I would like some time now before dinner to speak to these six women about our future here together, and, since you would be a hindrance to us in our talking, I would prefer that it be only us women present. And, do you not realize it is Sunday, a day of rest? So please leave us."

Soola knew the master well enough to understand what all this bluster was about. He had wanted to show his wife that he was the high and mighty plantation boss, especially competent and experienced in dealing with his slaves. He's an idiot, a child, she thought, as she had found from the very first day. But here, he's met a woman who will tell him off, tell him what's what. Now I can see that we must try every trick to make her stay and not let her flee back to town. We will be especially helpful to her, and we'll include him in that too, so he'll perhaps be easier and gentler, in fact be influenced by her ways. She looked first to Gertrude then to the master, fascinated by this confrontation. Tabitha and Judith, over by the barn, clutched their children to them and stared at the ground in terror. The surprise was that Massa Archie did not reply. He merely dropped his head, turned, and walked rapidly back to the house, but not before Soola spotted a trembling of his lower lip. Ah yes, she's taking the upper hand, she thought. I think he did pay her a visit last night, or perhaps she paid him a visit, yes that was it.

Gertrude returned to her seat on the stool and waved to the other women to come back and sit with her. She put her hand out and stroked one of the cringing dogs. "One of the first things I will do is teach you how to make soap and at the same time send a message to my friend in town who will help us dig two wells and install pumps. Those two steps will help you to clean yourselves and present a more pleasant and less odorous image to the world." Gertrude's speech was accompanied by intermittent smiles, but still, in order to determine whether this white woman was believable, the slaves kept sneaking glances at Soola, who, always aware of her leadership role, reassured them by saying, "We're listening, Miz Gertrude, we're listening."

The mistress started writing the list on her sheet of paper, and soon Soola couldn't keep her mouth shut. "Mistress, I venture to say that a big thing we need is a better place to sleep. I do not know what's possible, and I know Massa Archie don't never like to spend money, but all of us, men and women, sleeping on the straw ain't right. Where I grew up at the Pine Forest Plantation down the coast, we had cabins, each family had one. Me and my brother and mother were a family." She wanted to go on and tell how nice those cabins were, how Massa Jimmie liked his slaves to be comfortable at night, and even tell how Selma, Massa Jimmie's girlfriend, had the nicest house on the place, and that Selma was a brown skinned beauty, not black like herself. However, she had better sense than to say all that, so she stopped in time. But there was so much to tell this woman, who apparently wanted to hear. She watched as Gertrude wrote "cabins" onto her list, then added quickly that clothing and blankets were needed for the coming cold weather.

There were other ideas that Soola wanted, but she decided to wait until all items on the list were accomplished. The other women had not spoken. With every word put forward by Soola, they had nodded and whispered yes, yes, and even the newcomers, usually intimidated by Soola, had crept in, watching and listening.

When Gertrude McLachlan had written the main needs and ideas, she closed her notebook and stood. She had tears in her eyes. "Perhaps you are wondering why I came here. I shall tell you now that I came here, not only to be wife to Archie McLachlan, although that is true too, but also on a mission to maybe help put right the wrongs that have happened here. I will not quit in my purpose. But don't ever forget that I care about my husband too. And, as your mistress, I shall expect support and respect from all of you in our endeavors and shan't appreciate direct and insolent airs, nor insults against Mr. McLachlan." Her face was serious as she looked at Soola, turned, and walked up towards the house. Soola remained, sitting quietly, wondering about Miz Gertrude and listening to the caroling song of a robin high up in a tree. She had seen a pack of the red-breasted birds all over around the barn yesterday, pecking for the grains that had dropped from the straw last month. The robins' return to these parts always pleased her. She waited anxiously for Adam to return from the fields. Massa Archie had certainly never considered Sunday to be a day of rest.

Chapter 7

Soola awoke early the next morning, glanced at Adam beside her, and rose out of their straw bed in the far back corner of the barn. She was puzzled about the mixed messages she had received from the new mistress. The woman wanted to help them, yes, but also expressed loyalty to her husband, the source of their pain. And yet again, Gertrude had spoken harshly to him and had verbally put him down hard, twice. Of course, she and the other slaves knew how to deal with these unpredictable behaviors of white people, and yet...they had all remarked on the kindness in her eyes and in her smile. Maybe, they needed to watch the expressions of her face and her body language, more than try to interpret her words. She returned to Adam, sat down, and shook his shoulder. He woke up and turned towards her putting his arm around her waist. She explained her puzzling over the intentions of Miz Gertrude. He laughed and pulled her down beside him and assured her that the actions and intentions of white people were beyond all comprehension, true of every single one of them, and she was to concentrate on his intentions right now and nothing else before they all had to go out to work. "Next Sunday we can lay around all day if we like. Let's wait and see what she says about that. He gave us this new Sunday rule yesterday." He kissed her and held her down. "Your job will be to count the days," he added with a laugh.

"Adam, don't hold me so tight, you'll hurt our little baby, and your voice is too loud, other people will wake up," she whispered. "We need to concentrate on Miz Gertrude's promise to build cabins and water wells, then me and you can have privacy and me not to have to fetch water all the way from the creek. When you go to the fields, I'm gonna get Tabby and we'll go to the house to take breakfast, clean up, and find out if she's in Ole Archie's bedroom." She had to laugh at that thought, then looked at Adam's handsome face and stroked his chest and stomach.

"You'd better quit that, Baby, if you don't want somethin' big to happen right here, right now," he answered and turned over on his stomach. Then Adam raised himself up with elbow in the straw and head in hand. "Another thing, Baby, is that white people, we all know, for them the deepest thing is always gonna be money. Remember now, it's them gold and silver pieces or them little promise notes—that is what they love. And so, it is money that makes them love a woman, or love a farm owner with all his acres, makes them love their children, makes them make real nice to their slaves one minute then turn around and say the opposite the next. So, let's keep that in mind when we try to understand the new mistress."

Soola laughed, remembering her own sassy mouth when she was growing up. She told Adam that she had said the same to Massa Jimmie one day, had said that he and his friends talked about money at the dinner table all the time, and that she thought they loved money more than anything else on earth. "And I said, 'Massa Jimmie, I do believe that you go to that bank in Kingston, or Charleston, and worship money like you worship your God and Jesus in your church.'" She bent over Adams body, laughing about that memory. "And Adam, Massa Jimmie laughed so hard and told me I was smart and sassy and had imagination too and that he would have to tell those friends because it was the goddam truth. But I told him not to do that because they wouldn't think it was funny but would tell him to whup me. And he said that he would never whup me but would keep me to amuse him into his old age. And, Adam, that was only one week before he died."

"Soola, that Massa Jimmie was sweet on you, I guarantee he was looking you all over. I know because I'm crazy sweet on you and been lookin' you over myself."

And she answered in a serious tone now, "No my darlin', he was not sweet on me, I was just a kid, and he was big time sweet on pretty Selma. He had built a fancy little house for her and he loved her like crazy. She's the one taught me to read and write and do numbers."

Soola grew sad with those memories, knowing that conversation had marked the beginning of the end of the good times at the Pine Forest Plantation. So, she kissed Adam again, stood up, put on her head scarf, and went to find Tabitha. They needed to make sure Judith had the breakfast for two ready on the tray. But mostly they hoped to discover the sleeping arrangements in the big house.

Soola and Tabitha carried the breakfast tray around to the back door of the big house, went inside to the front and placed it on the table in the parlor. Massa Archie had told them never to enter through the front door, that was only for white people. That was at least six years ago, in the first week of their arrival there, and Soola had answered that she was happy to obey that rule because the front steps were broken and they might hurt their legs, for which she had received a slap in the face. Even the slap didn't close her mouth—she had answered in a sweet cautionary tone warning the Massa to be careful not to hurt his own legs. She remembered that now with some nostalgia for her greater sassiness in those days; for afterwards, Judith had been furious, reminding her of her promise not to aggravate the master, and so over the years she had toned down her rude voice.

Her memory was interrupted by Tabitha's elbow in her ribs. She raised her eyes up the stairs, and they both saw Massa Archie creeping quietly out of his wife's bedroom and heading to his own. Soola immediately called out. "Massa Archie, sir, we have your breakfast, a tray for two down here in the parlor, sir." He didn't answer, but they heard his door slam. She grabbed Tabitha's arm, bent over, and couldn't suppress a quiet laugh. "Now Tabby, we'll go in the back and be cleaning the house, then we'll go upstairs.

"No," said Tabitha, "we'll wait, we'll eat first, then, if we see them on the porch, we'll come back and do the cleaning. In that way we'll hear what they're talkin' about."

When Soola agreed, the women went back to the barn, ate their beans and corn without speaking, following an edict that had come through Tabitha from her mother that you should never talk while eating. Thus, it was after eating that Soola asked all assembled why they thought Massa Archie was so damn bashful about being with his wife. "Hell, he's not bashful about telling us to have babies."

Judith said, "Well, we never have known much about that man; he never had a woman here in seven years. Maybe he's scared of them and thinks that being with them takes him down a bit in our minds, that is, if we know that he truly is doing it with Miz Gertrude. I dunno, he's a strange one for sure."

"Do you think he'll go in there with her every night?" asked Tabitha, putting her hand over her mouth and raising her eyes in embarrassment.

"I bet not," answered Soola, "I bet she locks her door sometimes. But we'll watch and see. And we'll ask the men what they think."

"Jake won't have no opinion about that," said Tabitha smiling. "He'll think we're so stupid even talking about it. All the men will say the same. All they think about is doing it themselves, they're never worried about who else is."

"Yeah," said Soola, "Adam would be like that too."

Judith stayed quiet. She had no boyfriend. Most of the men had expressed fear of getting too close to her with her half white face. She had declared some years back that she didn't really care; Mittie was the father of her daughter Ida, and she had kinda liked him, so she wouldn't seek a replacement. Soola had believed that was her quiet way of defending her affliction.

Soola then changed the subject and asked the women what they thought of having a whole family in a cabin, that is, if these mythical cabins would ever be built. For instance, she would invite Adam to stay with her, her two daughters and their baby which was on the way. "What about you and Jake, Tabitha? Because, you see, I think it's us women who will be in charge of who's who and who's where in these cabins, then maybe the mistress too."

"Well, I dunno,", answered Tabitha, "he might not want to live with us—that is me and Lil Jake and George and new baby, Lord I hope she's a girl. I'll wait and see, wouldn't want to decide on any of that yet."

Judith shrugged, "No man will want to be in a cabin with me. So happy I have Ida, she's sassy and fun, and she's already learning to cook. It'll be the two of us, and we'll do fine."

Soola felt sad for her. Adam had been a solace, an arbiter, a go-between— between the two sides of herself, the crazy and the sane. She loved him in a way she had never loved a man. From that first time he had stared at her and told her his name, she had lusted after him and then loved him. But it had taken a while to vanquish his roaming instincts, a time when she had played the don't care game with determination…until one night perhaps four years ago, no maybe three, he had taken her in his arms over by the river and sworn that his passion for her had conquered all. She had never before known the desperate beauty of the act of love.

They had fallen on the ground, midst the weeds and pine straw, in desperation, groping, and crying out, there beside the river sweeping by. The mites had gotten under her skin that summer night, but Soola endured the terrible itching with smiles. She felt sorry now for Judith, in fact for any woman who would never experience that wild joy. Although, maybe she had, who knows?

The three newcomers were off by themselves and so didn't offer their opinions on families living in cabins. Soola had never thought it necessary or advisable to draw them in.

Later in the morning, noticing that the master and mistress had moved outside to sit on the porch in the shining early fall sunlight, Soola and Tabitha decided it was time for more sleuthing. It was certainly unusual for the Massa not to be out in fields by this time. He had come and told Jake to be in charge. They walked quietly behind the big house, gathered the cleaning tools from the back storeroom, climbed the wobbly back staircase and commenced cleaning in the two front bedrooms. Although the southeast front room was not in use and contained neither bed nor chairs, it was from that room they could hear the voices and see the chair in which the mistress sat. They could not see his chair, but by leaning sideways beside the window, they could stretch their necks and see his arm reaching over, holding his wife's left hand. The mistress' right hand held her knitting bag, which she then placed on the floor. Her head was turned towards her husband, but they could only see the back of it with the tightly coiled hair at her neck. Soola and Tabitha looked at each other in high amusement. "Lovey dovey," whispered Soola.

They heard Gertrude say, ever so sweet and polite, "Mr. McLachlan, do you realize that your slaves live in unimaginable privation and hardship, more so than any I have seen?" to which he replied that no, he did not realize that. He removed his hand from hers and asked what on earth she thought they needed that they didn't already have, after all they're slaves, ain't they? She reached down and took her knitting out of the bag and commenced klickety-klacking at a speed that astonished the two upstairs.

Gertrude then revealed to her husband the most pressing needs from the first lines of her list—cabins, wells and pumps, soap, clothing, blankets, and more nutritious food. Furthermore, she told him, fewer whippings and less fear. She then indicated that she would be willing and pleased to get some of her money from Bruce in order to finance these much-needed improvements. Archie wouldn't have to contribute a penny to the effort. "And, Mr. McLachlan, I'm a little bit surprised that you haven't figured out in all these years, one of the basic truths of slave-owning—a happy, well-treated slave will work harder and be more productive than one who is half starved, cold, and frequently whipped. Anyway, when these improvements are finished, you will see the change in productivity."

"Now, what makes you think I haven't studied this question and found that you are wrong, that the only thing that will motivate a slave is fear of punishment—whipping or a cutback on rations, or some other penalty that I can think up?" Archie was not rushing into anger at this point, but Soola could tell by his strained tone that he was struggling to hold it back. He went on in a reasonable voice to assure her that by law the master held the power, that a slave could not bring a legal protest against his master for bad treatment. In fact, a slave owner could not be accused of any crime if he killed a slave while in the process of using correction. If outright murder of a slave were proven, the master might get a year or so in prison, but such an outcome was rare indeed. "So, you see madam," he said, "the law is on my side, and gives me no reason to be gentle when I see slaves venture their own opinion or act rude and insolent, or in fact don't put their minds to their work as they should. By nature, these people are full of sloth. However, Mrs. McLachlan, if you want to pay for these improvements, then I won't raise any objection, so long as my men remain available for farm work."

Gertrude replied, "Thank you, Mr. McLachlan. But I must tell you I have lived with slaves all my life, which apparently you have not. And I have known slave owners to sometimes hold a sense of pity and decency, even affection for their human chattel. Since I've been here, I have been disappointed to see that you have not shown any kindness to them at all, indeed I have only witnessed the opposite in your treatment of your slaves. I thought from our conversations during the past year that you might be a kinder, more generous man, as you had indicated to me that you were." It seemed to the two slave women upstairs that this mistress was not only forceful and bossy, but also quite unafraid of the consequences of combat with Archie McLachlan. They continued to hear from this fearless woman: "And, Mr. McLachlan, the workers all need one day and a half per week off, and those days of course should be Saturday and Sunday."

Soola and Tabitha stood riveted to the floor as they listened to these words. They looked at each other, all giggling and amusement gone, both sensing that this conversation was a prophecy of the future for the newly married couple and for themselves. And there was more to come.

Archie could barely conceal his anger now. They could not see his face, but Soola knew exactly his expression as he spoke again, "Mrs. McLachlan, it is not your place to preach to me how I shall treat my slaves; this is my plantation, my buildings, my workers, my animals. I am the master here, and a wife should do her husband's bidding. She should not utter her opinions and should not dare to scold me on my behavior, should not tell me how to behave towards a wife. And don't think for a moment that you can continue to treat me this way. You have already told me to clean myself up in the most insolent manner and have not had the courtesy to compliment me on my efforts to do so. And now you say that I am not the man that you thought I would be. Well, I tell you that you are not the wife I expected; you are not the soft and loving wife who might aid me in my efforts to make a prosperous plantation with a warm hearthstone…in fact, not the wife that a man deserves." He paused in his tirade. Soola saw his right arm moving, indicating that he was probably wiping his brow with a pocket handkerchief.

She looked at Tabitha and whispered, "Warm hearthstone? Is the man dreamin'?"

And still he went on, "Madam, I will not tolerate any more disrespectful talk from you; in fact soon, if you continue, you might be feeling some of the same punishments that my slaves receive when they are insolent and out of line, like that aggravating and defiant Soola you were listening to so closely yesterday. Many men use their whips on rebellious wives like that too."

Gertrude put down the knitting on her lap, raised her hand with the palm outward towards her husband and said calmly, with good nature and a hint of humor, "Stop. Mr. McLachlan, I do believe you are not serious; but you must know that if you ever touch me in anger, you will have a real fight on your hands. I am as big and strong as you and accustomed to keep my brothers in line in that fashion." She returned to the knitting. "Furthermore, yes, I am familiar with the laws regarding master and slave, and with our new national government already at work, I hope and pray the delegates at Philadelphia or New York, or wherever they are now, will draft laws to protect these defenseless people from the tyranny that you describe."

Archie stood and faced his wife with one arm akimbo, which was visible to the two listeners upstairs. He told his wife he would walk alone through his plantation and survey the fields, especially those where the cotton still awaited harvest, and check to see if all were working. When he was on the steps, he turned around again to face Gertrude and said, "Mistress McLachlan, I would never strike you; my uncle Duncan told me a gentleman knows better than that. And, Madam, I have already told my slaves they can stay home on Sundays." He gave her a timid smile, and Soola watched him walk away down the river path kicking the autumn leaves into the wind, which was blowing that musty leaf smell through the upstairs windows. Tabitha looked at Soola and said, "Gentleman? More dreamin'? Sunday off?" Archie strutted a little as he walked away, making him seem like a bigger man; and his favorite dog, the one with brown and black spots, followed him, whining and trying to reach up to lick his hand. The master bent down and stroked the dog's head. But because in the past Soola had seen Massa Archie kick this dog, she wondered aloud if the stroking was for Miz Gertrude's benefit. Tabitha shrugged and they both giggled.

Soola and Tabitha moved swiftly to the back bedroom, straightened and cleaned, then performed the same job on Massa Archie's room. Neither of these rooms was decorated with items that collected much dust. Only the bed frame and a wooden chair needed wiping, then for the bare, unstained wooden planks of the floors, a quick sweep. So, in a short time they were back at the barn trying to impart to the other slaves the complicated conversation they had heard, trying to interpret its meaning for their future. Tabitha said quietly to Soola, "I wonder if she knows how hard that man is trying to please her, and to impress her, but how difficult it is for him to control his temper." Soola's only comment, as she watched those warden crows lined up again on the branch: "I do believe she wants to be a good mistress for us. We'll not forget the crows. I bet they'll accept her before the people do."

When Soola was listening to her master and new mistress discussing the regulations and practices in the slave system, she was unaware that the hope for abolition of slavery had, in fact, been present in the hearts and minds of some convention delegates three years before. At that time, they were toiling through the summer heat in Philadelphia to write a constitution for the new republic. For those believers, the rights of man and equality for all did not match up with the institution of chattel slavery. However, when the arguing and compromising were done, no mention of abolition of African slavery was written into the document. The dread of financial disaster in the southern states was put forward as the reason, but there were other unspoken factors as well. Soola, with her clear mind and sharp tongue, if she had been handed the final document, would have immediately understood the undercurrent of prejudice and assumptions about Africans in the hearts of many delegates at that convention. A statement, finally, did require that the foreign trade in humans could not be prohibited by the national Congress until 1808, but that was all—a glimmer of hope perhaps? Did that mean the idealists might vote to close the frightful Atlantic slave trade in twenty years' time? Soola would have laughed at that timid, and yet unyielding, twisted-around surrender from the slave-owners.

Soola soon discovered, too, that the mistress would never talk to the slaves at Inveraray Plantation about any subject that hinted at the institution of slavery itself. Treatment of slaves, yes, but abolition, no. Gertrude would never assure them that many of the new nation's leaders among the slave-owners—for instance George Washington himself, Thomas Jefferson, George Mason, Patrick Henry—were deeply conflicted about slavery, although unwilling to free their own people. She was certainly aware that Washington finally wrote into his will that his slaves would be free on the death of his wife, but to Gertrude, in 1789, there was no avenue that would lead to her embracing ideas of freedom for the Africans in her care. She rarely heard a white person speak about it. She never saw the letter written by Alexander Hamilton, who assured the reader that if freedom and education were provided to the African slaves, they would perform in the new nation as well as any white man. Nevertheless, over the years, Gertrude came to that same assessment, quite on her own.

What all at Inveraray did hear loud and clear was Massa Archie complaining about the higher price of slaves lately, all due, he was sure, to the new North Carolina import duty on humans brought in from the West Indies and Africa. It was stifling the foreign trade into Wilmington, he said, and was forcing people to buy on the domestic market. So, of course, the traders were raising prices. And South Carolina had temporarily stopped the foreign trade into Charleston, which considerably irked the master. "Mark my words," he cried, "they'll smuggle them in, up the rivers and into secret coves. Who's going to stop 'em?" And, as he predicted, smugglers did that, so powerful was the hunger, the greed, for cheap labor among the rice, cotton, indigo, and tobacco growers.

"The only thing the Massa's interested in is cheap slaves," announced Soola to the other workers, after they had finished eating one evening in November. "He's always bitching about the higher cost these days. And I remember how he dawdled around all day at our auction, then jumped in to pick us up after no one had bid on us. So, there's no doubt he'll be trekking to Wilmington soon and coming back with more flimsy women to satisfy all of you men; they may be the sick ones, or ornery like me." She placed a hand on her chest as if to apologize for that failing.

Although they all knew that the new mistress was negotiating with her husband daily, the cabins and wells had not been started. "I bet she's selling her body right now," said Soola, who went on to assure them that Gertrude would be telling him, not tonight, not tonight, honey, unless you promise you'll get more women or start the cabins." Her mimicry brought laughs.

On the next morning, as if to confirm the predictions of Soola, Archie called for Lil George to come and help him harness the horses, two of them now, to the wagon and load up the chains to tie in new slaves. He was wearing a new shirt that bloused out in the back and that Soola had seen the mistress working on the previous week. He walked to the barn and told all the slaves assembled there that they were to follow the orders of Mistress Gertrude while he was gone, for how long he did not know. He aimed to increase the population of females on this farm. Soon he was loaded up and told them he was heading to town and then on the road south to Wilmington. "Jake, I want you to help the mistress, especially with the last of the corn and first of the cotton and with the cleaning up of the fields. When I get back, we should be ready to walk around and examine the condition of the fences." When the creek of the wagon and the clippety clop of the newly shod hooves had faded, the slaves stood and cheered. Jake stood and announced he was the boss for two days, maybe more.

Then came the mistress to tell them it was time to get to work but that she also wanted a special favor from Adam. "Adam I would like for you to take one of the small boats at the dock and row as fast as possible to town and deliver this letter to Messrs. Brown on the docks. I would like for them to come here tomorrow, bring two pumps and sink two wells, one beside the barn here, the other down the path at the end of where the cabins will be. I shall also ask them to dig two latrines with wood partitions, one for men, the other for women, and these will be far away from our delicate noses. Please, Adam, take one, or maybe two, of the boys with you."

Adam jumped up in great excitement, grabbed one of the younger boys, then another, and took off down the river path. And so the work that would change living conditions at Inveraray was underway, little more than a month after Mistress Gertrude had arrived. Soola approached her with deeply felt thanks. "Mistress, you must know we are grateful and do you think that by the time my baby arrives we'll have a cabin to live in?" She always remembered that day because it proved she had been right these past five or six weeks to have trust in Miz Gertrude when some others, especially the men, had scoffed at those promises, insisting that little weasel would never give in to his new wife. They, of course, had no idea as to whether Massa Archie had agreed to the wells and pumps, or whether perhaps she was acting on her own. Soola said who cared whether he agreed or not, she didn't believe the mistress required his approval, hadn't she heard her say that she would pay for it with her own money? Anyway, Adam and his helpers were thrilled to pocket their pass and go to town, and the rest of the crowd became anxious to see what they had to report and whether the well crew would come on the morrow.

It all happened. By the end of the third day, the wells were dug, and pumps installed. Water was not far from the surface. The slaves of Inveraray clustered round, watched the water gushing out of the pumps, each waiting her turn to work the handle up and down, then picking up their skirts to run and try out the second pump. "This will be a big surprise for Massa," laughed Adam. "And folks, you saw them silver coins pass from her hand into the hands of Messrs. Brown, did you not?" They all agreed they had seen that happen, or at least they had heard the words from others that they had seen the passing of the money, or anyway, heard the clink. Soola believed this was a triumph over the master and especially for the mistress, whom she had seen encouraging all the slaves to work at double speed to get the fields ready for winter, the cotton fields ready for harvest, even start the cotton picking, and show the master that a happy servant was a harder worker. Some muttered negative thoughts about that, but they went along with it, just this once. Many had expressed doubt that the master would be pleased by any success on the farm achieved by Miz Gertrude. He would prefer to tell her that a woman was not capable of either running the farm or of sweating her brow in the work.

As a result of this habitual pessimism, there was some anxiety at the end of the next day when they heard the horses and cart approaching. Soola and Gertrude at that moment were walking down the path from the area they called the Turpentine Forest, where Soola had been closing the turpentine business for winter, the business she had organized over the years for Massa Archie. Gertrude had complimented her and told her that the master was fortunate to have her.

"Well, I thank you, Mistress, but the Massa, he never tells me that, he only cusses at me," answered Soola, who then saw the slaves clustered around the cart, heard Archie shouting, and finally could see four young women and two boys chained inside. One woman clutched a baby in her arms. Archie jumped down from the cart appearing gleeful and full of pride. "Got these two women free, and these other two cheap because one was a prostitute, you men should like her, and the other's weak in the mind," he shouted.

"My, oh my," muttered Gertrude as she peered into the wagon. "This one is real sick." Touching the smooth, hot face of the young girl, she added, "a pine box might be more appropriate for her right now than food and clothing. Soola, could you get someone to help me with this poor thing." The other "free" woman appeared to be already dead. Soola looked in the cart and saw that the sick girl still living was little more than a child. One of the men seemed not much older than that too. He said his name was Pete, and that's all he would say.

"Cat got your tongue?" asked Gertrude. The boy stared at the sky with malice the size of the whole world in his black eyes. Soola called on Adam to carry the girl to the barn and lay her on a bed of straw.

In the meantime, the slaves were watching Massa Archie's face and listening to his words, anxious to learn his feelings about the wells and pumps. At first, it was as if he hadn't even noticed, but then finally, just as Adam was laying the sick girl down on her straw bed, and as Gertrude was pumping a jug of water, Archie appeared at the barn door. He spoke to his wife as she walked past him through the door carrying the heavy jug. His words were obviously for all to hear, "Mistress McLachlan, I see that you have taken this matter of water pumps into your own hands and you're thinking that in the middle of all this ruckus I would not have anything to say about it. Well I will tell you now that I have seen your intrigues and plottings with these women and you have done the work behind my back. I believe it to be a sign that you think you can take over the running of this farm yourself. You have put my slaves to working double time in the fields, and I can assure you that I am not impressed by your trying to take over their daily schedule. I won't have my wife taking over, nossir, I won't have it."

Soola looked up, wishing a bolt of lightning would strike him dead, then stared hard at the mistress. Gertrude merely shook her head in amazement and replied calmly, "Why, my dear husband, we all thought we were aiming to please you, never imagining you would twist our intentions around in such misguided fashion. You said to me a few weeks ago that I could make these improvements. But come with me to the house, and we'll talk."

Jake said quietly, "See, what did I tell you?"

The next morning Soola and Gertrude sat on the floor beside the girl, trying to talk to her with sign language. The other sick one, they discovered, had died in the cart on the journey. Archie soon pushed the barn door open and looked in to see who was surviving. Pointing to the body under a cover, he reminded them that the auctioneer told him to "pick up the leavings" in the pen, they would soon die anyway. "I told him, I'd take that risk and that my wife and my other slaves would revive them," added the proud master, looking over the assembled crowd. "Now, you menfolk, git on out to the cotton field, we gotta git finished there." No thanks were offered for the extra-long hours they had put in while the master was away.

During the next few days, the sick girl improved, and Soola called on one of the men who knew some African words. Through him she managed to tell them her name was Bejida, which she had miraculously clung to during the fearful journey from Africa, the landing in the islands, and the second journey to Wilmington. In the language of her home, she told them, the name meant "born during the rainy season." No one had bought her, she told the mistress and the slave women; she had lain in the slave pen, refused by all. Soola and Gertrude and the other slaves became determined that Bejida would live. They petted her, taught her English words, fed her, smoothed her feverish forehead constantly, and wiped away the sweat when the fever began to diminish. After a week, she was standing, feeding crumbs to the birds, then helping to clean up the barn. A week after that, Gertrude said she could no longer hold her back from work in the cotton fields, work that even she, the mistress, participated in.

As she gradually picked up English words, Bejida brought to the community firsthand stories from the old country, from the village of her birth, of the slave "castles" on the African coast, then of the Middle Passage, and the terrifying white people. As they listened spellbound, it seemed to the people of Inveraray they could truly see the prison on the African coast, could actually hear and smell the fearful ship and feel the cracking whips.

Bejida became immediately, even at her young age, a foreseer of the future, assuring the people of Inveraray that she had been born with that gift, had started her predictions at five years. And before long, she proclaimed herself to be a midwife, had already delivered two babies back in her African village. She said she would be medicine and wise woman of the group and even predicted she would herself bear at least a dozen children.

"How rewarding is life on this earth, even surprising just to be a fish, a bird, or the smallest blade of grass," cried Gertrude Munro McLachlan, addressing Soola and the other slave women one evening, three weeks after the arrival of Bejida. "And we all live our lives under the loving care of our Lord God and his son Jesus." The people turned their faces to the mistress with hope and gratitude in their hearts.

Even the ever skeptical Soola was encouraged by the cheer in these faces, shining in the firelight. But then, remembering the moment on that boat when she had observed for the first time the white travelers, their finery and happy optimism, and at that time had realized the difference between a white life and a black life, she now glanced at the smiling face of her mistress, and her spirits sank. The mistress is from the white world, she thought, where happy smiles reign, where they sleep on feather beds and rule over their slaves. We are of the black world, locked in our prison, where all is dark and unfathomably bleak, where we sleep on the barn floor and live under the whip. But, surely, it doesn't have to be that way, surely not in the eyes of the mistress' god and his son Jesus? She checked on the unchanged line of crows, stood up, and went to lie down beside Adam.

Chapter 8

    Soola's reflections on those thoughts stayed with her during the next few weeks. Included in these reflections was a fear about Massa Archie, who seemed to be angrier than in the past, but that anger seemed now to be directed against his wife, more so than against the slaves. In fact, there were fewer beatings, even an occasional compliment on work done, for the men. But against Gertrude, and herself, Soola began to notice heavier doses of sarcasm, criticism, and ill humor.

    The worst occurred one day in early January, when, wrapped in a shawl against the cold, Soola walked up to the back of the big house to gather some dirty dishes from the night before. She had grown big with her child by now and was losing the swiftness of foot she had always been accustomed to. She saw a thin layer of frost on the dead leaves and pine straw and an even thinner layer of ice on the puddles from yesterday's rain. No birdsong did she hear and imagined they were tucked in the bushes hiding their heads under their wings.

    While walking slowly, she began to hear voices from the front bedroom, mostly from the master. Soon he was shouting at his wife that she had no business talking to his slaves about the crops, the cabins, the food. He never wanted to see a cabin on this place or to waste his money on fancy food for these black devils and didn't she know that they weren't complaining about their food, and as far as he knew none wanted a cabin to sleep in. Then, in the crescendo of his tirade, he repeated what Soola had heard many times, "This is my place, I bought it with my money and bought the slaves to do the work; nothing on this farm is yours and never will be, specially being as you deprived me of your property that was rightfully mine." But the crescendo was not the end because he immediately started in on another subject Soola had heard the past week—Gertrude's friendship with her, Soola. His voice dropped now; he was trying to sound more reasonable and gentler, but the message was just as mean. He didn't like his wife to be so chummy with that slave woman. What were they talking about and plotting together? He was certain it was something against him, the two of them probably cooking up a scheme to take over his farm. "You can tell her that she's never gonna have that cabin to sleep in." And so on.

This appeared like the talk of a madman, Soola feared. She knew the mistress well enough now to imagine the expression on Gertrude's plain face—quiet, serious, even a small smile, then some consoling words to try and calm him down. She would be standing there in her brown, or perhaps blue, dress buttoned up to the neck, her arms folded, and head slightly tilted. The only indication of stress would be the thin lips closed and drawn tight across her teeth with the right side slightly higher than the left. Soola quietly gathered up the utensils and was ready to leave when she heard the voice of the mistress, "My dear husband, I would like to tell you what one of the women said to me just yesterday. She said that she thought Massa Archie truly is happy to have the mistress here to help him and that behind his hard voice, he really loves her." Archie said not another word, and Soola slipped out. She remembered it had been Tabitha who had said that, definitely not herself. She wondered how Miz Gertrude was taking all this insulting shouting. Was it hurting her deep inside? She was aware, of course, that Archie was quite wrong—Mistress Gertrude never uttered a word of criticism about her husband to the slaves. It was all coming from his addled brain.

In February, it became time for the early spring planting—potato pieces and leafy vegetable seeds must be pushed and sprinkled into the ground. Jake took some boys with him to the upper barn and dragged out the sacks of seed potatoes from last year and commenced to cut them into small pieces for planting, gagging sometimes at the wicked smell of potatoes gone to rot. Another crew of men, women, and children was already hoeing the rows in two fields. Archie counted on these products to bring in the first money of the year, along with the turpentine, which would be starting production March/April, depending on the weather. Gertrude was out there too, working beside her husband. The women clustered behind her, bending down, straightening up, and using their fingers to break up clods of dirt that might impede the growth of seedlings. It was a cold day. The shawls wrapped around them did not protect their bones against the bitter wind.

Soola, little more than a month from the date of her delivery, was soon exhausted and unhappy and so asked the master if she could please be excused to go back and rest. He told her no, she'd have to wait until the lunch break. In the old days, Soola would then have retorted with a sharp reminder to Archie that she was carrying a future slave for him and that he'd better help her safeguard the child. But now, partly to protect Miz Gertrude, she said nothing, only slowed down her pace of work.

This protective feeling towards the mistress had been growing in Soola, especially as she had heard Archie's scolding voice increasing. She wondered again how big a disappointment was it for Gertrude, married only five months, and suffering almost daily the new husband's endless complaints and abuse. But for sure she would never ask about that. If only he would go away for a week; they might have a heart to heart talk, so great was her sympathy for her mistress. As her fingers pried down into the damp black soil, her mind was racing, thinking about Adam, the love of her life, and now Miz Gertrude, perhaps becoming the closest female friend she had ever known since Missy and Prissy. Friendship was interesting, it seemed to happen like a bolt into the heart, from one conversation, or perhaps a series of conversations, or merely a look of compassion in the eyes. Why had she become so close to Tabitha after that first meeting at the slave pen, but not so much to Judith? She liked Judith but lacked that warm friendship kind of feeling. Then she thought some more about her affection for the mistress that had come from her slow realization that Gertrude cared deeply about the welfare of the slaves, had already improved their clothing and food, plus of course installed the water pumps. And perhaps Gertrude had influenced the master more than he would admit—mostly, as Soola and the other women had been witnessing, less cussin' and fewer whippings on the backs of men in the field since the arrival of the mistress. On the other hand, that indefinable spark of friendship between the mistress and herself seemed to have triggered a new kind of anger against the two of them. She pondered yet again on Tabitha's words about Massa Archie—that he respected, and strove to please, his wife. Soola couldn't perceive much of that. Who could fathom the depths of this strange man? Soola knew too of Miz Gertrude's unwavering resolve to build the cabins, although how she might accomplish that in the face of Massa Archie's wrath, she could not picture. Her back was aching. She stood, stretched, and rubbed that old sore spot in the lower back.

Gertrude turned her head to see if Soola was all right. Soola smiled, giving no indication otherwise. For a moment, Soola watched the river, visible now through the winter trees, daydreaming of taking a boat with Adam down to wherever the current might carry them, maybe to that wide ocean she had seen eight years back, to freedom for them with their baby.

Abruptly, the mistress' voice broke through her thoughts. The voice was directed to the master, "Mr. McLachlan, I've been thinking about this farm and how well you have developed it from the beginnings that you told me of. But I know you feel a strong need for a cash crop you could rely on to bring in more money each year, particularly since the failure of the canals and rice cultivation and the difficulty of raising the most productive kinds of cotton in these counties near the sea."

With a sigh of impatience, the Master delivered his predictable reply. "I have told you already, Mistress McLachlan, that I do not seek your opinion about this plantation. No farm succeeds where a woman is allowed to speak on business matters. The female brain is not made for such thoughts. You stick to your knitting."

But this time, Gertrude seemed determined to pursue her idea. "Oh, you mean I shouldn't be out here in the field helping you?"

"Humph."

"Anyway, what you say about women is rubbish," she continued. "I shall certainly express my opinions whenever I wish. I am quite capable of doing a woman's work combined with that of a man. I've been doing that since I was ten years old. And, as for business, I have some excellent ideas for this place, sooner or later they will be implemented. You see, I know you are fond of money, and you will be grateful for the profits in the end."

They continued the hard work of potato planting in silence for a few minutes. But soon, Gertrude could not keep her mouth shut any longer. She disclosed that she had been hearing from her brother Bruce about recent failures in the famous Virginia tobacco business, which had been much injured by the war and by exhaustion of the soil. Eastern North Carolina might pick up the slack, so to speak. "The challenge will be to grow the same high-quality plants as the Virginia tobacco growers have been accustomed to."

Archie did not reply immediately, but in a few minutes, controlling his temper this time, in front of the slaves, mumbled that he had already heard about experiments in tobacco near the Virginia border and that she did not need to bother her pretty little head with the crops on his farm.

Gertrude responded quickly and sharply, "My head is neither pretty nor small, husband; I have a head for thinking, and that it will continue to do, I hope for the benefit of all."

Soola knew what the look on his face meant. He might explode to his wife later, inside the house. She wished that more of the men had been nearby to hear the mistress put him down. She realized she was probably the only one truly aware of Miz Gertrude's genius in dealing with Massa Archie. Miz Gertrude had raised this question of tobacco in front of all in the field for two reasons: to show the slaves she was still unafraid of her husband, and to introduce tobacco to him in a place where he might show hesitation in attacking her. Well, and maybe a third, more important: to give them heart that he might go away for a couple of weeks to investigate the Virginia tobacco markets. Soola laughed about it later with the women. And that same evening, after she had heard Miz Gertrude mention tobacco to the master, and when Gertrude was approaching the barn to talk to the women, she beckoned to the mistress to speak to her alone. "Mistress," Soola whispered, "I fear for you some evenings after you have spoken sharp to the Massa. I fear he'll hurt you up there in the house."

Gertrude jerked up her head in surprise. "Why, Soola, you are kind to worry. But our lord Jesus Christ died on the cross as payment for our sins. He hung there in agony, probably for two days or more, until death took him. The anxiety I might feel means nothing compared to that. Furthermore, it is nothing compared to what the slaves endure, all around these states. So, I can endure anything if there's the smallest possibility it would help the people in my mission. Please, my friend, you should not ever concern yourself with me. It is your hardships we must work with here."

She walked slowly back to the house, seemingly unmindful of what she had come to discuss. Soola, transfixed, stood quietly thinking. Mission? She was only vaguely familiar with the story of Jesus—from Sally, one of the new girls, the one with the baby, and from one or two in her childhood. Those words concerning the painful lives of the slaves touched her heart, helped her to understand the depth and breadth of Miz Gertrude's compassion.

Two weeks went by with Soola's baby eager to see the world, although it didn't seem to be as violently active as the others had been. Then she would warn him, No, baby, you're right to hesitate, you don't want to see your world, except that your mama and papa will love you. Adam, in the hard schedule of the slaves, still found time to spend with her, care for her as she began to feel like resting most of the time. She would look up at his face, so handsome, his mouth wide like hers, and the deep black eyes watching over her with love. It was that broad set of his jaw that she loved the best, and perhaps his tough and agile body. "Adam, do you still love me, when I'm so big and ugly?" she would ask, and he would reassure her that she was always beautiful, his wife, his woman forever, and then would lay his head on her breast.

At the end of the month, one Sunday morning, Archie entered the barn where his wife sat talking to the women and informed them he was going on a scouting expedition to see what other farmers were doing. He even expressed pride in having a wife who could take care of the place in his absence. The women looked at Gertrude in wonder that her husband had complimented her so. Soola whispered to herself that her wish had come true. She would have to ask Bejida if one of her many gods had granted that wish; never mind that the young girl had lost some of her faith in gods and spirits.

"So, Mrs. McLachlan, watch these slaves carefully, keep them working. We'll see how big and strong and smart you think you are after managing this place for a few weeks." He called for George to help him get the horse ready—bridled and saddled with the saddle bag behind and the hooves and shoes checked out. It is thanks to Miz Gertrude that the horses don't look starving no more, thought Soola as she watched the preparation. She had seen the mistress return from town with not only better food for humans, but also some rich feed for the animals. She then had instructed George on how much to feed them.

Archie announced to her now that he would go west first, along the river, then turn north, towards the Virginia border, where he would talk to strangers, examine their methods and tools and curing sheds, buy some seed, and return home prepared to plant a field of tobacco, if not this year, then next. Soola knew he would never admit, even to himself, that it was his wife who had planted this seed in his mind.

But Gertrude smiled as he rode away and told Soola and the other slaves that time was short, they had much to do, and Adam must return to town immediately to find the lumber men and the building men. "We will have our cabins," she announced in as loud a voice as she could muster. The slaves of Inveraray laughed that night to realize the clever wrangling and negotiating the mistress had struggled through in order to achieve this spell of autonomy. Soola told them Miz Gertrude had been waiting for it, had in fact fostered it.

The cabins were begun, with two carpenters from town doing most of the work at first, but also teaching Jake and two other slaves the basics of cabin building. They began by clearing a broad path from the first pump, which was located to the left of the house, then down in a slanting direction, almost parallel to the driveway, to just beyond that second pump and the dogwood thicket. They began two one-room cabins, with the mistress insisting that they leave enough space beside each and in the back to allow for future expansion and present-day vegetable gardens. Fireplaces in the cabins presented a problem at first because Gertrude had not thought of the brick work. She told Soola and the other women that she had failed to figure on brick chimneys and lacked the money right now to get the masons down here. As a result, during the first few weeks, each family made a fireplace outside the back door, created with scraps of metal brought by the builders. To Soola she explained that she would get the masons here next month, only sorry that this project had to be started during the cold months.

Near the big house and to the left was also constructed a kitchen shed with a huge brick fireplace in the front, erected as best they could by these newly trained carpenters. Bricks for the kitchen fireplace, Gertrude could just squeeze into her budget. The front of the shed was covered by a sheltering roof. The kitchen fire spread warmth around, providing comfort for those in the cold cabins. The hardwood for the fires was not in short supply.

Soola, Tabitha, and Judith told the women that each would have a cabin, and they could work out for themselves whether they wanted a man to share it with them and the children. "The women are in charge," said Soola. The left-over men would have to remain in the barn until a bachelors' quarter could be provided in the next few months. Soola immediately grabbed the first cabin, closest to the house, for herself, her two daughters, and Adam. Tabitha claimed the second, across the path, and Judith the third, next to Soola. The excitement was intense, as was the competition for cabins, and complaints by men who remained single. "Oh well," said Soola, laughing, "We'll set up a boxing area for the men to fight over the women and cabins." They placed a wooden post beside the path and hammered on a sign that read Dogwood Lane. The mistress explained to the children what it meant, sounding out each letter for little brains to absorb. Soola's younger daughter Mary Alice, growing to be a big girl, was the most eager to listen and to learn.

As the weeks went by, tension grew in anticipating the return of the master. What would he say? Who would be the object of his wrath? Obviously, his wife and Soola— the usual targets. A worried brow could even be seen on the face of Miz Gertrude herself and sometimes a crossing of her arms as she paced up and down staring at the ground—as if waiting for her death sentence, said Soola to Tabitha. Both were daily sending many anxious glances down the driveway, ears attuned for the sound of the master's horse. Well into March, they had six cabins built; the smell of freshly cut wood pervaded the place. The builders had instructed the men and had left a pile of wooden boards down the lane so they could continue the work. Gold and silver coins had been seen to pass from the hand of Miz Gertrude into the hand of the chief builder. And nature was on their side:

because of warm weather in February, the thicket of dogwood trees down the lane beyond the water pump had blossomed early, and a few of the flowers were showing a hint of pink. One of the men had seen this at his previous place of work, and he explained that Jesus painted those petals to show his approval of recent work done. And that was surely true here, the mistress assured them. The women loved the smell of the new wood. Soola liked to open her door, step inside, fill her nostrils with the rich smell of the walls and the floor, then turn around and welcome others into her home. She laughed and told the women they would all be ladies now.

"You crazy, girl," said Judith.

It was on an evening like this, on the first day of April, after work was finished in the fields plus an hour of building work, that Soola felt her first birth pains. She knew it was time. And, as night fell, she sent Patty to the big house to fetch the mistress. Of course, since Soola was anxious to test the girl's skills in childbirth, Bejida was summoned too. As midnight approached, the mistress came running down the new steps, nightgown and robe flying, to help with the birth. So Soola had plenty of advice and many hands to pull out the baby as his head emerged; although Miz Gertrude proved herself to be quite unskilled in the art of midwifery. In fact, she had to be instructed by Bejida not to pull so hard on the baby's head. It was not a hard or long birth; the baby boy slithered out easily, but all remarked immediately on his small size—like a little frog said Mary Alice, who was then chastised by her mother for such frank language about her tiny brother. "He will be named Adam for his papa," pronounced Soola, as the father took the baby, all wrapped in blankets, into his arms.

Baby Adam was puny from the start, rejected the breast at first, and appeared listless and slow moving. It became apparent that it was not only the breast he rejected; ultimately, after ten sad days, it was also life itself that the baby refused. During that ten-day period, Soola walked around with him, frantic for the baby to suckle, sat down, repeatedly trying to push the nipple into his little unresponsive mouth. She loved him so much, loved his smell, the milky smell when she did manage to persuade him to eat. She walked him up and down as the evenings grew warmer, Adam beside her with his long arm around her shoulders, then sitting on the steps of their new cabin beside the warmth of the outside fire. "Oh please," cried Soola, "Little Baby Adam, eat and grow healthy." But the baby over those frenzied days withered and grew more diminutive with each setting of the sun. Soola's cries grew louder in contrast to the baby's increasing stillness, until finally both uttered small whimpers, then silence.

Soola felt the aura of death, known to her from its constant companionship throughout her life. She clutched little Adam to her. No one, nothing could console her, not even Adam. She had so longed for their baby—for nine long months—and now he was gone. She walked down the path to the river. Jake had fashioned a small bench out of a tree trunk on the high bank overlooking the water, and there she sat beside wild cherry blossoms, holding the dead baby on the morning after he had breathed his last, Adam and the mistress, followed by Tabitha, approached and began the process of extracting little Adam from her arms. "I wish I could put him in a tiny boat and push him out into the current, let him float away to his new life, wherever it may be," murmured Soola, finally surrendering him and allowing Adam to pick her up. "Oh Adam, I wanted our baby, I wanted him so bad." He shushed her and promised they would have more babies. They buried little Adam beside the other departed souls in a clearing in the forest.

A gentle quiet descended over the farm. Because of Soola and Adam's standing in the community, the mourning was intense, more so than after any other death. For the first few days, the slaves walked slowly and without talking to the fields, for it was planting time and no days off could be tolerated. The grieving mother began to revive, and on the fifth day she approached the mistress with a request. "Miz Gertrude, we are still building our cabins, and our men are working fast now. Could we have a spirit house off by itself?"

Gertrude looked at her friend, puzzled. Soola smiled, "I'll explain. My mother told me that's what they had back in Africa— to be a home here on earth for the spirits of them that's died, especially for the baby spirits that's floating around here and worrying us at night. You see, little Adam's been doing that to me. It's a place we can go in and talk to our people who have passed on. Bejida too was telling me that we need it, and she will put her special things in there that will calm those spirits."

The mistress stopped and looked at Soola. "Soola, I know little about the beliefs of Africa, but I do know about our Lord God's gift of life to us his people, and that's what I would like to teach you. And yes, let me think about the spirit house, maybe we can do that; you are very persuasive, Soola, you're as good as the salesmen I knew in the town market, selling their wares to suspicious buyers. However, I do like your idea, and it would fit well with my thoughts about a small church here at Inveraray." Soola smiled to herself. It was Tabitha who had suggested the spirit house, and now, maybe they could have it, that is if they showed an interest in the white people's god, and his son Jesus. She ran straight to Tabitha's house, knocked on the door and told her yes, they would have the spirit house.

And so it was that Gertrude began on the next Sunday to introduce to a few of the slaves the concept of the one God and his son Jesus. She opened with stories of the creation, with the birth and death of Jesus, and the subsequent development of the Christian Church. The women heard the tales of Jesus and his mother with the deepest interest, the brilliant boy in the temple, the man of great leadership and wisdom, of magical powers, and finally they wept when she told of his crucifixion, picturing in detail the cruelty of the death and grief of the mother seated below him. Although skeptical of any such thing as a virgin birth, the slaves received the concept of magical powers without questioning. The birth of babies was part of their daily lives, well known and understood; miracles were events outside their knowledge, and thus acceptable as part of the unknown world. But the boy Pete would listen in silence, then leave in a rage, muttering this was all lies told by white folks. Several of the newly arrived slaves had heard of Jesus from previous mistresses, and a few told Miz Gertrude that Jesus was in their hearts every day through the hard life of slavery. They believed that he would eventually save them; they didn't use the words "free them," because they knew not whether the mistress would accept that word. Soola held back, reserving judgment, always pulling her mind back to her grasp of what was real, tangible, and true of her own life and imaginings.

The spirit house, which was built immediately, became a place of solace, hovering somewhere in the spiritual space between the old African gods and Christianity. Bejida decorated both the inside and the outside with pieces of animal bones, small and large, bunches of dried flowers, twigs and driftwood gathered up from the banks of the river, carried in almost daily at first by her delicate small hands and the revived strength of her tiny frame. She persuaded some of the men to help her with stumps and roots of old trees dug up from the new fields. These roots represented previous lives of all living things. The women contributed pieces of fabric from the edges of their garments. Gertrude handed to Bejida her deepest treasures—a small cross and a picture of Jesus that she had carried with her in the cart to Inveraray Plantation last October. Bejida also placed in a corner one of Soola's colonaware bowls containing a collection of fragrant plants, leaves and petals. The scents from this bowl varied according to the season, but, especially during spring and summer, it provided an added attraction for those who entered.

The most fearful object, displayed on the outside wall, was a dried six-foot rattlesnake. Its head was nailed right over the door with mouth open and fangs threatening, and the body with tail rattles intact, wound around on both sides. Bejida assured the anxious people that it would be a useful charm to scare off evil spirits. For the inside of the little house, Jake, at Bejida's request, had crafted some small stools so the people could go in, sit for a while, and have conversations with the spirits. Soola thought this girl had remarkable confidence for a person so small and so young.

By the middle of April, Inveraray Plantation was acquiring the appearance of a flourishing farm with comfortable quarters for some and fields filled with young plants. On the morning of the third Sunday in April, Soola opened her new cabin door in response to the tap-tapping of her mistress Gertrude. Her little cabin room was already taking shape with a log stool for each inhabitant and two mattresses. The mistress had purchased in town a pile of thick cotton fabric for making mattresses. It had been quite a task finding stuffing for these, but they had all succeeded in locating enough long grasses and weeds, bolstered by pine straw, autumn leaves, and many leavings from the cotton harvest, to create comfort at night. Although there was no fireplace yet, Soola had said she wanted to imagine one. So, with a piece of charcoal, she had drawn a line on the side wall, then across, then down the other side. On the floor she had marked the lines of a hearth and placed the stools in front so they could sit and talk or think, perhaps admire the colonaware. She had been taught by her mother to fashion these bowls from clay along the river.

"Soola, I am sorry to disturb your Sunday morning, but I have been thinking that I would truly like for you to show me today what you and your helpers have been doing to start the spring turpentine production, and perhaps Jake and Adam could walk with me around the fields and acquaint me with all the planting. I've been so busy with our building projects that I have failed to be a good manager of the farm in the absence of my husband."

Soola cried out with delight, "Why, Mistress, we will all show you everything, starting with the big trees. Ain't that right, Adam?"

Adam jumped up from his makeshift mattress, "Yes Ma'am, we'll do it for sure. Gimme just a few minutes."

Thus, they took a walk on that warm Sunday morning. Archie had acquiesced in his wife's request for the Lord's day to remain the weekly day of rest; although he had warned her that, in the future, she should be hesitant in asking such favors. She had made the request while stroking his arm early one morning. Soola led the mistress back along the path to the Turpentine Forest, which Gertrude had seen, but she wanted to hear from Soola exactly how the extraction of sap was done.

"You see, Mistress, most of these trees will be continuing to produce from where we shut down in November. You see this tree, we have made a long high gash in the trunk, and by now the sap is flowing down fast into the box at the bottom. But notice how high up this one is, and the men must climb up the ladders. But look, you see how this high up sap ain't so pure, it has bits of bark and all that from its journey down the tree, and from being scraped where it gets stuck. We call it scrape. So now I'm gonna show you that me and the men have cut into four new trees, and the sap that comes out is pure and a lighter color. This makes high quality turpentine." After showing them the special axe-like shovels used for hacking at the wood to create these great gashes after the bark is removed, Soola sneaked a look around, caught Adam's eye, and saw his smile of pride in her work and her knowledge. She tried not to act too big-headed. "So, when each box is filled, we pour the sap into those barrels over there, but don't mix the pure with the scrape, then fasten them up, and they're ready to ship to the distillery. You see, Massa Jimmie at Pine Forest, down there where I was born, he had his own still, and they made pitch and tar too, but that's real hard and dangerous. I never did that work; I just worked on the trees. But I was not much more than a child then, and I ran up and down them trees faster than any of the men, which made 'em edgy. So that's it, Mistress, that's the turpentine business. Well, one last thing to say—I keep reminding Massa Archie that these pine forests ain't forever. These old long leaf pines still produce the richest and most turpentine, but eventually when a tree is shed of its bark, it weakens and dies, and it takes a long, long time for a tree to shed its seeds and a new tree to grow. We saw that back at Pine Forest, which was a huge, enormous producer of turpentine."

Gertrude was quite impressed by this lesson and congratulated Soola on her skill. "But where is the distillery?" she asked.

"I dunno, Miz Gertrude. All I know is they load it onto boats over there at the river and take it west towards town. Massa Archie, he's in charge of that operation. He just wants us to get the sap out of the trees. But I bet Eddie knows somewhat of that because he has learned how to make the barrels and Massa Archie calls him the 'cooper' now."

"Soola, I do believe that my husband also owns a part of the pine forest further up the river, west of town. Has he ever mentioned starting the turpentine business up there? Because North Carolina is looking to become the biggest producer of turpentine and tar." Gertrude patted the trunk of one of the biggest trees, so huge it would take at least four of them with long arms to circle it holding hands. "Look at these trees, so tall and strong."

"No ma'am, he has never told me that. He doesn't like to talk to any of us like we're people." Adam poked her in the back to remind her not to start that. She switched her tone. "Tho' I will say that he's grateful to me for getting this business started, because nobody but me knew about it when we came here." She wanted to tell them about how she had felt as a young girl, out on those trees at night, and how those sensations were with her still—how the sounds of the night birds calmed her—the low whooo of owls, the quaint human-like words of whippoorwills, and the scratching and squeaking of the tiny black and white woodpeckers rushing up and down—and always the faraway howling of the wolves. She had never feared the sounds of darkness. No, those creatures composed her music of the night. But those were private thoughts that she shared with no one. As they left, her mind was full of memories of the Pine Forest Plantation, especially the night that Massa Jimmie died.

They moved on, out of the forest and into the fields, newly denuded of trees, only a few stumps remaining, but now planted in corn, wheat, potatoes, and other vegetables. In fact, some of these earlies were already being harvested. Jake and Adam explained that it would soon be time for the cotton field to be planted and the potatoes harvested. Soola was quite aware that Gertrude knew all that; the mistress had grown up on a farm and had worked in the fields since childhood, but neither she nor the mistress said a word, except a few oohs and aahs. On a day like this, it was the walk on a circular route around the fields that they enjoyed—feeling the warmth of spring and that fresh breeze blowing off the river. Two chickadees on a low tree limb were warbling out a chorus of short songs until a blue jay flew in and chased them away. Soola believed this was her happiest time since Little Adam died. She wished it would never end.

Chapter 9

But the end came. From the far side of the cotton field near the river, they began to hear voices coming from the big house. Then shouting. They looked at the mistress, whose head came up and turned in that direction, "We need to get back there," she said and started off at a run. Soola knew it was the master, returned home. He would not be happy seeing them all together like this, enjoying the scenery. And, as for the new buildings, well, he had pitched a fit over the pumps. What on this earth would he do now?

Soola saw from a distance Massa Archie standing up in a new cart, surveying his plantation with hand at brow to shade his eyes. Little George held the horse's bridle, and Judith with Ida stood nearby awaiting the master's orders. At a closer range, Soola realized that he was pale and shaking, watching them approach, his face twitching slightly, then uttering in a voice heavy with sarcasm as his wife approached. "Well, well, Mrs. McLachlan, what have you done to my farm? Tried to make it pretty, eh? Not satisfied with a down-in-the earth farm?"

Gertrude did not answer the question immediately. There were three minutes of silence and to Soola, it was a long three minutes, feeling the tension, the fear creeping through the gathering throng. Then the mistress stepped closer, looked at him with a clear and straight expression, and spoke. "Mr. McLachlan, I did mention to you that the cabins would be part of my plan, all paid for by me."

Archie jumped out of the cart and drew near to his wife. "Yes, and I recall too that I said you would never have them. But perhaps you have put that out of your mind. Perhaps, you decided to go ahead and do it while I was out of sight, whether I liked it or not. Perhaps you decided to disobey your husband and owner of the Inveraray Plantation." His voice was rising, along with the wind that seemed to provide a soft chorus of sound behind these two in their argument. It looked to Soola as if he might strike her. But surely he wouldn't risk a physical fight. She wanted to laugh, but good sense took hold of her voice at that moment.

Then, as always, Gertrude's calm voice dominated the conversation. "My dear husband, I thought you would be so pleased with my work managing the farm, as you asked me to do. You haven't seen the fields yet, or the turpentine trees with the sap flowing down, which will all bring you profits most certainly as soon as we get it all packaged, or maybe boxed, for you. Jake and Adam and Soola, this very afternoon have spent their day off showing me the great work performed by your workers in your absence. I know they will be proud to show you tomorrow morning. And, as for the cabins, this has been on my orders; the place will look more organized, more comfortable for our families, who will all want to demonstrate their gratitude by working ever harder, all at no expense to this plantation. And, husband, have you brought any fine gifts for us to share, in return for our dedication to your wishes? Or maybe after our meal, tell us some happy tales of your travels, to entertain us in our secluded life?"

Archie had tried to interrupt her as she spoke, to no avail. The mistress' voice was too strong, too steady. Finally, Gertrude smiled, turned away from her husband and went to sit in her rocking chair on the porch, where she resumed the new knitting project—a cap for Tabitha's baby, which was due to meet the world in a few weeks.

As for Gertrude's husband, he clammed up, causing disappointed looks in the men who had expected a real fight. However, Soola was watching his face and his fists; she knew that the fight was not concluded, only lurking beneath the surface. He shouted at George to put away the horse and cart, and George asked Lil Jake to help him. Archie, breathing heavily, stopped at the top of Dogwood Lane and surveyed the scene. He seemed to be settling down, and the women began a collective sigh of relief, when, in a sudden burst of ire, he grabbed hold of the Dogwood Lane sign-pole with both hands, pulled it out of the ground and flung it spinning away in front of the house, barely missing some of his slaves standing around there. The pole and sign broke apart upon landing, and Archie, brushing his hands together, went up the steps, not even glancing at his wife, nor at the new boards in the steps, nor the two rose bushes Tabitha had planted beside them.

Late in the day, Jake came and said to Adam the Massa had told him to gather the men at sunup, go out, and pull up all the new vegetables shoots growing in the far field, but not the potatoes. The vegetable field must lie fallow this year, the master had ordered. Soola said to Adam, "I've always said the man's crazy as them little stink bugs that creep around not knowing where the hell they goin'. And I think he's scarier when he keeps his tantrums inside. We'll see more of that craziness this summer, I guarantee. What're we gonna do with all the vegetable plants and all that muscle power wasted?" Adam couldn't disagree but did add that they'd wrap 'em up, get Judith to cook 'em, then they'd have a vegetable feast.

Before they slept that evening, Soola whispered to Adam, "I seen Massa Archie's eyes studying my flattened body, but he said not a word about not seeing no baby around."

"I'm thinking he's forgotten," said Adam.

Soola wasn't sure about that, "I doubt it, knowing his love of having more slaves."

The next morning, the people were called upon early by the master to get out in the fields and commence unplanting and planting anew. They all muttered and mumbled, complaining bitterly. Archie shouted at them that they had been spoiled by the mistress for two months, and now they had to forget about those holiday weeks. Soola saw him there on his steps and hoped she could slip away to the turpentine forest without his spotting her. But no, he came down the steps at high speed and addressed her with words both cruel and mocking. "So Soola, you weren't able to keep your baby for me, huh? I heard you did away with it yourself to spite me and do me out of a fresh young worker for the future. Where did you put it—in the pond back there, or perhaps in the river?"

Soola couldn't believe her ears. The death of her baby, her precious child, killed by her to spite the master? Thrown in the pond? She looked up at him with loathing. "Massa Archie, why don't you drain the pond and the river and find his tiny body? You're so crazy you might just do that. But, I will promise you, I wouldn't never think of my own darling child in the same thought with such a man as you, and I know that when dark falls tonight, the spirit of that baby will be hoverin' over your house to curse you for your evil accusations against his mother. May all the wicked spirits curse you for your life of evil."

Archie picked up a stick and started beating her over the shoulders and head until the mistress came running out of the house, dressed ready for the field with scarf and bonnet. She grabbed the stick from his hand and pushed him away. "Mr. McLachlan, stop it, stop it right now. Are you not a grown man, do you not know how to behave? Don't ever touch her again."

"But wife, you didn't hear what she said to me," replied Archie. He dusted himself off.

"First I want to know what you said to her," said Gertrude, helping Soola to stand and straighten her bonnet.

"You always blame me, wife, when you should be supporting me. Instead you speak up for this rebellious and treacherous darkie." He reached for his hat on the ground, shook it, slapped it against his leg, and placed it on his head. "I'll talk to you more about this later."

"Yes, we will both talk, Mr. McLachlan." Soola stood quietly, watching the man and wife walk together towards the field. She shook her head in wonder, just as a crack of thunder appeared out of nowhere. She smelled a coming rain shower, saw a black cloud hovering to the southwest with its ghostly shadow spreading across the pine needles, and heard the crows flapping their heavy wings in flight. She took off at a run along the turpentine path thinking she must ask Bejida what might have brought them a thunderstorm so early in the morning—both unseasonal and untimely. But when she later questioned the girl about the storm, Bejida answered with a laugh—she didn't think the gods cared about the weather much and anyway all weather in April was unpredictable, they could even have a bout of winter weather in this changeable month. One of the men had told her that about the temperamental nature of April. Soola liked that Bejida had been realistic in her answer. It made her occasional predictions on weighty matters more reliable and believable.

That afternoon, sitting under the tallest pine tree in her forest, Soola felt surrounded by gloom. She pondered on all the hard words this man had heaped upon her, with never a recognition of her skill with the turpentine, never a thank you for developing this money-making business. Since Adam and her two girls would not have returned from the fields yet, she decided she'd rest here a while, wrap herself in the aura of the spring day, and create a goddess who would whip the hated master for putting the hex on her that morning. Her mind wandered back to Massa Jimmie, a man in contrast to this master because, although he sometimes exploded in anger, the slaves at Pine Forest always felt that he cared about them, in fact probably preferred their company to that of white folks. Soola knew that he especially cared about her and had told Selma to teach her reading and writing. Now, staring high up the trunk of this king of trees, with hand over her eyes, she believed it had been her fault Massa Jimmie died on that awful night, her fault that the mistress and the Red Devil, Mr. Anders, had tortured some of the slaves and sold others, including her little brother Amos. Red Devil, too, had put her onto dangerous turpentine work, high up the tree work, and whipped the scars onto her back. Then later, he had sold her own little Kayla, Prissy too, along with Missy's girls, and had sent them on the cart down to Georgetown to the Britishers. Yes, Red Devil was worse than Massa Archie. She looked at her thumbs that had been weakened by the agonizing thumb screws and knew that Miz Gertrude would never allow such cruelty here. Her mind grasped something else: this aggravating little master was perhaps too ignorant to know about the bad tortures. But why did Massa Jimmie agree to have them? No answer to those ponderings. She looked at the sky and knew it was time to end the day.

Later, alone in her cabin, Soola heard a light tap on the door, jumped up and opened it. No one there. Looking outside through the shadows of the trees, she saw a figure, not even a definite shape, but a cruel vision resembling Mr. Anders, the Red Devil from her memories. She drew in her breath with a whistling sound and, looking again, realized the strange vision was Massa Archie standing there talking to Pete, that new boy who hated all white people, even the blessed Miz Gertrude. Well, why should he not? thought Soola, but, lump Miz Gertrude in with all them others? That's plain stupid. As her eyes moved to the left, she found Adam staring at her. He was wearing an old threadbare tweed jacket with a torn seam at the shoulder, and a narrow-brimmed hat cocked a little to the side. To her eyes, he presented a dashing, joyful sight which melted her heart. He came over, pushed the door back, pulled her inside with him, and she fell into his arms. Tears began to fall. When Paddy flew in a few minutes later, she asked her mama why she was crying, but Soola couldn't answer, couldn't explain why. Paddy said she would get their supper from the kitchen.

Late that night, Soola and Adam whispered together in their corner of the cabin. They had pulled the curtain across, the curtain that Adam had nailed to the wall to give them some privacy. As Adam pulled her to him, Soola listened for the heavy sleep breathing from her daughters, then turned to him. Although she didn't feel amorous tonight, she could never refuse Adam, and she didn't refuse him this night. It was he who stopped, trying to see her face in the dark. "What's the matter Baby? You don't want me?"

"I always want you, Adam, but the Massa cast a gloom over me this morning, and it's still on me." She didn't feel like explaining it, and yet, maybe he would understand and help her. "But mostly it reminded me of my days long ago at Massa Jimmie's place after he died."

Adam sat up slowly and whispered, "You never did tell me how he died and why you're always thinkin' it was your fault, which I'm sure is just your own mind talking."

Soola sat up beside him so her mouth was near his ear. "Oh Adam, I hate to burden you with this junk from way back, but it keeps coming back to my mind. Massa Jimmie died when his heart stopped beating one night in bed with Selma, his beautiful girl friend."

"All right, but I can't see how you was to blame in that." Adam raised himself up on his elbow.

"Well, you see, my love, I had upset him real bad at dinner that evening. You remember that me and Amos, my little brother, used to work in the dining room, serving the plates, cleaning up, and all that, helpin' our mama, specially when Massa Jimmie had his white friends from Kingston to come and eat and drink with him. Well that night, I reckon I was about twelve years, maybe thirteen, they was all talkin' about freedom and independence from England. He said to his friends that soon the Britishers would be telling them they couldn't even make their own rice pudding anymore but must send the rice over there and order the pudding from their pudding factory, or something like that. I remember him saying that like it was yesterday. I remember his face was red from drinkin' and talkin', and he was somewhat tipsy. Because he turned to me and said Kanky— remember that was what they called me back then—come over here to the table and tell us what do you think of all this freedom talk. And I told all those men sitting around that table that I thought freedom to make your own rice pudding was kind of silly, but if it was freedom for me and my brother and my mother too, then I would like that kind of freedom."

Adam had to use great self-control to stop from laughing loud and waking up Paddy and Mary Alice. Soola put her hand over his mouth and continued her story. "Well, Massa Jimmie went into one of his fits and shouted out that I was an insolent black brat and for me and Amos to go to Selma's and wait for him there. He would take care of me real good and would shut my mouth up for a long time. As we were running out, I heard him apologizing to those white men for my uppity behavior but that he liked to show off my smartness. I heard Mr. Rawlin's voice say that Massa Jimmie should take care how he encouraged that kind of independent thinking in his people cause for safety he should keep them ignorant and scared. Well, we waited and waited at Selma's house until we finally crept back to our house hopin' he was drunk and would forget about it. But this is the sad part, he did go to Selma later and his heart stopped while he was in her bed. She screamed and cried in the dark. Her and Taylor ran away in the morning cause they knew the mistress would come from Charleston, and her and the Red Devil would treat Massa Jimmie's favorites real bad. And that is what happened. My growin' up was rough after that. So that's why it was all my fault—for not keepin' my mouth shut when he asked me about freedom. Getting real angry was not good for his heart."

"You don't know that's what caused him to die, Soola. In fact, any person would say that too. Massa Jimmie probably had a bad heart, no matter what. But, Soola, who's Taylor?" Soola couldn't see his face but knew that expression when jealousy crept in.

"Taylor was Massa Jimmie's right hand man. He was a sly one; most of the slaves didn't trust him for a minute, but he was my friend."

"Well, I bet he was sweet on you too," said Adam in a tight voice.

"No, Adam, stop being jealous," she answered stroking his face. "The only person Taylor was sweet on was himself, always sly and self-serving and seeking special favors from the master. Years later, he came back there with the red coat Britishers, but we never saw him again after that. I hope them British took care of him."

Soola snuggled up with Adam then, and they slept. She had not told him about the most terrifying incident in her life at Pine Forest, in fact, had no intention of remembering it with him.

The hot weather came, and the men working on cabins had to help families create windows on the back to allow in the breezes that might blow through. Complaints of the heat and stuffy air in the cabins abounded, which didn't help calm the fights and disagreements that continued to trouble these families at Inveraray. Gertrude had to frequently step in as mediator. Often, the source of a disagreement was between a man and a woman, and the result would be the man's expulsion from the nest. Soola had said from the start that the women were in charge; and as the months went by, this became more or less the rule.

One evening, Mistress Gertrude stood laughing in the middle of Dogwood Lane in discussion with Soola and Tabitha, all wiping their brows and hoping for a brief storm to come by and cool them off. They could hear the distant thunder and see the faint flashes to the west, but sometimes this relief from the heat passed them by. As the women gossiped on the subject of yet another expulsionof a man down at the end of the lane, Gertrude bent over in merriment with hand on her head, "Well, this is the opposite of what's supposed to happen," she said. "The man is supposed to ask the woman to marry him and beg her to come live with him."

Soola replied, "Well, this be a place where not supposed to does in fact happen, because slavery ain't supposed to be, it's freedom that's supposed to be, and yet it's the opposite here."

Gertrude looked at her in surprise but only nodded her head and said nothing. Lord, should I be so friendly with these women who are in my power? Maybe that's not the way it's supposed to be either. That old fear of rebellion sneaked in to give her a shiver, but contrarily, she'd been sensing a growing closeness between her and Soola ever since Archie had departed on his long trip. She finally replied, "This has always seemed the natural order of things to me, but perhaps not to you folks." And that was the first time she had spoken of slavery in general terms directly to the slaves. She had certainly always lived and worked with slaves but had never imagined before this year that a slave would become her closest friend. And it wasn't only Soola. She enjoyed the company of Tabitha and Judith, and the men like Jake and Adam too, also Bejida, an amazing young girl. But here she was, a white woman, in a secluded place, with no white friends, finding greater and greater difficulty in speaking to her husband about almost any subject, let alone her most precious and deeply held beliefs—her faith and her reverence for the teachings of Jesus. When all is said and done, thought Gertrude, my mission to help these people is the highest of my aspirations, and their friendship has attached itself to the mission in order to help and encourage me through almost insurmountable strife. The hysterical singing of the cicadas high up in the trees seemed to support her ambitions. The songs of these insects, and of the chirping crickets, provided a constant summertime chorus, permeating the atmosphere and providing an almost unnoticed but essential element of the warm weather season. At this moment they entered her conscious thoughts, and Gertrude felt the need of listening to those thousands of tiny voices.

She touched Soola on the shoulder and said she would see them on the morrow, then turned and walked up to her rocking chair, her knitting, and the concert from the trees. She thought about Tabitha, who had borne a baby girl in June. The new mother had asked permission to name the baby Gertie. Gertrude chuckled to herself as she rocked, remembering her brothers' teasing nickname for her. Anyway, little Gertie would need some warm garments in a few months.

Gertrude's thoughts moved on to Archie. She grew puzzled and fatigued at the very thought of the man. Surely, aiding him to get through life should be an important part of her mission, but here she had failed. Since his homecoming from the tobacco journey, the attacks on her had increased. Two subjects seemed to hold deep bitterness in his withered heart—her treachery in building the cabins, which she had refused to cancel, and her friendship with Soola, which likewise she had told him she would not give up, that she could not live in a place so unnecessarily impoverished, so destitute of either comfort or human kindness, couldn't live here without friendship. She soon suspected that he would eventually accept the physical changes to his plantation because she kept reminding him of possible profits from healthier and more satisfied workers. But, resentment over her friendship with Soola, he would never put aside. He asserted that she was lowering herself by that friendship; whereas she believed he was jealous of her closeness to another human being, be it slave or free, man or woman. And how do you deal with jealousy? Finally, Gertrude admitted to herself that she truly didn't care whether he forgave her or thanked her, or neither. Indeed, he had never shown any hint of gratitude for all she had done, nor had he admitted her role in his investigating the tobacco business. As a result, Archie was becoming separated from her mission; no help for him seemed possible.

She hardly remembered now those few moments of pleasure she had felt with Archie in the early months here, when he'd been an ardent lover, smiling at her, a young and active man in contrast to Hermann. It was with a smile and affectionate feelings that she sometimes arose from his bed; although, even from the start, his impatience, his fits of anger and suspicion, his reminders that she had stolen her money from him, had interrupted those sensual reveries.

Lately, with his increasing verbal harangues against her friend and herself, she would fall silent and ignore him. If she questioned him about his pessimism and want of any joy in others, he would turn it around against her with sarcasm and sneers—"and so, you wish me to find gladness in my heart, as you have, for these hopeless creatures?" or "I suppose your perfect father and mother taught you these absurd notions?" She wondered what had happened to her attraction to the man. Had there been clues early in their acquaintance? Bruce had tried to warn her. Then, recently, Soola had told her that the slaves marveled he never beat up on his wife the way some husbands, both white and black, did. Gertrude had laughed at that and said no he wouldn't dare.

Anyway, she could never abandon these people now. If she left, they would have no one. Plus, she was godmother to Tabitha's little Gertie, who would be her first pupil in Christ. No, her mission had launched and was underway, and Gertrude saw fulfillment in her future. The song of the cicadas grew more intense in encouragement as darkness fell. And the crows added to her sense of belonging: they no longer escaped to the treetops upon her approach. But her husband's anger seemed to be always present, always her fault, becoming rooted in her mind.

1792

Chapter 10

    In April of the next year, Tom Adams, a salesman of household goods, in fact of just about any goods a country person might need, was spotted by Gertrude as he drove his horse and wagon up the long driveway at Inveraray Plantation. She and Tabitha were cleaning up the front porch, sweeping, dusting, and shaking out the floor mats beside the door. Gertrude asked Tabitha if she knew who this might be, and Tabitha answered that he was a salesman who had stopped by here a couple of times in years past. "It was Judith who spoke to him and told him what they needed, but then she had to find the master to get his approval," she added. "And he had always told her not to buy much, said we was all getting fat at his expense."

    Tom pulled his horse to a stop by the steps and jumped down. He doffed his hat revealing a mop of thick black hair, and a pair of bright blue twinkling eyes, then replaced the hat and gave a slight bow. "Madam, I am Tom Adams, and I have visited here a few times in the past and would like to speak to the person in charge of household goods."

    "Well, sir, that would be me, Gertrude McLachlan, the mistress here, and I am pleased to meet you. Please show me what you have," replied Gertrude, wiping her hands on her apron and descending the steps.

    Tom looked around and smiled. Gertrude thought he had a sassy air about him. In fact, he then commented on the state of the farm, remarking that the place had changed for the better since he was here last. "The all-pervading stink is gone," he said, grinning, "and you got some cabins for the Negroes, I see, and I ain't never seen a white woman here before. Is there new ownership? Man alive, the aroma from this place was picked up, even by boats going by on the river."

    "No, my husband is still the owner, and I now would prefer to look at your wares rather than listen to your insolent remarks." She went to the back of the wagon and quickly picked out some crockery, linens, cooking utensils, notebooks, paper, feather pens, ink, and staple foods.

She paid with cash from her apron pocket and asked him to come back again in six months. She could tell that he was pleased with the large amount of her purchases, guessing he would be back in that time period. "So where do you come from, Mr. Adams?"

"We've recently moved to the new city of Raleigh, which will be our new state capital. We plan to expand our business over this whole part of the state, that is, if we can find the salesmen, for it's a long distance. However, we'll try to be back as you wish. He touched his hat, pulled the horse around, and moved off down the driveway.

"Wait," cried Gertrude suddenly, "When will Raleigh become the new capital city?"

Tom didn't stop but looked back over his shoulder, "Nobody knows exactly, ma'am, but it looks like soon."

She thanked him again and stood there for a while, feeling sad that the eastern part of the state might decline in importance with the removal of the capital from this region. She looked down among the underbrush around the trees, listening to the song of the gentle towhee, its voice rising at the end of its song. They moved in pairs, with the female merely brown, dull compared to the bright black and white and red of the male. Was that usually true of birds? The female dull and unnoticed? That seemed to be what Archie would like to see in his wife too, she thought.

Archie had kept silent with Gertrude during the winter months about his plans for tobacco. A few days after his return from the tobacco trip the year before, she had asked him when he planned to plant his tobacco seeds. He had mumbled a little then assured her that it was too late at that time to start the tobacco, it must wait until the next spring. "But, Mrs. McLachlan, I have told you before that I do not choose to speak to a woman about my plans for this farm. All I can say now is that I'll tell you next year when it's time to start." He had not spoken another word on the subject since.

Now, a year later, he came running to the house after Tom Adams left and asked for her help in transplanting. "We have the young plants crowded together in a sunny spot," he said, all excited and breathless, "and tomorrow we will transplant them, spread them out in the two fields. That's gonna be a big job, and all on the farm, even the children, must help. We've been collecting the manure, and now it must be spread around. Tobacco plants need a lot of encouragement from the soil in old fields; they like new ones best. I need you to help git these women goin'."

"Why certainly, we'll see how it looks tomorrow." she replied acting quite cool, even reluctant. "But Soola might be too busy with the turpentine, and I might be needed with the children. Judith can't be cooking all day as well as watching the children. Anyway," she added giving Archie a sly look, sitting on the rocker and looking down on him on the steps. "You have given me to believe I am not competent to help with the tobacco. Why don't you give me a job washing clothes or something womanish like that?" Gertrude looked at his usually stubborn face lit up with anticipation, thinking him to be the silliest, most ridiculous, also ungrateful, person she had ever seen. He had never acknowledged for a moment that it was her suggestion about tobacco that had led to his trip and to this beginning. And now when he needs everyone, even us foolish women, he doesn't think we're so incompetent.

Archie stamped his foot. "Why can't you just do what I ask you like a normal woman without ruffling my feathers and tryin' to put me down all the time?"

"Don't stamp your foot like that on the wood step, you'll break up the hard work Jake put into those steps last year while you were gone. I bet you've never thanked him either." Gertrude watched him turn and walk back to admire his tobacco plants.

He didn't speak to her again that evening—all during their meal, silence. But, of course, the next morning, she did round up every available woman and child to get out early and help with the transplanting. Gertrude was excited and even persuaded Soola, despite her friend's sulky looks, to abandon turpentine in favor of tobacco on this breezy spring day. Soola had said many times how much she hated field work but then made up for it by working alongside Adam most of the morning in the fallow field, the field that was closest to the river and ringed with pines and dogwood trees, now at full bloom. Having developed an elaborate set of rules for field workers, Archie would be enraged, thought Gertrude, if he saw this forbidden activity, what he called fraternizing, which meant, flirting, laughing, fooling, and slowing down the work. But since Archie was working in the other field, he failed to see this subterfuge evolving until he noticed it after lunch. Gertrude played innocent, keeping busy with the planting, bending over, standing up, until the pain in her back felt like ten large daggers implanted there.

Archie dropped his tools, picked up the whip that was always nearby and ran over to the couple, brandishing the whip, "Git over there with the women, you thrice damned bitch," he cried in a rage. He brought the whip down on Adam and Soola both, the fringed end of the "snake whip" curling up and catching Adam's face. The other workers cringed and shrank near the ground. Gertrude hurried to the rescue, snatched the whip out of her husband's hand, and threw it with all her might into the trees, then took Soola by the arm and pulled her over to work with her. Adam seemed to crumple up in humiliation, while Soola yelled cuss words at the master. "Hush, hush, you'll make him worse," urged Gertrude. She despised the ugliness of these outbursts by her husband and looked with yearning at the dogwood blossoms on the edge of the field. So delicate in contrast.

Archie wasn't finished with his anger. He turned his attention to his wife, accusing her of treachery, deceitfulness, counting this slave woman as more important than himself. "You wait, the both of you—I'll git back at you, you won't know when it's coming, but it will come." His face seemed to take on an aspect of madness and confusion, an aspect which frightened the slaves. Even the mistress felt a sudden dread, but not Soola, who merely looked on the master with loathing. Gertrude wondered what on this earth would ever put fear into the woman's heart. Finally, declaring in a shrieking voice that she was a bad influence on his workers, Archie expelled his wife from tobacco work, told her to get out of his field and never return. She walked in dejection back to the house, while word raced in whispers around among the workers, even into the other field on the tongue of the water boy, that Massa Archie had kicked out the mistress from the tobacco fields, had treated her like a slave, although, yes, she had thrown away his whip.

That evening, Archie sat down with Gertrude for dinner after Tabitha had carried up the food. He seemed quieter, the anger gone. He attempted to make conversation about his pleasure with the tobacco fields, even commented on the fine aromas floating up their way from the kitchen. He felt they had made excellent progress today, and she knew that silver and gold coins were clinking in his mind. She agreed with everything he said, too exhausted for another fight, stirring the food around on her plate, scooping up another spoonful of beans and pork, and wondering how his face would look with beans dripping down it from hair to neck. Archie even made a slight hint that she might return to help him on the morrow.

"No, Mr. McLachlan, I think maybe it's better if I stick to housework and leave the fields to the men."

Furthermore, Adam appeared broken up by this latest outrage from Massa Archie, He remained subdued and ashamed for the next few weeks. He spoke to no one, except one of the dogs who had befriended him. He had no words even for Soola, who whispered to the mistress that he was turning his back to her. Gertrude understood this to mean that he was turning his back in their bed at night. The mood of the place had changed—back to the constant melancholy and mist of anxiety that had hung over the people before her arrival, Gertrude thought. Several of the slaves attempted in subtle ways to please her, performing special favors without being asked, like carrying extra water up those steep stairs to her room and ironing her clothes. Ironing was something she had always done for herself, the iron being an implement she had brought with her to Inveraray two years back and had placed at the disposal of all near the kitchen fire. Judith took to preparing spring vegetables in butter, which she knew the mistress liked. And, sensing this gloom among their masters and mistresses, even the dogs walked more slowly, frequently looking up at the human faces with unease in their eyes.

Gertrude accepted these little favors with warmth and affection for the people and witnessed a kind of healing taking place. As she watched the pale green shoots push themselves out on the trees, heard the birds singing, and smiled at the kindliness of the spring sun, she reminded herself of her mission, watched the people moving about in greater comfort and trust, and understood yet again that her presence was undoubtedly a necessity in this place. She watched Adam begin to recover, saw him put his arm around Soola and felt relief that their love would survive. As for Archie, her puzzlement continued as she walked around the plantation performing the usual chores of sweeping, raking the dirt in front, pulling weeds around the house, knitting, and checking on the sick. She deemed him to be calmer but could discern no clues as to his future behavior. Desiring to soak up the warm air and resume the bond that drew them together, she and Soola commenced sitting together on Sunday afternoons under the dogwood trees at the far end of Dogwood Lane. Soola would shell peas or split beans, and Gertrude would all the time knit like a whirlwind, creating clothes for the children. She not only knew this bond continued to be a conversation topic among the slaves at Inveraray, she also pondered over her husband's silence on the subject. Gertrude guessed it was stored up inside him, awaiting another outburst.

1794

Chapter 11

In the months and years following that miserable brawl in the tobacco field, Gertrude stayed away from field work, even took to spending a day in town with her brother Bruce a couple of times a month. There she would talk to him about her money and accept from him a payment, which represented her share of their business profits. In September, four years after her wedding, she got Adam to row her upriver to town to see her brother and his wife and their two little girls. She relished the calming effects of the rippling current and occasionally of a fish jumping out of the water. A huge bird flew over and alighted at the top of a tree on the far bank. Osprey, she thought, or even a bald eagle, but no, there was no white head visible. "Thank you, Adam, for rowing me up to town, I am grateful to you for this effort." He tipped his hat and said he was glad to be of service.

When they pulled up at the dock, Adam said he would help with a loading job and make a little money while she was visiting. "But where will you sleep?" she looked at his dark face, the furrows running down each cheek, and the deep-set black eyes. Maybe he was older than she'd thought. No telling the hard times he'd experienced in the past, no telling the mysterious, powerless life of a slave. Thoughts flashed through her mind of her own life and that of her brothers, wide open, the oral history known to all, details written on land deeds. Adam assured her that the shed over there was waiting for him and that he had years of experience sleeping in barns. He smiled and touched his cap again. She reached in her bag and gave him some bread and cheese, and on second thought, two coins.

Later, as she negotiated her steps along the rutted muddy street, Gertrude questioned to herself the wisdom of leaving him there alone with such ease of escape. What if he took the boat and sped down the river with the current, out into the sound, and escaped on a ship going north. Adam, betray them and abandon Soola? No, that didn't seem possible. She thought she knew him well enough, but does a slave owner ever really know a slave's mind? Pushing these suspicions away, she walked on, reached her house, and greeted her brother, who sat on the porch smoking a pipe, surprised to see her.

Remembering that Bruce had been hesitant in handing over her money lately, Gertrude decided they would get that business done first, leaving time later for visiting. He was reluctant to hand over any piece of the shipping company profits, which had been increasing since the time of her marriage.

"But Baby Brother," she said in a voice of authority. "it was the profits from Hermann's business that we both invested in the shipping company before I went away."

"But Gertie, it was my idea and anyway you're just going to spend the money on building more cabins or barns on that hopeless farm of your husband's." He began walking up and down the room with hands clasped behind his back.

Gertrude said, "My goodness, you look so much like Father when you do that way. And I bet Priscilla spends a lot of your money on fancifying this house too."

"No, she usually spends her own money on that, money which she demands of me every month from her dowry. That's all people want from me, money, money, money. I get confused about all this money which I'm holding, and which isn't mine— you and Priscilla both, and I have to admit, the farm business is not as strong as it used to be. And, with two little ones now, and Aurelia's increasing family, my expenses are on the rise. Plus, we want to build a new house of our own. In that event, of course, we'll be moving out of your house, and you'll demand the rent from tenants, or you'll want to live here again when you have had enough of that madman you live with." Bruce was getting worked up, wringing his hands.

Gertrude was concerned that maybe he was having financial difficulties. She was ready to let him have the shipping business money and be satisfied with the smaller amount from the farmers. "Oh, Bruce, don't insult Archie. None of this is his fault. In fact, he's always at me for signing over to you all my property, which of course has been nothing but a boon to you. But maybe I'm willing to surrender my share from the shipping this month, that is if you really are short on the earnings lately." She would look at the books and check on that, she thought.

Bruce went in the house to get her money, and she followed. "Let me see your accounts, Bruce," she said, then studied each page carefully. "Why, brother, you're making a fortune. There's no problem here, but what are these big payments to a Miss Abigail?" Looking up, she saw that her brother was sitting in a chair with head in hands. "Why Bruce whatever is the matter?" she cried and ran over to him. "I don't care about the money, you can keep it all."

Looking up at her with tears in his eyes, Bruce told her he had recently had a misadventure with a young woman in town and she had given birth to a baby boy, who already could pass for white if separated from his mama. Anyway, he must pay for this mistake for the rest of his life. And he added that Priscilla had not forgiven him and perhaps never would.

"Oh Bruce, I'm so sorry, but you are right that you must support them. Are you sure it's your son?"

"No question about that, Gertie. Can you imagine—he has that same little fragment of extra toe on both feet, like me and Father." He touched the toe of his boot, looking up at his sister with a rueful smile. "I am full of regrets."

"Bruce, we will look to the positive and imagine that he might be a fine son for you as the years go by. But who is her owner? Or is she free?"

"She's free, Gertie, she lives with her mother and works at the market setting up and cleaning up at the end of the day. The town hired her. It's difficult because I see her there frequently. But I've told her it's over, and I'll help with the child. But here, Gertie, I'll not hold back on the money I owe you, nor will I go back on my promise to you."

He took out a handkerchief and blew his nose and wiped his eyes. "I love my family and will honor my promises to Priscilla. Always. This happened when she was carrying our second child."

Gertrude laid an arm around Bruce's back and rested her head against his shoulder. "I know you will, brother, because you are a good man. If she loves you, Priscilla will forgive you, that is if it never happens again and you never fuss at her, always act loving." She then suggested that today would perhaps not be so good for spending time with Priscilla and, that she would be on her way. Bruce assured her that he was already doing all those things she suggested.

Gertrude hurried away, not wanting, for sure, to be witness to the disagreements of this young couple while knowing they could only help themselves. Why had she even come to town today? Oh yes, to get her money, and get away from Archie for a day while she pondered on the question of how to tell him her big news. She was glad that yet there was only a small thickening of her body, almost unnoticeable; although the nausea and vomiting might have been obvious to Tabitha and Soola. She fretted on the question—would her husband like this idea of being a father? She needed to tell him before he noticed her increasing size.

Not wanting to deprive Adam of his opportunity to earn money, Gertrude wandered around the shops for a while, bought some badly needed household goods—fabrics, scissors, needles and thread for Susan, their new seamstress at Inveraray, as well as new headscarves for all the women. All these she found at the new dry goods store. Then to the bakery, where she bought some small apple pies, as many as she could fit into the carry bag. She ate one to hold her appetite at bay until they reached home, biting into the delicious pastry and apple juice until it ran down her chin. Rushing away, ashamed that someone might see her gluttony, she grabbed a large damp leaf beside the path to wipe her face.

Adam sat reclining against the wooden lean-to on the dock having apparently finished his job when Gertrude arrived. He jumped up, "You're not staying over, Mistress?"

"No Adam, there wasn't much for me to do here, so let's go home." She noticed that he exhibited more than the usual care in helping her down into the rocking boat with waves lapping. It came to her that of course her secret condition was more than rumor on the farm, more like a newsflash of fact. She must tell Archie tonight. Oh dear.

So, tell him she did, while eating supper that evening, blurting it out quickly—"Archie, we have something exciting going to happen to us in the future. Our child is on its way." She studied his face as he looked up at her with a puzzled expression, the spoon stopped halfway to his mouth, frozen there for a few seconds. Then resuming his usual sarcastic bearing, he asked her the question guaranteed to insult any woman, "Well, my dear wife, are you sure that the child is mine? I never do know what you're doin' roamin' around up there in town by yourself." A little smile played across his face.

Quite forgetting that she had asked Bruce the very same question that morning, she felt the shock of his words sear into her very being, as painful as any real flame. My God, words will not suffice against such an indictment. In that moment, before she fled upstairs to her bed, all Gertrude's senses became enflamed, almost like the hallucinations that come with a high fever. The shape of the beans on her plate, the fork dropped haphazardly beside it, the rough contours of Archie's hand resting on the table, the smell of roasted pork, and a crow's commanding voice outside the window, all melted together to form a small pageant of horror that would ever remind her of this, Archie's ultimate betrayal. He knocked timidly on her door later, but she told him to be gone.

The next morning, Gertrude went looking for Soola in the turpentine forest, and as her friend's tall dark figure emerged from the giant trees, it struck her that Soola was also with child. The mistress embraced the servant, and her voice expressed joy, "Soola, I am mighty pleased and gratified. We will both have boys who will become the best of friends like their mothers, and they will bring together the people of this community and make us a true family. And for the present, it is your friendship that will bring me through this ordeal." Gertrude recognized on that morning that her love for Soola was greater than for any other human being. Her lifelong reservations and belief that there must be a separation between servant and mistress were evaporating.

After Soola understood for sure that both she and the mistress were with child, her first thought was to consult Bejida. But knowing that Gertrude would never tolerate any voodoo charms or foretelling the future with heathen customs, she told the mistress that she would talk to Bejida alone that evening. Gertrude's brow wrinkled, but she nodded, touched Soola's arm and promised they would sit together on Sunday and talk about their future, a future that she considered to be God's prerogative, not that of Bejida's superstitions.

At the end of the workday, Soola walked with some foreboding to the cabin that Bejida shared with the young boy Pete, who had come to Inveraray in the cart with her. When she answered the door, she immediately acknowledged that she understood why Soola had come, took her by the arm and made her lie face up on her bed. She touched Soola's stomach, murmured African words, and studied some pieces of bone, rocks, twigs, dried flowers, stirring them around into variegated shapes and colors. Soola looked up at that striking black face, thin and angular around the jaw and chin, the eyes large and hooded, and a nose unusually sharp for an African face. It was a face to always attract a second glance. "Ooh, Soola, I see boys, arm in arm, but also a girl, can't see her color. They're in a thick mist but the message is clear, they will bring happy times to this place. But there's some dark shadows too and troubles; do not sass the Massa during your time carrying this child. If you manage it right, he will grow up to be a great man, a man respected by the slaves and by the white world too."

"What's inside those dark shadows, Bejida?" Soola felt uneasy. She had faith in Bejida's living connection to Africa and believed her revelations.

"Can't see clearly, it's too dark in there, but there's a chance of trouble, that's all I can say." Soola suspected that the young girl did see something, perhaps a vision too fearful to reveal, and that old feeling of dread struck her as she walked back to her cabin, that dread that had shadowed her now for at least a dozen years, ever since those bad times at the Pine Forest Plantation. She wished she could unburden herself, but who could be a trustee of her past? Whom did she know that might stomach such a story? Only the mistress, perhaps, but still Soola postponed taking that risk.

Chapter 12

By the turn of the century, it looked to many white citizens of the new nation that the liberty promised in the Declaration of Independence and in the Constitution, was approaching fulfilment. And a year later, in 1801, with the triumphant inauguration to the presidency of Thomas Jefferson, the promise seemed even more likely to be delivered. Surely, the new president represented liberty and equality because that's what he had written in the great Declaration. The old established leaders, the Federalists, were finally defeated in the closely fought, almost disastrous election of 1800. They had fought for freedom from England, yes, but in writing the Constitution, they had perhaps never believed in the democratic ideals that Jefferson spoke for.

On the other side, Soola and a few of the other Africans at the Inveraray Plantation could see that any dream of freedom the slaves had ever believed in was disappearing. Word came to them in clumps and assorted stories that yes, the northern states, one by one, were passing laws prohibiting slavery, but the southern folks held in bondage would never be freed, and worse, this new President Jefferson owned over a hundred slaves himself up in Virginny. President Washington had willed that his slaves would be free upon the death of his wife, but not Jefferson; he was holding them tight. So where was the equality of all men?

There were other frightening tales making the rounds, said Soola. Up near Richmond, in August,1800, some slaves had plotted to kill their masters and take over the city. While these culprits were caught and executed, more plots to massacre the whites came to light in Virginia and in North Carolina near the state border. In their Sunday chats, Mistress Gertrude never discussed these rumors with Soola. It was around the campfire by the big barn after dark that the slaves whispered their fears and their loss of hope. Soola assured them that these rebellions were causing stricter laws against the bondsmen and women, that the groups of whites who believed in abolition in Virginia had packed their bags and abandoned the state, and that even Negro freemen were being forced to leave. She said the noose was tightening around the collective neck of the African people in America, and that Miz Gertrude's god and his son Jesus had again abandoned them. Those two were looking down and separating dark skin from light, curly hair from straight. Didn't matter slave nor free. But why on earth would those white gods be so busy fussing about skin and hair? Why, the gods back in Africa had kinky hair themselves, and surely, somewhere up in the sky all the gods from all over the world were sitting around, all mixed up, chatting just like the people here.

"Soola, where d'you hear all this," asked Bejida one night.

"I hear it from the master and the mistress talking, and from her talking to the salesman from Raleigh. From the newspapers they leave layin' around, and from that man who came here last year, that runaway who the paddy rollers came after. And from you, Bejida, you've told us about African gods. Some from my poor mama too, tho' she had few words. Anyway, we don't know the half of it; it seems that the black people took over a whole island out in the ocean some time back and killed all the whites, but not sure about that; it doesn't seem likely." She added that the whites were getting scared, and that didn't bode well for "us slaves."

Adam told her she needed to quit talking about all this. It could lead to big trouble if Massa Archie ever heard of it. "He has his head full of mean thoughts about you already. And don't never mention it to the mistress." So, the fireside night talks came to an end.

At the McLachlan place, life went on under the shadow of a more immediate fear, the fear radiating from Massa Archie's intermittent tantrums and threats of sale. His wife had put the hex on him about the whippings, which now were rare, but the terror that he could sell family members continually raised the bar of menace in the community, especially among the women. Even Soola was not immune from the fear of such a danger. It was now almost eleven years since the birth of her son John and a few days after that of Mistress Gertrude's son Robert, and over the years, Soola had relied on her friendship with Gertrude to protect her family. But during that time, she had also seen a gradual, ever more unyielding severity in Massa Archie's stance against his wife. Could her mistress be counted on forever? Mistress Gertrude did not like to talk about it, but the slaves all noticed and gossiped among themselves on the subject of the master and mistress.

And there was another subject for chatter which worried Soola. That was the close friendship between the two boys, one white, the other black—Robert and John, born within a few days of each other, grown up together, trapping wild animals, searching the woods and fields for the perfect sticks to make the perfect bows and arrows, and finally at the age of eight years walking like grownups to the fields to work alongside the men and women. From the start, each competed to be the most efficient hoer and planter, the fastest picker, and the strongest hauler of manure, potatoes, and other heavy goods from field to barn and back. From George, they learned the lessons of animal care and of the tricks to persuade horses to behave. From their mothers they learned the secret language of educated people—reading, writing, and numbers. The problem that made Soola fret was Massa Archie's rage when he saw his son close to John. Soola had tried hard to figure out what went through the master's mind when he let out a tongue lashing against the boys. But no one, not the mistress nor any slave, not even Bejida, could delve into the circuitous and unpredictable mind of Archie McLachlan.

On a Sunday morning in early summer, these two women, Soola and Gertrude, sat in their plain wooden chairs, which after eleven years were now starting to look like old ladies, sagging on one side and splintering on the other. Sometime during those long-ago months while Gertrude and Soola awaited the birth of their babies, Jake and his son had made the chairs and plonked them down at the end of Dogwood Lane. After all this time, the chairs seemed to have molded to their bodies, the boards of the seats being noticeably curved and smoothed, and underneath in the small squares protected from rain, cold, and sun, the weeds remained, even climbing up the legs, all winter long.

On this Sunday, they were talking idly, mostly about their worries. Gertrude again was knitting some small garments for the children of the plantation, Soola cleaning the last potatoes from the slaves' garden. It was a cool day, but unstable with weather moving in on the wind, the pines bending and swaying; even the hardwoods with their full-grown greenery were tossing around. Soola's little son Lucas, her third child with Adam, played around the cabins with the other children, digging up the mud, making rivulets, constructing cabins of twigs. The two older boys had walked out along the cypress pond path to check their animal traps. The clicking of Gertrude's knitting pins soothed this new anxiety of her friend. Somehow the sound reminded Soola that Mistress Gertrude would always be there, interested in the slaves' welfare, knitting items for their comfort, ever standing as guardian angel with her shielding wings.

"Well, Soola," Gertrude assured her friend, "I am always watching them carefully, and I have already urged Robert to not show so much of this friendship in front of his father. However, I do not think the master would hurt John in my presence or in Robert's. And John is always respectful and attentive when Archie's around. But Soola, it's you I'm more worried about. I'm still wishing you would look at the ground and just say yessir or nossir when he yells at you. Then he would have no good reason to attack you; although I admit he never needs a good reason to become violent, and that problem seems to be considerably worse than it was in the early days of our marriage."

"I wish I could do that, Miz Gertrude, but it seems my nature doesn't allow it. My mama always told me I need to show fear, but that feeling I never did understand. I've never been a fearsome woman. If something needs to be said, seems like my mouth just opens right up. Adam keeps telling me what you said too but that's hard for me to follow."

Gertrude told her the story about the "Boy That Knew No Fear" her mother had told her from the wealth of old stories from far back in the oral history of their people. That boy completely lacked the feeling of fear, so when he was out in the forest, if bears or wolves threatened, he ran at them shrieking, growling, waving his arms, and they ran off. Gertrude could not remember the turn this story followed, but it certainly involved the lesson that fear is a protective instinct, usually to be obeyed, almost as if a person were deaf or blind, the lack of those protections would be dangerous.

"That's interesting about fear. Fear seems like such a natural thing, Soola. But you mention your mother, which reminds me that in all these fifteen years I have known you, I have never asked you what she was like, and was she a good mother for you and your brother? Did you have some happy times with her?"

Soola smiled slightly, nothing surprising that a white person would be unaware of the unhappiness of a slave's life, maybe she truly believes that slaves like being slaves, she thought. Miz Gertrude might be an unusual mistress, but not all of her is different from the others. "Excuse me, Miz Gertrude, but not many slaves have happy times when they're children or ever. There's mostly hard times and sad times filled with violence and injustice. Maybe that's why we don't never talk about those old times. We just try hard to make it through each day. That's why it pleases me to see my John and your Robert so happy, even when they're working, except when the Massa's round about. Oh, Miz Gertrude, yes ma'am, I do know fear when I'm afraid for my John." She went on to say again that hers was not a pretty story on the Pine Forest Plantation, where she grew up, especially towards the end when it became unbearable. In fact, she wasn't sure whether she should tell it, didn't think the mistress would want to hear about that. "But you asked about my mother. She was a sad woman, had never recovered from the boat ride across the water. She wasn't loving, but she tried. Then too, she was one of the cooks on the place, so she worked hard over them stoves all through the heat of summer."

"Well then, I truly want to know the end time at Pine Forest, Soola. I'm not afraid to hear an unhappy story. I want to know as many details as you remember, and I aim to write it down and give it to John when he's grown."

Soola's frown increased, and she grabbed Gertrude's arm with urgency. "No mistress, you must not write this ending part down. No one must ever know it or read it, especially John. If I decide to unburden my soul of those happenings, they will be only for your ears and no one else, not even Adam. And if I do tell you, it will be because I trust you and know you to be a kind and tolerant person and hope that you will not judge me with harsh thoughts. You see, only one soul in this world knows what I did, that only one being me."

Gertrude stood and put her hand on Soola's head. "My dear friend, Jesus said, 'Judge not, lest ye be judged,' and it will be with that spirit that I hear your story. Meet me here next Sunday at this time of day, and you must tell me what happened back then that has so haunted your mind. But right now, please go inside and close your door, so you don't encounter my husband. Even I sometimes feel a tightening of the stomach when I hear him coming these days, and, indeed, I can hear his heavy footsteps now."

Soola swung the basket of potatoes up onto her head and walked with a swaying motion up the path to the kitchen. She turned for a moment and saw Gertrude smile with admiration. As she ducked into the kitchen and handed the basket of potatoes to Judith, she heard the master slam the front door of the big house, then his voice yelling at Gertrude, so loud she could hear him even through the closed door. She looked at Judith whose face filled with fear and whose hands covered her ears. Archie was shouting at Gertrude—he had told her to stay away from that damn bitch Soola, why wouldn't his wife ever do what she was told, he was the master and owner here, but no one seemed to give a damn about him. Just wait and see, he would show them his power and get his revenge, on and on, more invectives, then finally silence. Soola looked at Judith and laughed, "He's got that speech by heart now, ain't he? Remember what I said on our first day here years ago? The man's crazy. And I'll add that he's gotten worse each year of his miserable life. And I think the mistress suffers more from it than she lets on."

"This surely is a fine time of year, but then I think that in every season even the hottest days that are coming soon seem appropriate at the time," said Gertrude as she took her seat the next Sunday morning beside Soola at the end of Dogwood Lane. Soola had been sitting there musing for the past thirty minutes, taking in the scent of a wild azalea bush nearby and listening to the incessant birdsong, which Miz Gertrude had told her brought back memories of the church choir in her childhood. Ah, the life of a white girl, thought Soola ruefully, imagining a childhood where the sun shines in perpetuity and where neither pain nor harsh words rattle the feelings of love in the family. Well, she's about to hear about a slave girl's experience, if that's what she truly wishes. She was half a mind to tell Gertrude that her story needed to remain locked inside her, like the frozen lump of ice it had been, stuck in her craw for these twenty-five years, maybe more, she couldn't remember. But, too late. The mistress sat down and told her to start. That ice was about to melt. There was no turning back. Gertrude did hold a new pencil and a notebook, bought from Tom Adams. No knitting this time, but Soola remained adamant that she not put her words into writing. As if to herald the start of her story, a wood thrush overhead raised its open beak and sent its lilting song into the air. She looked up and saw the bird, seated on a dogwood branch.

Soola had found some very late peas and was shelling them into one of her colonoware bowls as she readied herself to speak. She often referred to her memory of her mother teaching her how to gather clay from the riverbank, then mold it into bowls and bake them. She hesitated. Where would she begin? The mistress knew all about Massa Jimmie and how he died and how the mistress had come up from Charleston. So she started from there, telling how the mistress and the Red Devil conspired to sell half of the slaves, her little brother Amos among them. They were carted away midst the screams and cries of their families. Her mother lost what was left of her mind and eventually hung herself in the punishment shed, a most unusual action for a slave woman, Soola said with a tense and hurried voice, eager to get this done but also to help the mistress know some details. She herself was put out onto the big trees and learned all about the turpentine and pitch and tar business. She would tie up her skirt so it looked like trousers for the climbing, and soon she became the most efficient and fastest worker up and down the trees. But she made the other workers furious because whenever the Red Devil came around, she cussed at him and also, they said her fast work was making them look bad and lazy, which they were, Soola said, and told them so. She was maybe thirteen, fourteen, during those years but wasn't sure about that. "But these scars on my back came from cussing at Mr. Anders," she added. Soola trembled as she reminded the mistress quickly about her attachment to one of the turpentine boys, then, nine months later of the birth of her baby, the little girl she named Kayla. Over the following years, she stayed away from all the men, even if they were paying her untrue compliments and begging her to lie down with them. She only wanted to spend time with Kayla, determined not to create another baby.

They lived with the twin sisters Prissy and Missy and their children until the terrible day came. The Britishers, who, they had already heard, had arrived in their ships and taken over Georgetown, came up the river with traders looking for slave women to buy. The Red Devil and his vicious giant helpers went around the cabins picking up the girls and many young women. Soola said she screamed, and Missy screamed over the loss of the little girls, and of her twin sister. They couldn't believe the traders would take little girls so young, but they did. Kayla was only five years old. "Her little face haunts me, Mistress Gertrude. She sat in the cart with tears streaming, holding out her little arms to me and crying for me to come with her. I looked up at the big trees on that day, and, swearing revenge, I began to make my plan. It took a while for me to recover from the blow to my head that Mr. Anders delivered with a big board on that day, but plan I did." She turned to Gertrude at that point with a little smile, "They said I was hard-headed, so mebbe that's what saved me from the blow. Miz Gertrude, since that day, each morning as the sun rises to the east, I hold Kayla in my mind. I wonder where she could be, whether she remembers me, where she lives. She must be near about twenty-five years old now, or more. She most likely has children of her own, which makes me a grandmother."

The first part of Soola's plan, she continued, was to modify her behavior. She became quiet and polite with Mr. Anders, Yessir, Nossir. The workers believed that board blow had changed her brain, but let them believe anything they want, she had thought. Soola knew she was coming to the heart of the evil she had committed, and so her voice lowered to a whisper, slow and hesitant.

Gertrude said, "What's wrong, Soola dear?"

"You'll see in a minute, Mistress. The words are stopping right there in my throat because they know how bad it's gonna be. But I won't stop now telling the words to come out because that block of ice will melt in just a few minutes, and I do believe the burden will be gone, and my soul will know a new light and warm feeling."

Gertrude smiled, reached over and touched Soola's hand. "I'm listening, and remember there will be no judgment, if that is indeed what's worrying you."

"Yes, Mistress, and thank you kindly." Soola continued, explaining carefully how she found a good length of a "voracious" vine, so called by Taylor, Massa Jimmie's right hand man. "I chose one that was thick, long, and full of them tough, vicious thorns. I worked on it for a week, bending it, cutting off the thorns where my hands could grab it tight, soaking it, then leaving it in the sun to dry. Mistress, that voracious vine is evil, like you know it around here. I concentrated and thought of every detail. In those days, long after the mistress had hightailed it back to Charleston, the Red Devil was drinking up Massa Jimmie's whiskey as fast as he could, sitting out there on Selma's porch every night, then staggering around in the morning searching for bad behavior, then calling for his wicked helpers to give the beatings. But I was giving him only yessir and nossir and scrambling up and down them trees. Then I crept into Selma's house when he was out away and checked on which boards was creaky. Then there came a Sunday evening of the almost full moon, and there was that devil out there drinking from the bottle."

Soola glanced at Mistress Gertrude, whose face had grown tense and more serious than
she had ever seen. Oh my, I should not be telling this, but well, I can't turn back."

Gertrude broke in, "Soola, where is Selma now, what happened to her?"

"She ran off after Massa Jimmie died. She hid in our house under the bed for a coupla days, then ran off. She said she'd find her way to Georgetown, cause she knew the mistress hated her and Red Devil would kill her. When Taylor showed up with the Britishers several years later, he said he had seen her there living in a big house, getting gold and silver from the soldiers, but you couldn't always believe what Taylor said. I hope he spoke the truth that day. Now, I'll finish—I had to wait until the full moon and no clouds so's it wouldn't be black dark, and that was a week away, but I was ready and waiting on that night. Missy and the two boys didn't hear me leave the cabin in stealth. I reached under the house and got my voracious vine. I bent close to the ground and stepped slowly and with care, over to Selma's, and went inside by the back door. There was Mr. Anders sitting with his back to me on the porch, snoring away, bottle spilling on the floor, the smell of whiskey and stale pipe tobacco strong. The smoking pipe was on the floor too, smoldering tobacco spilling out, looking like it might set the house on fire. Now, Mistress, you still want me to go on?" Soola was wringing her hands, swaying back and forth in agitation.

"Yes," said Gertrude.

"I crept real close, my heart was feeling like a hammer pounding against my chest, I could truly feel the pain. Finally, I stood right behind him clutching that voracious vine with its vicious big thorns. Then he stirred. Oh Lordy, what'll I do now? I backed up and hid behind the door. So, mistress, now you know I do feel fear sometimes. He bent down and picked up the bottle and took a gulp of whiskey even though there wasn't much left in the bottle—most was on the floor. He settled back down, but damn, I had to wait another few minutes before I heard them sickening snores again. I almost lost my nerve. Now you see, Mistress how these memories have made a deep rut in my brain with all these details. Then I went for it, throwing out my arms over his red head then pulled back with all my strength and crossed my arms and pulled both hands together, strangling his throat, and letting the thorns dig deep into his neck. He gave a moan but couldn't cry out much cause that voracious vine was doing its work; there was blood, and I kept pulling and tightening. He tried to fight but I was strong as him. In fighting back, he was knocking about, falling off the chair, and I wished he would hurry up and die." Soola immediately put her hand over her mouth and looked with fear at Gertrude, who stood up in anguish, pale and trembling. "Oh my, Mistress, I should never be telling you this, it is so terrible what I did and me hardly more than a child, an angry child, and a wicked one."

"But, Soola, you must finish, you must tell me what happened," cried Gertrude, so shaken was she, "You must explain how it ended." She sat back down and folded her hands to stop the trembling.

Soola became frantic too and anxious to flee back to her cabin. She continued at a faster pace. "Mistress, he died right there on the threshold of Selma's front door, his body half in and half out, his greasy hair awry, his dead face a mask of horror. I dragged him to the back door. At that moment a cloud covered the moon, and I was thankful for that because it became pitch dark, and I was hidden from sight. I had been wrong to wait for the full moon. Anyway, I was stumbling around and had a hard time wrapping his body in the canvas that I had there ready. Before taking away the body, I wiped up the blood on Selma's front porch. Well, then, to tell this quickly, I dragged him down the path to the lake, but in the dark could not find the metal weights that I had hidden, ready for me to tie them to the body, and so I had to do some more dragging him on down to the river so maybe the currant would take him away. I couldn't put him in the lake cause he would float to the top without the weights. You see, there weren't no rocks around there. All I could do was tie him up better with the extra rope, pull him out into the river with water up to my chest, push him under, wait for bubbles to gurgle up, and then I sent him on his way to hell, pushing him out into the currant. I was convinced the body would be found, such a sloppy job I had done. There weren't no lightning bugs that night because they could hear the thunder coming. It began to storm, and I was soon wet all over, and honestly, I was hoping the thunder god would take me away or at least the lightning would strike me dead, like the man who was struck and fell from high up a tree the past year.

"Mistress, Missy wondered why I was so wet the next morning, but I blamed the storm, and no one ever discovered what happened to Mr. Anders. I was lucky with the storm cause the rain covered up the drag marks on the path. And certainly, no one could have imagined a young girl like me had murdered him. He disappeared and that was that, and there was no one around to investigate. His wicked drivers went off too with the Patriot soldiers who came through or with the British soldiers who came later. They were promising freedom to them who helped as guides through these endless forests. But some of us knew not to believe what white men promised, and for those who went away with the soldiers, that freedom was in doubt to us doubters. So, I remained for the next coupla years, and we were near about starving and surely sorry sights by the time Mr. Rawlins came to get us and take us to Georgetown to be sold. Oh yes, but one of the redcoats told us they had found a grizzled body, very decomposed, he said, with remnants of red hair on the bank far down the river and did we know who it might have been. We just shrugged and said there was a lot of dead bodies around with this war goin' on."

At the end of her story, Soola had one more thing to say to her mistress. She told Gertrude that she understood she had done the worst to another human being, that her punishment would always be the sense of guilt that hung on her, and that furthermore, if you do violence and murder, the same will happen to you. Look what happened to the Red Devil.

Gertrude in a strained voice assured Soola that she was absolved from the guilt by admitting to her what she had done. And as for the prediction of violent death for herself, she held that was mere superstition, not true because the overseer at Pine Forest had been a wicked torturer and murderer and deserved what he got. Soola grew silent, then told Miz Gertrude that she gave her permission to write down her story, if she promised to keep it hidden. They both went away to lie down trying to dispel their mutual sense of foreboding, a foreboding that hung around, perhaps triggered by Soola's story, more likely by Archie's increasing rage.

Early the next morning, a woman from down Dogwood Lane came and knocked on Soola's door and told her to come. They walked to the end of the lane, and the woman pointed to the chairs. But there were no chairs, only roughly chopped up pieces of wood strewn on the ground. Nearby lay the heavy axe that had chopped them.

"Was it the master?" murmured Soola. The woman nodded.

Chapter 13

In the early hours of a hot morning in July, Soola and Adam were both wakeful, lying face to face on the mattress behind their curtain. She stroked his face and ran her finger down the wrinkles of his cheeks, which Adam reminded her were his marks of old age coming fast upon him. She answered immediately that these were the marks of a handsome face that each year made it more lovable to her, and to emphasize those words, she pushed her whole body hard against him.

"No baby, we'd wake up the children if we do that now," he whispered.

She didn't care and put a long leg across his pelvis. He couldn't resist. As he covered her with his body and pushed inside her, she moaned quietly, and he told her to hush. It was intense and deep; she smiled and stroked his back while gazing into his eyes. "You're the finest woman I've ever known," he whispered. At the moment they pulled apart, there was a hard and insistent rap at the door. Soola untangled herself from Adam's body, grabbed a rag and a shawl for her shoulders, and went to open the door. There stood the boss, her least favorite sight on earth.

"Tell Adam to git out here, I need his help today, why's he lounging around in bed?"

"Yessir, I'll tell him, but it'll be a minute cause he's naked right now," she answered and closed the door. She knew that if Adam kept Massa Archie waiting too long, he would suffer all day, so she told him to hurry. He did hurry out there, and she could hear them talking. Soon, he poked his head back in and told her the Massa wanted him to drive the cart with him into town and help with something the master was picking up at the new hardware store. They'd be back that afternoon, wouldn't take too long. She pulled him inside and hugged and kissed him. "I don't like you being away, Adam, but still I know you like a trip into town, so be good and don't be lookin' at all the pretty gals." He laughed and, vowing he would keep her own beautiful face in his mind the whole day, ran off to get the horse and cart ready. Soon, she heard the clop, clop of the horse's hooves and went out to watch til they were far down the driveway, the two men sitting side by side, Adam holding the reins. They were talking and laughing. Adam always had the knack of sucking up to Massa Archie without seeming phony. Hmmm, she thought, why did he need Adam with him, and what was it he was picking up? He was in town alone only yesterday. Oh well, you could never tell with that crazy man.

The place was smelling of breakfast, so Soola turned back to her house to get her children up and out to fetch the food. Maybe Jake had instructions as to their tasks to accomplish. After breakfast, she went to the big house to find the mistress and see if she knew what was going on. Jake had received no instructions from Massa Archie before he departed with Adam. Soola was beginning to feel a little worm of unease inside her.

After searching upstairs and down, she found Gertrude over near the trees behind the house on her hands and knees in careful examination of an interesting beetle she had found inside and had removed to the back. "Mistress, do you know why Massa Archie took Adam with him into town this morning?"

"Why no, Soola, I didn't know they'd gone." She stood up and rubbed her knees, shook out her skirt and wiped her hands on the apron. "What'd he say he wanted him for?"

"He didn't say nothing except he needed Adam to help him pick up something at the new hardware store." The worm of unease uncurled itself and began gnawing at Soola's gut, and at the mistress' next words, the gnawing became a big bite.

"Why, that's odd, the new hardware store ain't even open yet, won't be open until end of the month. But Soola, why are you worried about this, the master don't know everything, and he's forgetful, he'll get there and have a tantrum because it's not open yet. As my grandfather used to say to me, 'dinna fret, wee bairn.'"

"But Mistress, he never takes Adam into town with him, it's always Jake, and he do know about the hardware store cause Jake says they were there last week, and Massa Archie pitched a fit when he saw it weren't open yet." Soola put her hands over her face and bent double in anguish. "Oh Mistress, I should not have let him go, I know it now. But we didn't think."

Gertrude was now paying close attention, getting a little anxious herself, trying to calm her friend, "Soola, you can't say that. You know that if the master wanted Adam, there surely wasn't nothing you could do to stop him. You hear?"

The two women went to find Jake, who spoke again the words he had earlier given Soola—the master had not told him he would be away and had not given him instructions. But Jake knew what to do; they rounded up the workers, men, women, and children and spent most of the day hoeing around the corn stalks and picking beans. Soola wandered off to check on the turpentine trees but soon returned to the field, all the while checking the driveway and listening for the comforting sound of wagon wheels. She had never, since Kayla, experienced such a day of desperate apprehension.

When all began to trickle back to the cabins in late afternoon, Soola at last heard the wagon wheels crunching on the shell gravel driveway. She looked out and saw the horse and cart approaching, but as it drew near—oh my, only one on the driver's seat, and that was Massa Archie. Maybe Adam was in the back. She rushed forward, no sign of Adam in that cart. Soola cried out for the mistress, and Gertrude came running. "Oh please, Mistress, ask the Massa where is my Adam?"

But when Gertrude asked her husband the question, he only stuck out his chin and told her Adam had run off. He and the sheriff had been searching him out all day. "See," he added, addressing Soola, "he don't give a damn about you and your pack of brats. He's run off and left you, and he one of my most valuable hands, and nowhere to be found. Now leave me be, get away from me." George appeared from nowhere, waited for the Massa to get down, then led the horse away. Massa Archie looked around at the others, then gave a weak laugh, "yessir, you ladies can see now that a man doesn't feel the need of his family. Adam never did have any liking for the settled life or for work. We'll see tomorrow if the paddy rollers bring him back all beat up, yessir half dead is what I mean. Or I'll kill him myself if he shows up here." He laughed again and walked up to the house.

Soola sank away from the Massa with panic in her heart. He was the gaol-keeper who had them locked in a cage, and, furthermore, he had thrown away the key. They couldn't kill him and grab it from his pocket. But is the mistress in here with us, or outside with him? She knew not where to turn, where to look, what to think. Oh Adam, I know you would never leave us, something else has happened. What has he done with you? She looked for Gertrude, who had backed away too, then saw the look of horror on the mistress' face. It came to her like a revelation from faraway through mist and cloud, slowly. Soola knew finally what Massa Archie had done, what he had been planning all during the past weeks since he destroyed the chairs. The fear that came to her at that moment was mixed in her mind with her loathing for the man. He has sold Adam to devastate me, and he knows I am powerless to get him back. But the mistress will help me. They had failed to read his destruction of the chairs, failed to deduce that his obsession of jealousy and anger at her and Mistress Gertrude had led to an act that would destroy them both, perhaps even to delusion and insanity. She took Gertrude's arm and whispered, "I know what he has done Mistress. He has sold Adam, I know it."

"Yes, Soola, I was thinking the same thing. His thoughts and his deceits are quite transparent." Soola had remarked to herself this year that Mistress Gertrude had quite forsaken her previous custom of trying, albeit weakly, to defend her husband's reckless behavior. As she looked at the mistress, she shaded her eyes against the sun setting over there on the river. Gertrude formed a dark silhouette against that backdrop.

At that moment, their two sons came running, carrying two dead rabbits, excited that they had provided meat for Soola's family. John was now a head taller than Robert, and his dark skin provided a contrast to Robert's pallor. John was a mix of his parents—long face, with broad mouth and nose, like his father, but possessed of deep-set black eyes and a tall, strong frame, like his mother. Robert was somewhere between average and tall, no match for John, who at age eleven was already near six feet. And Robert bore a strong resemblance to his mother's family, the thin pale face, blue prominent eyes, narrow lips and straight brown hair flopping in his face, usually in need of his mother's scissors and capable hands. Indeed, the two friends together resembled a blackbird and a white dove, so different were they, each a prototype of his inheritance.

John spoke to his mother, "Is Papa home yet?"

"No, son, and we don't know where he is, but we'll find him tomorrow somewhere up in town. We'll go there tomorrow with the mistress and see what happened there. Robert, your father came home alone; he says Adam ran off, which is a lie." Robert looked quizzically at his mother. Gertrude nodded. Soola knew that Robert had already at his young age developed a low opinion of his father, had even considered Adam and Jake to be better men, had looked to them for advice in personal matters. Especially Adam, he thought of as a father, and John as his brother. He had told Soola that his mother Gertrude served as mother and father, since he felt nothing, neither affection nor trust, for his own father. Archie had never made much effort to earn the boy's respect, the result being they avoided each other most of the time. When he did approach Archie, Robert usually received a caustic, even derisive reply or a suggestion that he go ask his mother. "She thinks she's the boss around here." The avoidance technique had seemed to be the most convenient. Soola had always, throughout Robert's childhood, retained enough good sense, even when she felt the deepest hatred for the master, to never insult Massa Archie to the boy; although he had occasionally witnessed those overt insults himself. And, if Adam were present, he would put his long arm around Robert and tell him not to pay Soola no mind, she always had it in her heart to give a boss a hard time, then would give his big laugh. Soola watched over Robert as if he were her own son; Robert adored and revered them both. Thus, his horror at Adam's disappearance was as keen as John's.

For Soola, the world turned dark and frightening. She had now lost the one man, the only man she could ever love and who had loved her the same. Everything in their cabin reminded her of him. So, she had to drag the mattress over beside the girls. But then the mattress itself had been hers and his, so she had to move it back to the corner and lie on the bare floor to sleep. The memory of his voice, of his large hands and strong fingers, his laugh, and his body against hers, kept her awake most of the night. And, as the chorus of birdsong heralded the morning, even those delicate voices turned sour in her ear.

When the master knocked at sunup, she slammed the door in his face. Then opened it again and shouted at him that the devil would find him and punish him, that she knew he had sold Adam, that she knew Adam, that he would never leave his family. Then Gertrude appeared, told Archie to be gone. "We will go into town Soola, you and John and Robert and I." But when Lucas heard that he would be left with Tabitha, he cried and said he wanted to be with them and find Papa. Gertrude said to bring him along. And when Archie tried to talk to her, Gertrude brushed past him on the steps and told him to speak not one word. They took off down the drive with the same horse that made the trip to town the day before, Robert and John jogging beside the animal with hands on his neck. Soola watched her son with pride knowing that his kind heart extended to all living creatures and remembering the words of Bejida, predicting his future greatness as a man.

Soola had, on a few occasions in the past, much enjoyed a trip into town to help the mistress doing business at the market and in the shops. It encouraged her to dream of living as a free woman, travelling along roads, driving a horse as she pleased. On this day, however, she held her mind and body taut, her hands clutching the reins, looking straight ahead, desperate to reach town and find Adam. She asked Gertrude if she had knowledge of where to search first, and Gertrude assured her that she did. "Soola, dear, we will first go to the sheriff's office and make sure Adam did not run off as my husband said."

"Why, mistress, surely you don't think he really did that?" Soola cried out in fear.

"No, of course not, but we want to set the stage for the sheriff to help us if he can. The sheriff has been on this job for many years and knows my husband well, and not favorably I believe. On second thought, we will talk to my brother Bruce first, then the sheriff."

At the dock, they pulled up the horse in a small thicket of holly trees overlooking the river, where Gertrude climbed down and tied the horse to a tree branch. Bruce had built himself an office and boat landing there some years back when he gave up the farmers' helper business and concentrated on the shipping. "My brother does well with this business," said Gertrude. Bruce was Robert's favorite uncle, and Soola knew Bruce too from his occasional visits to Inveraray. She had noticed his friendliness and fun with her son and Robert, albeit understanding that she would never be recognized as Gertrude's friend by him, nor by any other white person. What bewildered Soola, when she reflected on this endless and intricate slavery/skin color puzzle, was that even a kind, nice man full of fun like Bruce Munro could never consider her to be a truly human creature. Always she would remain half woman half beast, or so she thought. Was there a white person on this earth who had thought this question through deeply and who had come to the opposite conclusion and had acted upon it? Well, maybe Mistress Gertrude, but even she had her limits. Soola had noticed those limits and had stored them somewhere in that observant brain of hers. Now she looked up and down the wharf thinking to catch sight of Adam. But nowhere did she glimpse a man half so handsome as her Adam, no, not white nor black. During this time, Soola sat quietly, good as gold, without a trace of discomfort showing on her face, not a hint of attitude which might roil the delicate feelings of her white superiors. The lady in lace on that boat coming into Wilmington twenty-three years ago popped into her mind—as a reminder of what was to be expected.

Gertrude and Bruce came out of the building, wiping their brows in the heat. He had his hands in his pockets, his eyes looking down at the cobblestones. When he looked up and saw Soola, he came immediately over to the cart, reached up, and touched her shoulder, "Why Soola, I am always glad to see you, my sister's friend, but today I wish it were not under this fearful shadow. You are both aware, I'm sure, of how difficult it is to retrieve a man who has been sold like this, but I do believe the sheriff can give you good advice and guide you to find that drunken slave trader Tim Blakesley, the man who likely paid money to Archie for your husband."

After all her gloomy thoughts, Bruce's words had surprised and pleased Soola despite the pessimistic outlook for their search, and she grabbed his hand in gratitude, "Thank you, Mr. Bruce, you are a good man, just like your sister. Well she's a woman, but you know what I mean."

"Indeed I do," said Bruce.

The sheriff's office was close by, so they went straight there through the thick oppressive heat. But the sheriff was disappointing. For one thing, he was new to the job and knew nothing about Archie McLachlan or the Inveraray plantation;

furthermore, he appeared not to care. "If your husband sold a slave yesterday, he would not have needed his wife's or son's permission to do so, madam. But if you head west on this street, then turn left away from the river, you may find Tim Blakesley. He would be the one to give you the information you need."

"But, Sir, did you not spend hours yesterday with my husband searching for a runaway slave?" Gertrude stepped forward insisting on an answer,

"No ma'am, yesterday I was right here in my office reading up on the law, and, like I said, I do not believe I know your husband," answered the sheriff, somewhat mystified. As proof of Adam's sale penetrated her mind, Soola cried out in rage and sorrow.

They found Blakesley's ramshackle establishment, where a few young men hung around awaiting heaven only knows what. Upon Gertrude's request to see Mr. Blakesley, one of the louts mumbled he ain't here. "Where is he, and when will he be back?" she then asked in lofty tones.

Another answered, "Well ma'am, we don't know, never do know with him. All we know is he pulled out yester eve with a full load of darkies to sell and don't know which way he headed out. I thought he went south, but Bobby here thought he crossed the river. But, as I said, you never know with that fella."

Gertrude asked if they remembered her husband coming in a cart yesterday morning with a tall dark skin man in prime of life named Adam. The man assured her that he did remember him because he was a passel of trouble, but he didn't know his name. "Well, then, could I have a look at your books and see if Mr. Blakesley did buy a slave named Adam?"

"Ma'am, Tim don't like no one to mess with his books."

"I never said I would mess with his books, but I do need to know right now if our Adam was sold here yesterday." Gertrude climbed down while Soola sat in the cart descending into deep despair, ready to scream and create a scene. Although the mistress had kept urging hope and calm, those two emotions were becoming more and more impossible, ineffective too. She, the mistress, had reminded all in the cart that they would be dealing with the worst trash in the way of human beings to be seen in this town, and they wanted always to remain on the right side of the law and civility, especially now since the old sheriff was no longer around.

Yes, thought Soola, the laws and civility apply only to the white side of life but then reminded herself not to continue in that vein right now. Finding Adam was their goal—conquest of a specific evil, not general, not historic. She sat up there on her best behavior allowing Gertrude to deal with these people. The place was disgusting, the ground littered with the detritus of slavery— pieces of chains, locks, whips, wagon wheels and chunks of wood, along with giant screws with rings in them and piles of rope. An all-pervading smell of sweat, dirt, and of human suffering hung above and around the place. What is the smell of human suffering? she wondered. Surely it was more a feeling from her imagination than a clear odor in her nose.

Gertrude followed the man into the shed, and when she emerged with a face of distress and tears falling, Soola knew the worst. Had she ever before seen the mistress cry? She didn't think so but couldn't remember clearly, so distracted was she by the throbbing sting of pain and tenderness filling her mind.

Gertrude climbed back up beside her. "He is named in the account book, but no word of where he would be taken is written there. They said they never know where Tim Blakesley goes with a load of slaves, nor do they know when to expect him back. The man is unpredictable and often gets bogged down with his susceptibility to the bottle. And Soola, this one said he thought the wagon headed upriver along the river road. We seem to have three directions to investigate. The man told me also that it took three of the biggest men to pin Adam down and tie him. The trader paid three hundred in the new dollars for him. And Soola, he was calling out your name." The two women embraced and wept together. John and Robert, who had not uttered a word since they arrived in town, now stood behind their mothers, trying to comfort them, to no avail, while Lucas clung to John's hand.

Gertrude said they would stop again at Bruce's office on the way home. Maybe he would have some ideas. Unfortunately, when they spoke to Bruce, he could only promise to send out feelers over the next week and attempt to find news of the slave trader's whereabouts.

Soola dreaded returning home, to the tiny cabin without Adam. Midst the heat of summer, she felt cold, desolate. If it were not for her children, she would lie down and die; there was nothing else for her. But it was not only the sorrow for herself, she kept thinking over and over of Adam fighting with those thugs, shouting out her name, then finally being overpowered. And now, where was he, what cruel and hateful fate had they tossed him into, what refuse heap was his bed this night, and what cage for his keep in the morning? The cage with white men's faces. He was suffering the definitive fate of the slave's life, what each one feared for himself and for his family. The visions of Adam kept her awake at night and rendered her near useless all day. Even Mistress Gertrude could not rouse her, nor could she bring comfort, so devastated and enraged with her husband was she herself.

Chapter 14

In the first days of August, after another melancholy day
helping Soola with the turpentine trees and in the tobacco fields,
where this season she had returned to work with the slaves,
Gertrude climbed the stairs to her room, then changed her mind,
and returned to the front porch. She knew that Archie would stop
by the kitchen, eat something, enter the big house at the back, and
sit in the back parlor. She hoped that Judith and Ida would have
something to his taste. If they didn't, he might go into one of his
wild fits; although he had been quiet, subdued, in the days since
the sale of Adam, had even attempted a smile at her, had even
spoken a few kind words to Robert during the tobacco harvest.
What is going through his mind, she wondered, what other scheme
to cause misery? Surely, he has done his worst; although there
might be an ultimate crime, of which he is capable. A pall lurks
above us, the foreboding is still with me, she thought, then rubbed
her hands together, feeling the rough calluses. The hands of a
farmer's wife, yes. She liked that; although, she did not like the
farmer. What a dismal fate: to dislike your own husband.

As for motherhood, Gertrude had never thought she would
be a mother. For most of her life, she had been guided almost
exclusively by commands from on high; but now, at the age of
almost fifty, she found herself closely tied to three other human
beings. The emotions involved in these ties sometimes prevented
her from clearly hearing or understanding the voice of God. Her
nature was to be orderly, reasonable, clear, but now, in recent
years she sometimes lost her head—in anger, in fear, and in love.

Gertrude reflected again that her husband Archie was not
one of the human beings to whom she was emotionally tied. Even
before the vicious sale of Adam, he and she had become distanced
from each other. He had little interest in fatherhood, which
surprised her. His enduring self-interest would surely have led him
to treasure a son who would carry part of himself, Archie, into the
future. But no, she had noticed the increasing jealousy and
sarcasm which Robert had himself described. With Gertrude, his
behavior was difficult to fathom. During the past year, she had
suffered under his spells of staring at her with crazy eyes. In fact,
since Robert was born, he had entered her room only occasionally,

and on those rare occasions, he had knocked, entered, and performed his duty quickly, even roughly. Furthermore, he had long ago quit worrying about the body odor and clean hair. She endured these quick visits out of marital obligation, and recently she had been feeling relief that he apparently was bringing an end to all that. Amazing to recall, she had at first been mildly disappointed, even waited for his gentle knock on her door, had interpreted his avoidance to mean he didn't love her anymore, or probably never had. Love? What did that mean to her husband, she wondered now, recalling only too keenly his disappointed anger upon discovery that he could not get his hands on her money. In the end, she believed that if it weren't for Soola and John, she would long ago have taken Robert and moved into town near her brothers. Gertrude knew she could certainly trust Bruce to give up renting out her little house on the river and tend to her some shares in the shipping business. However, it wasn't only Soola, it was all the slaves—many would suffer if she left. Her constant return to that outcome did bring consolation.

So, on that muggy evening in the first week of August, a week or more after the disappearance of Adam, Gertrude sat in the rocking chair on the porch, knitting as usual. She had made another trip into town to search out Tim Blakesley, to no avail. No one knew where he was, and Bruce had fared no better. She was near to fearing he would never be found when she saw Archie approaching from the river path. She had opened up the neck of her dress and rolled up the sleeves to the top of her arms in a vain attempt to dispel the heat. She knew Archie wouldn't like that but made the conscious decision not to button nor unroll. Archie sat down in the other chair, and with a voice that attempted politeness, addressed his wife for the first time since the loss of Adam.

"Mrs. McLachlan, I want to talk to you about your so-called friendship with that woman Soola who, let me remind you, is one of my slaves. I have asked you politely, many times over these past years to stay away from her and that boy of hers. As the father of your son, I do not approve of his friendship with a slave boy. But I see you're not disposed to take these thoughtful suggestions from me. So, my dear wife, it is time finally for me to issue you a warning that if this goes on, I may be forced by your obstinate disobedience to take strong action. You see, there is something unnatural in the fondness you hold for her." Archie was studying and rubbing his hands when speaking to her, carefully avoiding her face. "And furthermore, I wish you would not expose your flesh in this way, you should cover your arms and throat. You look like a common woman on the street."

"In what way unnatural, Mr. McLachlan?" She knitted a little faster and rocked a little harder, studiously avoiding his comment on her clothing.

"Well, you know what they say about the love between two women, or between men? Neither of them improper attachments is approved by that God you set your heart on."

Gertrude looked at him with extreme puzzlement. "I know not what you speak of, improper attachments? You are a strange man, separated from all human longings and joy, unable to feel kindness or love. What happened to you to create this venom that spreads from you as from a snake? I will not try to defend the love I have for Soola and her son John or the friendship between the two boys. Such feelings are honored in the sight of God, and I will never change no matter what you say. Furthermore, she has helped you in many ways on this farm. You can see her influence through her leadership—in the work of the other slaves, in their greater language fluency, in the cleanliness of the place, in the frequent repairs and improvements in all the buildings. And let us not forget how she has brought you profits with the turpentine. She and Adam took over all that until you sold him away from her, just to spite her I think, or perhaps to spite me. They were a fine family until then; in fact, you have damaged your own best interests by your dislike of Soola."

She glanced at him and saw with alarm that his face had turned red and his eyes wild. His mood had changed in a flash. "How dare you, how dare you speak to me so." He screamed and shook his fist at her. "You sniveling, power mad woman. I wish I had never laid eyes on you and wish I had never given you a son. No other man would have touched such an ugly, devil marked woman. You will regret your words to me today, you forever goddamned bitch. Snake venom around here cometh not from me but from others I could name." He left the house in an ungovernable rage, with a great stamping down the steps, took his horse from the stable, saddled it himself, rode off down the long oak and dogwood lined driveway, at a gallop towards the highway.

This was not the first time Gertrude had been alarmed by Archie's behavior, but now she felt deeply afraid. Perhaps he really was losing his mind at last. She feared most of all for Soola and John. He had already done everything he could to ruin their life here. What else could he now plot in order to destroy them both? And what about his own son? These were fearsome thoughts. She walked slowly through the dusk to Soola's cabin, her eyes drawn to the twinkling lightning bugs in the bushes. They reminded her wistfully of how the two little boys had spent hours trying to catch them in order to locate the lights in their tiny bodies.

Soola sat, as usual, silent on her front steps. Every day after work she sat there, still convinced that Adam would be walking up the driveway. This evening, Gertrude suggested urgently that Soola take her children, at least her two boys, and go to sleep at Tabitha's tonight. "Soola, you need to stay out of the master's way. I think I have gone beyond what I should say to him, and he might be very angry against you. He has ridden off, I know not where. I think he is covered with madness at last" She added again that she was truly fearful this time and that tomorrow she would walk with them to the tobacco field.

"Mistress Gertrude, that man don't worry me. But I'll do what you say since you're so upset. I'll wait for the boys to come home, then we'll go. I've known that man was crazy since the first time we were here, but I've never seen you this worried about it before so that's why we'll go to Tabitha's." She touched Gertrude's arm with affection. Maybe this is like loving a man, thought her mistress, so strong was her love for Soola. She had never loved a man, well perhaps Archie at first, before they were married, before showing his rage against her regarding Hermann's properties; anyway, love was hard to gauge. But is this what Archie meant by unnatural?

Gertrude returned to the big house, and soon Robert appeared. "What's going on, Mother?"

"Please come and sleep in my room tonight, put some cushions on the floor, or you can have my bed if you like. Your father's acting very strange, in a towering rage, he went off on his horse and has not returned. We'll put the dresser across the door. For some reason I am deep afraid but maybe foolish to be so concerned." Robert was puzzled, having never before seen his mother afraid of his father.

There was a foreboding, even a premonition in the air the next morning, and it wasn't just the master's rage. The sky gave proof to the close humidity of the atmosphere. Uneasy clouds were moving fast, and more gathering in the southeast, the trees bending, the horses, even the new mule trotting around the paddock tossing their heads, and the dogs searching to hide under anything they could find. "Well, Robert, we have storms of all kinds coming, I do believe," remarked his mother. "But in the absence of your father, we need to ring the bell for all hands to the fields. We must get as much tobacco as possible into the barns before a deluge arrives." Gertrude and Robert, intent upon getting the slaves out to the closest field, did not notice Archie's horse trotting riderless up to the stable.

"Hey, Miz Gertrude, looks like a big storm comin', we need to seek shelter I do believe," Jake spoke up. "I can feel the air real thick."

"We will, Jake, but we have time still to get a portion of the tobacco into the drying sheds. If we don't, we'll not eat much this winter; a big storm could wipe out the crop. But I promise we'll take shelter before the storm hits." Gertrude scanned the sky again, turned, and caught sight of the great dark clouds to the southeast, much bigger now, more menacing, the storm approaching from the sea, she thought. Jake asked her where was the Massa, but she didn't know, only asked him to help her get the workers out.

Once in the field, despite the increasingly close, smothering air, they worked fast, eager to save the tobacco and then take shelter. Gertrude was thinking they should shelter all together in the biggest barn away from the trees in case the wind grew too strong. People could be trapped in their little cabins or crushed by falling trees. She saw Soola way down behind her in the field next to the clump of trees, the little copse, their two boys near her. The wind was now creating enough noise to drown out voices, but about twenty minutes later, she suddenly heard shouting, and looking back, she remarked that Soola and the boys were gone. An urgency, near panic, was taking over the field of workers as the wild weather grew. "Jake, get the folks up to the big barn, take the primed tobacco with them, get going now fast."

She started running in the opposite direction, towards where she had last seen Soola and the boys, pushing against the wind, all the while urging the people to follow Jake up to the barn. Then Gertrude heard a shot coming from the trees. A terrified woman grabbed her arm and shouted that was the second shot, mistress. Gertrude took a deep breath, two shots, oh please God, help me, looking up to the sky where the clouds were ever darker. Then came the rain, immediately, in great sheets almost horizontal. She could barely see into the copse, but finally, see she did. A great cry came from her throat for there was Soola on the ground, her chest a bloody mess, Robert and John standing in a state of shock, covered in blood, and her husband in a crumpled heap not far off with half his head blown away, the brains falling out. On the ground near Archie lay the three-barrel flintlock pistol that his father had brought with him from Scotland in the last century. Robert turned and vomited into the bushes. John fell to his knees beside his mother, sobbing and sobbing, "Mama, mama, oh mama." There was no sound, nor movement from Soola.

All Gertrude could say was, "Please, Robert, go and get Bejida, and we need two big men."

At that moment, Jake stepped in among the trees, and, perceiving the dreadful scene, fell to one knee with his face in his hands. He suggested in humble tones that it wasn't safe to bring in help now, trees were falling, and all needed to get in the two tobacco barns up the field. But midst the confusion someone had told Bejida that she was needed, and she arrived to make her pronouncements. Standing over Archie's body, she declared that the devil himself and all the bad spirits of the universe had taken possession of the Massa's body. No one should touch him. Others too were gathering despite the dangerous weather, and someone brought a tarpaulin. They gently wrapped up Soola's body and carried her to the spirit house, where she could lie in peace until the storm should pass and they could give her a fine African burial. However, Gertrude, half crazed with grief, would not herself leave the body. She would stay all night in the spirit house on the bare wooden floor but insisted that the boys go with Jake.

"Please, please, all of you go and leave me here til morning." So, they did, and the mistress lay there, on the bare wooden floor, with a hand on the body of her dead friend. She wept from time to time, blaming herself because she had heard Archie's warnings, had recognized his madness, but had not blocked his behavior, had not prevented this bitter crime.

For the remainder of that day and into the next, Archie's body lay open to the elements in the little copse, while all others crouched in shock inside the shaky shelter of the tobacco barns. Barely audible whispers traveled among them informing all that the Massa and Soola were dead. When they emerged, bleary-eyed and sore-limbed from the sheds the next day, the gaze of forty-two Africans and a white boy met a shocking sight—the huge old oak tree lay smack across the roof of the big house, while the third field of tobacco plants lay spread out with leaves pounded into the dirt, carpeting the ground, quite spoiled. Much of the pine forest between field and river was jumbled up in ruins. However, most of the dogwoods maintained their delicate beauty, and the gods of storm and wind had spared the cabins. As if to comfort the crowd, the air smelled fresh and fine, and the terrified birds, having sought out new perching places, were singing solace to their brothers and sisters who had died in the tempest. Dead feathered creatures were to be found scattered throughout the fields.

Finally, three bold men dug the hole for Massa Archie's unwrapped body. Because of Bejida's pronouncement, they managed this feat without touching the hated master, using only the shovels to roll the body into the grave, followed by all the blood-covered earth around, which then covered him. Worms would have quick access to the body. The little copse remained tied off, forbidden ground for the next century. No one mourned the master's passing.

Very different for Soola, whose funeral three days later was a heartbreaking affair, a tragic celebration, loud with cries of misery and sadness. Jake and his boys carried the coffin along the path behind the big house that led to the graveyard, which at that time already contained too many graves, especially children. Every inhabitant of the farm came in the finest apparel they could find. They must honor their fallen heroine, the one who was never intimidated by Massa Archie, the one who had brought many benefits to them through her friendship with Mistress Gertrude, had asked for the cabins and for the spirit house, had yelled and shouted at the master when he mistreated a slave, and in the end had been felled by that mad, enraged, miserable man.

Bejida spoke frequently in the African language of her home, perhaps calling on the old gods to come back and help them in their grief. Although few understood the African words, all accepted the spirit in the tone of her voice. Only one person, the woman named Sally, the one acquired by Massa Archie, with her baby Joanie, some years ago, could translate some of her words. Sally explained though, that, coming from a different region of West Africa, where each tribal group spoke a different dialect, she could not be relied upon to translate clearly. A few old timers understood that, while others expressed surprise, having thought that Africa was a unified place with one language, one culture, one set of gods, and one king.

Gertrude, with her arms around Robert and John, could not stop the tears coming. Jake and his children had made the pine box out of two of the fallen trees, and the people of the plantation brought flowers, leaf bouquets, and gifts of all kinds to decorate the coffin. Their faces seemed gray and their minds haunted, unable to accept that their great leader was gone. When Gertrude said in a shaky voice that she would like to say a few words, most were pleased because they would hear from her what she planned to do now without her husband. She did not disappoint. She spoke of her own grief, the loss of her best friend, of her hopes that they would accept her now as their owner and manager, and that she, with the help of Robert and John and of Jake, would lead the people to form a better plantation with a kinder atmosphere. She appreciated their work and loved them all, "And we will all comfort each other in our grief. Everything we do here will be for the memory of Soola, our dearest friend and leader, to whom I promise today, before God, will not have died in vain. She died, yes, for all of you, so that you will have a gentler, kinder life. I assure you that after we clean up the place and finish the tobacco harvest, what's left of it, we will make plans for the future." She added that all residents of this little community will be invited to come to school at the big house every Saturday afternoon to learn reading, writing, and numbers because, as you know, Soola and I have for many years been busy with teaching, but most of you were fearful to take part because of the master. I admit that I was fearful to encourage you. Now, you are all free to come if you wish. I therefore have two pronouncements before I close. We will honor Soola by making this a kinder, more generous place. And from this day forth, this farm will have a new name: The Dogwood Plantation. It was the dogwood trees that sheltered Soola and me in our talks. It was their beauty that survived the storm."

She made no mention of Massa Archie or his death. They all knew already that he had died a murderer and would suffer in whatever kind of hell they could envision. She gave them two days off before they began the cleanup, and the people started home. Gertrude asked John and Lucas if they would like to come and stay with her and Robert in the big house, but John thanked her and said no. He wanted to be in his mother's house with her things. "When I look at her pots and baskets, I can see her hands." He said too, "I want to stand guard over our mother and father's corner behind their curtain, so it will be ready for Papa when he comes home." Robert stated he would share his time between the two houses.

The exact sequence of events that happened in the two deaths that terrible morning remained a mystery. A few people were bold enough to question Robert and John, but all the two boys could do was describe the grisly scene that greeted them when they entered the copse. This they repeated to the new county sheriff, who didn't arrive until after the bodies had been buried. The mistress explained to him that, in this hot weather, it was not wise to leave a body above ground for more than three days, and he agreed. After snooping around and asking questions of Gertrude and Robert, he scratched his head and marked it down as an overzealous correction of a slave and a suicide. Perhaps, indeed, he added, it was a "crime of passion, and these two had killed each other." Most who knew Archie were quite certain his was not a suicide, nor was his nature capable of the kind of passion written in the sheriff's report. Gertrude alone had a glimmer of understanding that Archie's killing of Soola might indeed have been a crime of passion, one that resulted from a passion of rage and from his increasing madness, one related to his last weird harangue against her. But who had shot Massa Archie? No one could figure it out. Finally, they shrugged—who cared?

What they all did eventually know was that the hurricane of August, 1806, had dawdled around all day and night, causing damage up and down the east coast of North Carolina and Virginia, finally, before turning out to sea, creating a new sandbar island—Willoughby Spit—at the mouth of Chesapeake Bay.

Amid all this pain and grief, no one thought to press Miz Gertrude about the whereabouts of Adam. His loss intermingled with the greater tragedy of the moment, not forgotten, but also not dwelt upon as an isolated incident with a possible solution. It would be the two boys who began thinking truly of the future, but even they didn't mention Adam until some weeks had passed.

Chapter 15

It seemed that autumn came early in the weeks following the "Terrible Day". A gentle sadness pervaded the air at the newly named Dogwood Plantation, the horror of the much loved Soola's death being tempered by unhindered joy at the passing of the hated Massa Archie. Although that in itself was horrifying—to be mourned by no one on this earth, disliked by all. As the first hints of gold and russet began to creep into the trees, the lengthening shadows enhanced the colors of the season. But this year the signs of autumn seemed to accentuate the melancholy more than the beauty. Gertrude was surely on the side of grief, to the point where she couldn't get her mind straight. How would she tolerate this isolated place now without Soola, the pleasure of seeing her every day having been the highlight of her existence here? Then she thought of the two boys, who would need her more than anyone. She swore to be mother to both.

Gertrude was grateful that Jake, who had shown leadership qualities on the terrible day, was especially helpful to young John and Robert. It was apparent that Robert showed the most anxiety, while John just wanted his mama back. For the next month, Robert helped by staying with John and his little brother Lucas in Soola's house. Then, in September, while attempting to salvage some remaining shreds of the tobacco leaves, he told his mother of John's worries.

"John was just yestre'en wondering who's gonna stay with them now, who's gonna be in charge of their family, maybe his sister Patty would come back from her boyfriend's house, or maybe Mary Alice, but she's so loud and bossy, she'll make him tired.

"But Mary Alice is a fine and good girl, Robert, and she would be the one most likely to help," answered Gertrude immediately, while knowing that Mary Alice with her great size and noise had not walked out with a young man yet. "But, Robert, tell me more about John's mood. Is he feeling more collected in himself? It's hard for me to tell because he is so polite, you're the only one to really understand him."

"Well Mother, he's mournful, just sits there contemplating the fireplace, stroking and touching his mother's things—the special stoneware, salt glazed pots, the colonoware Soola loved, the gifts given to her by you, the baskets Soola carried on her head. And then, what about his papa? John's wondering where he might be. And you know, Mother, John truly understands now what it means to be a slave, to be owned by someone else, to be sold away by a master, to be utterly powerless. He, and me too, we've been wandering around together all our lives, never thinking about slavery or about the privileges I have and he doesn't have. Now, he's contemplating all of that as well as the terrible loss of his mother."

Gertrude straightened up, groaned about her stiff back, tried to stretch her legs and arms, hesitating in her answer. "Son, I know you are helping him with your kind understanding of these things, and it reminds us of the downside to slavery. But it is the law of the land, and we're stuck with it, at least for the foreseeable future. But, please, tell John to come and talk to me tomorrow morning."

The next morning, now almost a month after that fearful day, as Gertrude slowly descended the steps from the big house, John approached her, "Miz Gertrude, I wonder where my papa could be now. I know he was sold to the trader, but where'd he go and do you think he still lives?"

Gertrude's response was immediate. She had heard the day before, again from Bruce about his investigations into Tim Blakesley's whereabouts. He had crossed the river with his load of slaves that day, and Bruce's source had thought that he very likely was headed north towards slave trading possibilities along the Albemarle Sound. This second letter, newly received, had simply said no further information had been found. Now, John's questions awakened her as if from a slumber. Why had she not followed up and searched for Adam? She blamed herself, but there was still time, and she became determined to act. "John, honey, if we can find out where he is, we can buy him back to come here and live with you. I am most grateful you asked me that. Yes, I think I've been asleep, so covered with sadness, but now I'm thinking again, and if Adam is alive, we'll find him."

First, she leafed through Archie's endless account slips, carefully organized inside his desk upstairs in the hallway of the "big house." Fortunate for her, the tree had fallen over the back of the house, the desk and papers safe in the front; although the dampness from the damage could be felt all over the house, and mildew would be setting in soon. Slave dealings he had clipped together in a folder in the bottom drawer, and one small receipt told that Archie McLachlan had sold a "prime field hand" named Adam, age about 45, for the price of $400, July 10, 1806, to Mr. Tim Blakesley of the Eastern North Carolina Trading Company. Hmmm, euphemisms are certainly popular throughout this slave business, thought Gertrude. And with another hmmm, she remembered the price listed in Mr. Blakesley's accounts—lying to himself in his own books? Or maybe Archie was lying? No, her husband was not a liar. Who knows, who cares? What mattered most was the accounting. It gave no information about where Adam had been taken.

Gertrude found another piece of paper in Archie's desk that day—a paper folded four times and worn from opening and handling. It was a letter from his father at Cross Creek, North Carolina, dated June 1783.

Dear Archie,

I received your mocking, sarcastic letter, and I willna send you the smallest penny for your always ill planned and overblown ventures. I'll let the loan sharks bear the burden of loss with these new ones. Ye have ever been a burden and a sorrow enough to me and Duncan, and the only money ye'll get from me will be in the estate of me or your uncle when we're dead. I didna think I'd ever say that, but I've reached the breaking point. Remember, being a gentleman doesna come only from money in your pocket. Furthermore, I would never lend money to any venture that includes that abomination from the devil—the bringing of darkies from Africa to do your work for you.

Your father, Douglas McLachlan

She folded the paper and placed it carefully back in the drawer, hidden under other papers. It seemed sinful to read letters of the dead; although this letter did give her further insight into everything Archie had told her about his father and their affiliation, or lack thereof. She reflected for the rest of the day on the damage done to the child by the actions of both his parents.

The next day, she took off with Robert on horseback to town to find Mr. Blakesley's office. "Robert, we must all make the effort to recover from this terrible tragedy and start looking forward again. I have emerged finally from my stupor and will endeavor to be both mother and father to you now, and we must both help John. Our first step will be to find Adam. John's mother was a giant figure in all of our lives; it wrenches my soul to think of her; but it will help your friend if we can bring his father back here."

"Dear mother, you are everything I need in a parent. My father, I can honestly say, played no part in my thoughts. In fact, I always endeavored not to think of him at all, so he is no loss. I think he pure hated me, and I spent a lot of time figuring how to stay out of his way. But it is John I'm worried about, and I'll help you in every way I can. He is so smart, and he must learn lessons with me, whatever I do, I want John to learn too. Can he go to school with me in a couple of years? That will help him recover."

"Son, it is painful for me to say this, but the law would not allow that. I am, in fact, breaking the law when I have taught him reading and writing, a slave is not supposed to be educated."

"All right, that's easy, we can give him his freedom, then he can go to school."

"Not to your school, but if he's free, we might find a school for him. You're right."

As they entered the town, they remembered the Trading Company's address, found the street and number but no sign of the slave traders they sought, only empty shacks.

"Tim Blakesley moved away from here two or three weeks ago," a man told them. "I plan to open a hardware store in this space, but Jed Smith round on the next street owns this lot and he might know where Tim went." Gertrude couldn't resist a rueful smile at the words "hardware store," for here was the spot, but a store, not even built yet.

They found Jed Smith behind a desk in a rundown shack beside the river. Right away, he told them he knew something about Tim. "For one thing, he was drunk all the time and never paid his rent, then his slave business was declining because folks around here would be going down to Wilmington to trade. After a few months of failure to pay rent, I had to boot him out, and Tim

said he was going up to Plymouth to try it out there." Jed knew
that Tim had sold a few Negroes to the Canal Companies who
were needing more and more workers, both on the plantations
along the Roanoke River and Albemarle Sound and up to the
Dismal Swamp areas on the Virginny border. He sold quite a few
young men up that way to help with that digging and building,
"But that's a mean business, yessir, a dangerous business on the
workers. They don't live too long with that kind of work, for one
thing the sickness is bad—malaria and yellow fever's common,
and we won't even talk about the cotton mouths and rattlers. You
cain't git a white man to do that work, so it's mostly slaves, some
free Negroes too. If I was you, I'd try up there. If he's still in the
business and not dead from all that drink, Plymouth, or maybe
Edenton, or could be all the way to Suffolk, is where you'll find
Tim Blakesley. And how ya'll doing at Invary, Miz McLachlan?
I was sorry to hear about the recent disturbance down there."

"Thank you for asking, Mr. Smith, we're coming along all
right, and the name's changed to Dogwood Plantation."

"Oh, sure, that's easier to say, anyway, sounds better."
They noticed a boy about Robert's age hanging around in the back
doorway. "And I'd like you folks to meet my son Francis here, in
a few years he'll be taking over my property business, so you keep
him in mind if ya'll ever need anything."

"Pleased to meet you, Francis, and this here's my son
Robert." They shook hands. "Mr. Smith, what do you know about
the stagecoach that carries the mail north along the King's
Highway into Virginia?" A daring plan was forming in Gertrude's
mind.

Jed wasn't sure about that. He knew there was a
stagecoach, not much more than a wagon though, but Francis
would show them to the inn where it stopped and where they could
find out the ticket prices and time of day to expect it.

"They put the mail on that coach when it comes, but the
roads are bad and the drivers a bit wobbly," added young Francis
Smith, pleased to have an opinion. The boy had a friendly face and
a broad smile, which put Robert at ease, for Francis' clothing—
superior to his own—had inserted a tiny worm of shame into his
usually tranquil mind.

Gertrude thanked them with great sincerity, took Robert's arm, and when they were outside, whispered excitedly, "We'll find him, Robert, we will. I know now what that scoundrel, that sorry sot Tim, did with our Adam. We'll rescue him, no matter what it costs. My regret is that I didn't follow through on this a month ago at least." Robert tried to reassure his mother that they had been much preoccupied. She mustn't blame herself.

Francis led them down the street also leading the horses, to the Post Office and the filthy old inn beside it. By way of making conversation as they walked, Francis asked Robert if he would be attending school in town soon. No, Robert replied, they lived too far down river
back in the woods, but his mother had been his teacher and teacher of his friend John, and he believed his education had been as fine as any school could offer. "From her, we know as much as any schoolboy, right Mother?" She smiled and assured both boys she had done her best but acknowledged too that school had to be in Robert's future. "Just not sure when since we've experienced some difficulties lately. And we need Robert." She tried hard with her eyes to signal Robert to tell this boy no more about teaching John, but luckily, they were arriving at their destination.

At the post office, they discovered valuable information—the post stagecoach went from here along the old King's Highway north through Washington, Plymouth, and Edenton, as far as Suffolk, Virginia, then another company took the mail further north. There was space for seven or eight travelers, nine if there wasn't too much mail and baggage, and the price between five and ten dollars in the new money to Suffolk. It ran Tuesday and Saturday, leaving at eight of the clock in the morning. "Now it's not an easy route, roundabout through wild country across lotta water, a dangerous trip across Albemarle Sound on a ferry under sail, no trip for a lady, but for a tough young man, he could manage it all right," said the man in charge, looking at Robert, who appeared to be older than his eleven years. "From here to Edenton's about two days with plenty of stops, less if the weather's good, and I will tell you that over the next two months, this is the best time to travel, not so much rain. At Edenton, you best take a couple of nights to rest at the inn there, then the next stage when it comes, on to Suffolk. But you need to be aware, ma'am, that the times and days ain't reliable. Every trip on that stage depends on the weather, the horses, the carriage, and other hindrances. "How many tickets you want, ma'am?"

"We'll take two please, but we don't know when we're going. It may be this next Saturday." For Gertrude, the warning about the ladies only served as a challenge.

"Well, we don't save no reserved seats in the wagon. Y'all just show up; and come early so's you can get space."

On the way home, Robert urged his mother to take him with her. But she said no, he must stay and be the boss at home. "There's no one else now, Robert. Jake's good, but he's not the boss."

"Mother, then take John, he can be your 'servant' and help you. It's not safe for a woman alone. And it would be good for him to seek out his father. Anyway, you got two tickets, who're you planning to take?" She said definitively and without hesitation that she would be taking John. Robert looked at his mother and told her straight out that he would be mighty jealous of his friend for going with her on an exciting journey, a journey into parts unknown, to rescue a man who indeed had been like a father to him.

Gertrude then reminded him again of her need for him to stay and manage the farm with Jake. "Furthermore, my own dear son, as my mother told me long ago, jealousy be one of the worst sins but, like the sting of a hornet, it hurts for a short time, then disappears. The person hurt is yourself, not the person who created the jealousy. The hornet happily flies away. So, forget it and think only of the value to John."

"All right, Mother, but what would my grandmother have said if I told her I am nursing a bitter hatred for my own father?"

"Son, not ever having made the acquaintance of a man like your father, she could not make a judgment on you for that. And I do believe that God, understanding the mitigating circumstances, has already forgiven you, so put that thought behind you, after you have looked in the dictionary for the word *mitigating*. It is a latin word, not so much used in everyday speech." Ever the teacher, she smiled and patted his shoulder as they turned towards home.

A week later, before dawn, Robert drove the two travelers into town in the wagon and deposited them at the post office to wait for the stagecoach. Despite his disappointment not to be included, he wished them well, turned the horse around, and trotted off. The sun had barely risen over the trees as he jiggled the reins to go faster. He was nervous and uncertain about whether the workers would follow Jake's call to start out to the fields, and he lacked the confidence to lead others at such a young age, with neither father nor mother to turn to. Remembering Adam and Soola, he could almost hear Adam's loud laugh and voice reassuring him—"Come on, boy, you'll be the best boss in Culbreth County, just like your mama, and for her they will turn out." Soola, too, always with some saucy remark to make him laugh.

His gloomy thoughts melted away like icicles in a spring thaw when he reached home. Despite the drizzling rain, most of the workers were out in the fields, finishing the tobacco cleanup, hoeing weeds midst the cotton, and there were even three men on the roof of the big house, sawing at the fallen oak tree. He almost wept with relief. George appeared to take the horse and wagon, saying he would take the animal, Sir. They both laughed, "George, please, don't call me Sir, my name is still Robert. It was my father always demanded Sir." He then rushed to find Jake, who was leaning on his hoe, wiping his brow with a filthy kerchief. "Thank you, thank you so much, Jake."

Jake replied with some weariness, "Boy, did you think we was gonna sit around all day because your mama's gone to find Adam and help your friend Johnny? Hell no, and now you're gonna help us too."

Robert's heart filled with pride as he set to, determined to have the Dogwood Plantation in perfect shape when his mother returned. Both his grief at the loss of Adam and Soola and his dislike of his father became channeled into his resolve for the future.

Day after day the Dogwood people came out to work for Robert and for Gertrude. Jake told them what to do in order to complete the cleanup and ready the cotton for picking. Robert, with fortitude and grit, inspired them to follow him, without realizing that perhaps he was becoming a leader. He enjoyed working with these lifetime friends, especially the sons and daughters of Tabitha and Bejida. Little Gertie was a funny teasing girl for whom Robert had in recent years developed a special fondness.

Every day his mind reverted to his mother and John, where were they now, doing what, and when would they be home? As the days turned into weeks, anxiety took the place of wondering, then fear as the weather turned chilly. The smell of early falling leaves, the aura of fall, was in the air, and he thought of his mother sleeping in dirty inns, eating disgusting food, boldly approaching rough men who dabbled in the slave trade. Robert spoke to Jake and Tabitha about his worries and Tabitha reassured him. "Robert, no one will mess with your mama, she is a tough and impressive lady, she will be sending you a message to come get her in town soon. And we will be shocked if it's only them two, Miz Gertrude and John, who come home. They will have Adam with them, mark my words."

Chapter 16

    After Gertrude and John had said farewell to Robert, they examined the "stagecoach," which they realized was not worthy of the name—"more like a stage cart," whispered Gertrude. The only way to enter the vehicle was over the driver's seat in the front, then a climb over three benches to the back, where they could rest against the back end of the wagon. But soon, the driver appeared carrying a sack marked US MAIL. He told John he must sit on the front bench with him, to watch the mail, and to help him in other respects when needed, Gertrude guessed, and, of course, not sully the air around the other passengers with his black skin. She muttered to herself that John was surely a better man, yes, man, than any of the others here. Her supposition was confirmed when the driver added that the benches, each of which accommodated three travelers, were for the white folks. John obeyed without hesitation; Gertrude had cautioned him to speak little, keep his head down, put on his best manners with yessir and no ma'am to all. "We may encounter some tough behaving white people, you never know, and we don't want to give them food for complaint," she had said. John had answered that was easy.

    A woman's clothing makes this maneuvering over the backless benches quite awkward, thought Gertrude, wishing for a moment that she could wear men's trousers. She certainly dressed with the utmost simplicity and modesty—the plainest possible brown cotton homespun dress, no low neckline, bonnet and shawl devoid of lace. For extra modesty, she wore a cotton collar tucked inside the neckline of the dress, easy to remove and wash frequently on the journey. She had packed only her one other similar dress of blue in her small bag. Gertrude McLachlan always wished to dispel any thoughts of frivolity or vanity in her clothing. She looked up and saw that most of the benches had filled up. The driver called out, "We're ready to move out, push your bags under the benches, please, and I'll keep these curtains raised unless it rains." Gertrude noticed for the first time the leather curtains rolled up and tied at the top on all three sides. Late September, into October, should be ideal weather, but on this day the air was still—close, muggy, and warmer than usual. Clouds were gathering to the west, probably backed by a chill wind. Gertrude wrapped her shawl around her lightly, and at eight o'clock sharp, the driver called out the command to his four black horses. They took off, clattering down the oyster-bolstered street, eager to display their strength and new iron shoes, which were surrounded by thick white "feathers." People, especially children, came out of their houses to wave at the coach and four, a regular spectacle anticipated by the townsfolk.

They traveled a few miles north of town to the ferry, where the entire wagon, horses and people, were loaded onto a flat-bottomed ferry boat, then pulled by the ferry man along a taut rope that stretched across the river. He asked John to step down and help him. Gertrude watched with excitement, proud of John's behavior and willingness. All went smoothly, the horses appearing accustomed to the river crossing, while the passengers sat motionless and somewhat fearful. The river was wide, black, and deep here, and Gertrude guessed that most, like her, were not strong swimmers. The driver called out "This here ferry is where our nation's first President George Washington crossed on his journey south back in '91. I was just twelve years old and my mama took me out to see the President ride through town on his splendid white horse, surrounded by what looked like his courtiers." Ah, we get some history lessons as a bounty on this trip, thought Gertrude. I hope John's listening. She remembered hearing about the great hero's visit to their county at the time when she was struggling to adapt to life with Archie.

When they reached the steep river bank, the horses had to strain to pull this heavy load; then, since the road bed was smooth and dry at this point, they took off at a fast trot north along the Old King's Highway, the coach swaying gently to the rhythm of the horses. The possibility of seasickness did enter Gertrude's head. Then, the driver reminded them that this was not the original "old" King's Highway; it was a newer road straight to "Little" Washington.

"How's it up there, John?" Gertrude called out, trying to rise a bit to see him.

"I'm well, Miz Gertrude." He kept his head bent firmly down. The coach gave a jounce, and Gertrude was jolted back down and almost fell off the bench. The man on the bench beside her put out his hand to steady her. "Thank you, sir."

"Well I'd help a lady anytime, ma'am. I would like to introduce myself. I am Matthew Heinz of Suffolk, Virginia; I've been down here trying to extend my trading business into North Carolina. But I can assure you this journey is not for a lady like yourself."

"I am pleased to meet you. Gertrude McLachlan is my name, and what kind of trading do you do? And, if this journey is not for a lady like me, what kind of lady is it for?"

Mr. Heinz looked startled at both questions, "Well my trade is in iron goods of all kinds, hardware for home use especially." He obviously didn't know how to answer her wisecrack about what kind of lady and so remained silent on that one.

Gertrude smiled, "That's interesting, I'll try to be your customer when John and I return home to Culbreth County. I am owner of the Dogwood Plantation south of town on the river. And do you sell iron goods like chains for recalcitrant slaves and for slave drivers, Mr. Heinz?" She could see John's head drop even further and heard the deeply uncomfortable silence that fell among the other four passengers, all men. A wave of disgust went through her—they all deal in the slave business, the hypocrites, but only hushed whispers will recognize, or say the words.

However, she was surprised when Mr. Heinz spoke up, "Madam, I do not deal in the slave trade in any way whatsoever, nor would I buy or sell any of its equipages. I have seen the very worst of this wretched business around Suffolk with the building of the Dismal Swamp Canal."

A tall, distinguished-seeming man on the second bench looked back at them. "Please do not continue this conversation in the hearing of others. Surely you must know this is not a subject for open discourse."

Gertrude: "Beg pardon, sir." And she left it at that. But inwardly she was overjoyed, excited, by the comments of Mr. Matthew Heinz; she smiled at him again. John was getting soaking wet. There were many creeks and small rivers to be forded, and for the most part the driver seemed to speed up through them splashing everything and everyone in the front of the wagon, especially the huge canvas bag of mail under the driver's bench. Gertrude made him hand it back to her to cram into a back corner. And it was not only fording streams that caused the soaking, for much of the territory they traversed was swamp, the road covered in water even in this drier season. Sometimes, in low patches, the water came up almost to the wagon floor, and the road through these patches was full of holes, or sometimes fortified with logs laid horizontally across the road. Well, she had been warned. "You getting wet, John?"

"No ma'am, I'm fine." His head leaned down, down.

"Well, I'm pretty wet myself," she called back to him, "But I was warned, wasn't I?"

Gertrude imagined that John wished she would shut up—if his skin weren't so black, his face would be showing red.

She was happy though that the leather curtains were not lowered because she had the opportunity to observe the wild uninhabited country they traveled through and to feel the soft warm, humid air in her face. The almost unbroken forest of huge ancient pines, followed by swamps of grand cypress, followed by vine thickets almost impossible to pass through, then suddenly a few wide-open fields, all this bestowed upon Gertrude a feeling of immense freedom. She was reflecting, too, on the men who had built this road, or what passed for a road, when the voice of the tall man in front of her broke into her thoughts:

"I do find the endless forest without any apparent habitation to be extremely dismal and tedious. And oh my, the smell of decaying vegetation can be added to the horrors of living in any vicinity near to this wilderness." He spoke to nobody in particular; the other passengers seemed to be bent forward with heads upon knees attempting to doze. So, of course, Miss Gertrude could not refrain from answering.

"That is interesting to hear, sir, because I was just now reflecting on the intense beauty of these unspoiled forests and the varied perfumes, we derive from them; and you mention no habitation, whereas I was thinking of the wild animals which do inhabit here. Where we live on a forest plantation, we are surrounded in the summer by bears, deer, bobcats, snakes, red wolves, foxes, rabbits, raccoons, possum, and many more." She counted them off on her fingers. "Our children derive much pleasure in sometimes catching the little ones and alas keeping them in captivity."

"But are not these dangerous animals?"

"Well, most are fearful of humans, but the snakes are perhaps most worrisome. Every year we have a snake bite of some kind."

At that point, Gertrude looked outside and noticed they were slowing down, having crossed a shallow creek, and now approaching a ragged and scattered settlement of small farms, most equipped with an oft dilapidated wood frame house and a tobacco curing barn. Right at a fork in the road there stood a recently erected, it seemed, square wooden building, the steeple of which perhaps indicated a church. From the appearance of the autumn fields, all the tobacco had been primed and stored safely inside the barns for smoking and curing.

Gertrude thought of Robert and hoped he and Jake were finishing up at home, saving a little more from the flattened fields, already so late in the season. And are they chopping up the big fallen tree? She then remembered that she had been the one to suggest the tobacco to Archie, which he had never thanked her for, indeed had never acknowledged her part in this quite successful venture. She could see here that stubborn stumps were still poking up in these rich, black fields, and the great banks of trees surrounding the settlement threatening at any time to take back the open spaces so recently wrested from the forest—true, too, of many of the fields at Dogwood. She remembered her own grandfather Hamish, who had emigrated here from Scotland, commenting on this aspect of the landscape of North Carolina. In Scotland and England, he had told her, all the ancient forests were gone now leaving those islands bare of trees except for patches here and there of little woods quite tamed, combed, and contained. All but the lords and ladies, who kept them for their hunting and shooting, were excluded from these remnants of old forest. He had loved the wildness of North American forests, had appreciated that the native people here had not the equipment to destroy large swaths of wooded areas. He even feared for the future of these natural wonders with European tools now available.

These thoughts which had rushed through Gertrude's mind in a matter of seconds, were now interrupted by the driver, who called out, "We just crossed Swift Creek back there, so now we'll stop at Durgantown for a short rest and a change of horses before the rain comes; it's lookin' pretty black over there to the west. The farmers hereabouts like to help the stages when they come through and perhaps make a little money off the passengers. There will be some ladies with biscuits and corn pone for maybe 25 cents in the new money, but they'll take old coins too. The people also do not mind if we use the back rooms of their meeting house here to freshen up a bit—on the left side for gentlemen and right side for ladies. There's water barrels and privies out back, pitchers and bowls inside. And please don't leave any rubbish."

As Gertrude entered the building, she noticed the dearth of decoration, few seats, and doors leading into the rooms at the back. She was happy to have the ladies' room to herself. She peeked over at the men's place, couldn't see John anywhere. She called his name, and he appeared outside the window. "Would the men not allow you to use their room?"

"No ma'am," and when she started to look angry, "Please Miz Gertrude, don't say nuthin'." John looked very handsome, she thought, dressed in Archie's best britches, frock coat, shirt and tie.

Pretty soon, a slave girl with matted hair, dirty, poorly clad, appeared, followed by her mistress, not so dirty but dressed in mended rags. This is a hard life, thought Gertrude and happily gave the woman fifty cents for two plates. "John, come get something to eat." He took the plate and sat on a stump a distance away. "Thank you, Miz Gertrude." She heard the swishing of the pines and saw them bending—warnings of the rain and wind to come.

The driver got into a hurry. "All right folks, time to move along, we got some new horses, they ain't so purty as the others, but they look sturdy enough. We're halfway to Washington, that's Washington, North Carolina, not the new federal capital up there in Virginny. We take the right fork here straight north, and these fine horses should make good time, so if we're lucky with the weather they'll put us there by five or six or soon thereafter. There'll be a hot meal at the inn for you, and beds upstairs, that is if we can make it across the Pamlico/Tar River. It looked bad the last time I came through here. But, then again, if we run into a lotta rain and mud, that'll slow us up too." He turned, grinning at the passengers, no doubt hoping he'd put some little needles of fear in them. Gertrude had heard there was a new bridge across the Tar River at Washington. Yes, she thought, the rivers have perhaps been high from that hurricane a month ago, but she had already noted only minimal damage along the way; their hurricane must have passed over the coast and out to sea.

A great weariness came, accompanied by a queasy feeling from the swaying of the coach; her head dropped to her knees, and she dozed for the next thirty minutes. Suddenly, the coach came to a rough and awkward stop with the horses snorting, trying to rear up. Just ahead, crossing at a bend in the road they could see a large black bear accompanied by two smaller ones behind her. The mother bear looked up startled, stood there tossing her head, pawing the ground, and giving out short blowing sounds. The horses tossed their heads, danced around. This is where we need George, or even Robert, thought Gertrude, but before she could utter a word, John had jumped down from his seat, picked up some big sticks and was throwing them at the bears. He also grabbed the left front horse's bridle, talking, trying to calm them down and to the amazement of all, the bears took off at a run into the trees. They could hear them crashing through the underbrush for some distance. John jumped up to regain his seat, and the driver urged the horses to continue despite their snorting and still showing the whites of their eyes. For the passengers, John was the hero of the hour, "Good boy, well done, young fella, we're fortunate to have you with us."

The driver said, "Humph, thanks for your help, boy."

"Yessuh, yessuh."

Gertrude filled with pride and couldn't stop herself from adding, "See, I told you our children know the wild animals, and the horses too." She thought of John's mother, wanted to go forward and put her arms around him, to be his mother, but, realizing his embarrassment in front of all these strangers, she held back. However, at the same time, she recognized again that she now had two sons and would follow up on that when they returned home. In a minute, John had to step down again to lead the horses past the spot where the bear smell was most intense, so strong that even the humans caught a whiff. Gertrude said to herself maybe they'll let him use the washroom next stop, but on second thought, she knew that would never happen, principles always being triumphant. Tears filled her eyes as she knew that Soola was watching over her boy.

As they continued north, heavy drops of rain rattled the roof of the wagon, and the drops soon became a deluge. They stopped in order to lower the leather curtains, then started up again, much slower now because of the pouring rain and the less reliable horses. The road became muddy, slippery, and at times frightening, as the wagon skidded to one side then the other. The driver had to call out "passengers lean to the right please," then "passengers lean to the left please." Finally, as the wagon slid off the side of the road, he cried "All male passengers must get down; we need to lighten the load and push to help these animals. The lady can stay inside." At that moment a great crack of thunder filled the skies, one of the horses began to rear, and John had to use his magic again. Dear Lord, thought Gertrude, there are some benefits to being a woman. However, yes of course, she did step carefully down from the wagon into the mud. One foot sank between two log road supports and she was only just able to pull out her foot encased in its boot, now covered in black mud. The men were surprised to see her putting her strong back to the wagon to help get them going.

"We're gonna have to take it real slow now, folks, and I'm asking my young helper here to walk with the front horses to keep them in line. It may be midnight before we reach Washington." John was drenched by the sheets of rain, but, as he told Gertrude later, he was truly thankful for the warm temperature and to be out of that coach filled with unfriendly strangers, all white and probably unsympathetic to a black slave; although he was aware that he had absolutely no idea of what was in their minds. "I only suspect that they're not like my friend Robert, nor like you Mistress Gertrude."

The darkness of the storm moved straight into the dusk of evening, then night. The hours went by. The air cleared. There wasn't much conversation among the wet and uncomfortable passengers. Will this difficult day ever end? wondered Gertrude. And there's poor John exhausted and soaked, his shirt clinging to his body. "Sir, I think John needs to ride for a while now, please," she called out to the driver.

"Yeah, sure, get up here, boy." And John, ever obedient and silent on this journey, climbed back up onto the bench, put his head down and went straight to sleep.

Her friend on the bench beside her agreed with that, "Ma'am, I'm glad to see you watching out for your young boy; he seems like an excellent type."

"Oh yes, he's the finest young boy you could find, has a quick mind too." Gertrude felt another swell of pride, almost as if he were her own son. She looked at Mr. Heinz' face and saw his eyes watching John. She felt fortunate to have a genial travel companion.

As they finally were approaching the little town of Washington, the passengers voiced their wonders about the size and dangers of the Pamlico/Tar River and how they might cross it. But, lo and behold, there was the wooden bridge Gertrude had heard about, crossing the river into Washington.

"Yes, folks," said the driver, "we have here the latest in bridge building. It was built about ten years ago I believe, using the hardest and finest local woods. Now, Mr. Grimes, who operates the bridge, will charge us 50 cents for this four-wheeler to cross so I would appreciate you coming up with that sum. Thank you all mightily. And, boy, please get down and help me again with the horses. Some don't do well with their hooves drumming on the wood, and I never know how they'll take it."

As they approached the bridge, the horses did indeed show resistance, with a little snorting and shying. John got down, talked to them, hummed a little tune, and they set off. Suddenly, about halfway over, a loud blast from a bugle, followed by several more blasts, almost panicked the horses again. At that point, all passengers descended from the carriage and, breathing more freely, walked the rest of the way across. The driver explained, "that boy with the trumpet, he's telling the innkeeper how many mouths to feed for supper." Gertrude noted to herself that John was in the count. John led the horses while Gertrude noticed a shabby looking inn, and their driver continued his discourse about the town of Washington: a new river town it was, named as the county seat quite a few years ago, with a few houses and businesses huddled along the wharf. It had then been renamed after the nation's first president. The original name was Forks of the Tar. "We'll start up again at 7 in the morning," he cried out as the bedraggled passengers traipsed into the inn. "We've a long way to go tomorrow to reach Plymouth, then get across the water to Edenton, but we hope for fair weather and four fresh horses to hurry us along."

Upstairs in the women's room, Gertrude found water in a large bowl, some ragged but clean towels, and five small, sparsely covered beds around the walls. She changed into her blue dress, hoping the brown would be drier in the morning, then descended the staircase, realizing how happy she would be to lie down on one of those plain little beds. But how silly to be so tired when all she'd done all day was sit in the wagon.

When all were seated at the "dinner" table, Gertrude looked around, "And what has happened to my young servant John?" she asked, looking around at the bare furnishings and the walls devoid of decoration except for one picture of a coach and four stopped in front of an inn with the name The Two Swans on a sign. On the pictured inn's wall was the same picture of the coach and four with the sign. Hmm, Gertrude smiled as she glanced up at her hostess.

"Oh, he is well taken care of in the back, Ma'am," replied the extremely plump landlady while ladling out the chicken stew and rice. This fare looked delicious but on trying to chew the chicken, Gertrude asked herself whether the bird had been forced to fly back and forth in its cage in order to toughen up its muscles.

One of the passengers addressed Gertrude, "Where, may I ask, Madam, are you headed on this wild journey?"

"Well, my ticket is for Suffolk, Virginia, but it may be that I'll be able to cut it shorter. I'm searching for our Adam, John's father, who was sold by my late husband up there somewhere to work on the canals. I'm hoping I can find some good advice about where to go." She looked sideways at Mr. Heinz.

That gentleman immediately said, "Mistress McLocklin, you will have a hard time in this search, but I can certainly point you in the right direction and to some people who might help you."

"Have you heard of a slave trader named Tim Blakesley? He may be working out of Plymouth and may have sold Adam in that vicinity," asked Gertrude.

"No, I am not acquainted with any in that business, ma'am; however, I seem to remember hearing that name up around Suffolk during my business dealings, so that's a good place for you to start your search. I'll be honored to help you in any way I can." He bowed his head politely.

She looked at him with the deepest gratitude, noticing again the kindness in his eyes and that amazing bushy hair, sprouting around his face and neck. She did privately wonder how a man could partake of his dinner with so much hair near the mouth. There followed a general discussion of the difficulties in getting these much-needed canals dug and maintained, and the impossibility of keeping a labor force to do the work. White workmen wouldn't touch it, only occasionally a free black, and so it had to be slave laborers, but then that was hopeless too because of the terrible death toll and the runaways.

"Where do they run to?" asked Gertrude.

"Well, some make it to the coast and hide away on ships going north," remarked one of the stage passengers. "Others stay on in the deep swamp forest camps, where not even the dogs can smell 'em out. Some of these 'maroons' stay there for years living on fish and vegetation they find. Some join forces with a few remnants of Indian tribes around there. Sometimes they raid isolated settlements, murder, rape and pillage, they say. It's a dangerous and frightening situation for the poor farmers and their families who live around there. These wild men make up bands of the worst kind of criminals—they won't work on a farm, won't follow orders. What they like best to do is steal the products of other men's work. We would need a local militia to go after them, but who's gonna do that? I know I ain't. We're indeed hoping the new national government will help local folks catch these runaways. It's shameful that the Yankees on the boats will take em." The man lowered his head to better get a spoonful into his mouth.

And from the dignified man who loved civilization, "Well I am thankful we do not have that kind of trouble in our part of South Carolina near Charlestown. We have no runaways because our servants are loyal and for the most part treated like family. I cannot imagine that any would prefer to live out in such detestable places when they have comfortable quarters in town." After listening to that piece of nonsense, Gertrude excused herself and climbed the stairs to her room. Silently, she thanked God that she was not a pretty woman. These men seemed to include her in masculine conversation, without any flirting or attempts to grab her attention. It would undoubtedly be difficult for a beautiful woman to travel alone as she was doing. And yet even she, of ordinary appearance, could entertain offers of help from these gallant travelers. She laughed to herself.

In the morning, while waiting for the coach to be readied, Gertrude found John surrounded by a group of young girls, one of whom, he later whispered, had painted a fearful picture of canal work. Few men survived the agony of digging the canals, she said, and she hoped his father was not part of that misery. Afterwards, as the stagecoach moved east along the Pamlico River, then northward towards Plymouth, Gertrude's anxiety about Adam's whereabouts settled into a steady tightening deep inside her body. Her hopes had centered on finding Adam working in a tobacco or cotton field, but more and more, she was learning that canal building was just about the only reason to bring new slaves for sale into this northeast corner of North Carolina. It was becoming obvious what had been on the twisted mind of Tim Blakesley.

The weather cleared, and it became colder. The country changed, more cleared land with a few small farms here and there could be seen, each centered around a two story, square wooden house with brick chimney on the outside and a kitchen building in the back. Each also showed signs of a privy, a well pump, and a pit for rubbish. A few even had a couple of slave cabins and tobacco-curing barns out back. Gertrude knew the hardships these families suffered, their crops dependent on the weather each season, always a danger of fever, the line between life and death so fragile. Many had moved south from Virginia following the War for Independence, always seeking land and better opportunities for their children. But she wondered what kinds of opportunities were truly awarded to these new settlers in such wild country. The tiny settlements, eagerly calling themselves towns, did offer more amenities to newcomers, especially along the rivers, which although difficult and dangerous to cross, brought a better opportunity to travel and buy a variety of trade goods. Thus, each new community proudly announced its name and population on signs beside the road for approaching vehicles to see. But at no place could she see signs of slaves working in wide fields. With these thoughts wandering in and out of her mind, Gertrude decided to strike up a conversation again with the tall self-important man in front of her. She tapped him on the shoulder but soon wished she had stayed silent because all he wanted was to continue his discourse on the beauty of South Carolina in comparison with these wretched hamlets and lonely landscapes.

"Why Sir, I have been under the impression that a gentleman of South Carolina would be full of good manners and consideration of the feelings of others. But I am hearing from you nothing but insults and disparagements directed towards our new and struggling farmers. I consider this to be extremely bad manners." Gertrude delivered this little speech in the most polite and gentle tones. She bent her head in the direction of Matthew Heinz but saw that he was pretending not to listen. She gave a little smile. After all, he had already indicated that his home was in Virginia, another region where the inhabitants considered themselves superior to all others.

Suddenly, one of the up-until-now silent passengers raised his head, "Thank you, ma'am, I agree with you. I hail from Edenton, and there is no place more agreeable on this earth than my town and the surrounding country."

"I apologize to all of you for my insensitivity," muttered Mr. Charleston SC, and he said no more for the remainder of the journey. This journey, of course, continued through much of these same landscapes, with the horses sloshing along swampy roads, crossing creeks by fords or makeshift bridges. At one crossing, the passengers were requested apologetically by the driver to again step down and walk across a frightening bridge ahead of the horses. Gertrude considered this to be the greatest adventure as she looked down through the wooden slats at the murky water below. She did not even glance at her fellow travelers, not wanting her thoughts to be ruined. To be outdoors on this amazing, and she hoped fruitful, journey was a gift to her imagination.

They skirted the old town of Bath and were heading along the newer road to the little village of Plymouth, a trading post inland a way from the mouth of the Roanoke River, and thence northeast to Mackeys Ferry, which traversed the Albemarle Sound to Edenton. Most of this route was part of the ancient post road which, before the opening and fast growth of the town of Washington, had run north from the Middle River, along old Indian paths which followed Little Swift Creek and swampy barely passable roads to Core Point, and thence on the ferry across the Pamlico Sound to Bath. Their garrulous driver assured the passengers this new route was more comfortable by far than the old road via Bath.

After a brief stop at Plymouth for a change of horses, they continued, hurrying fast, northeast to Mackey's Ferry. There, in midafternoon, they saw the flatboat ferry with sails attached already loading up to take them across the water. On board they saw a large farmer's cart pulled by oxen, and soon another cart pulled by mules joined them for the six to eight-mile trip across the Albemarle. A deep and filthy creek joined the sound at the ferry landing—with dead fish floating, vultures and gulls hovering, and the strong odor of salt marsh thick in the air. John volunteered to help the ferry man with the rudder and sails, but he assured John he did not need an inexperienced darky child to help him.

"Yessir, I mean nossir," answered John, eyes down. He told Miz Gertrude that this must be like the ocean, but she assured him it was only a bay, not much comparison with the great ocean. The ferryman hoisted the sales, which caught the wind to carry them across to Edenton. Gertrude saw John's face fill with wonder. She smiled and wished Robert were with them too. They all felt more relaxed after such a long trip and assured each other that Edenton wasn't far, and they would sleep well that night no matter how uncomfortable the accommodations. Matthew Heinz turned to Gertrude, "Madam, I admire your bravery in making this difficult journey and assure you that you will find Edenton to be more to your liking than anything we have seen thus far."

"Thank you, Mr. Heinz, but at this point, my bed could be a hay loft, and I would not complain." They laughed; she believed they were of like minds and indeed hoped to solicit his aid and advice in searching for Adam in the Great Dismal Swamp. Gertrude was therefore somewhat surprised and disappointed, upon their arrival at the Edenton Inn, to see this charming gentleman give her a little bow and announce that he had a change of plan and would have to wait until the next week to proceed to Suffolk. He did not even stay with the other passengers at the inn but took off down the street carrying his little bag.

Gertrude now turned her attention to making sure that John would be well taken care of for the night. She spoke to the landlady who assured her that the servants' quarters were quite comfortable and would be safe for a young boy like John. This lady pursed her lips and wrinkled her brow when Gertrude insisted that she inspect these quarters; nonetheless she showed her guest the dirty and miserable shed assigned for servants. Gertrude covered her face—more bad smells, poor John. John whispered, "It's fine Miz Gertrude, it's all right." She patted his shoulder and said she'd meet him out in front of the inn early in the morning.

Gertrude was happily surprised to find she had a tiny room to herself with a bed covered by a straw mattress and even a pillow, not to worry about the tiny mouse that scurried into its hole as she entered. She saw a porcelain bowl and pitcher filled with, she hoped, warm water on the dresser and upon inspection behind a curtain, a chair with a hole in it and a chamber pot underneath. Oh, my goodness, I had expected to traipse downstairs and outdoors for that, she thought. This is luxury. It was 9 o'clock before they were called for supper, which wasn't much better than the dinner of the past night, and after that a deep sleep for almost eight hours.

In the meantime, John was thankful to eat a plateful of beans with a chunk of pork for his supper, then settled down on a bed of straw for the night, with only a small lantern to provide a dim light until morning. Something about this place made him nervous; he wished it was closer to the inn where Miz Gertrude was sleeping. Around midnight, his anxiety increased when the tall South Carolina man from the coach entered, dragging a boy about John's age by the arm. Mr. South Carolina spoke to John, "Here boy, watch this boy for me til dawn. Someone'll come by for him then. Don't let him leave."

"But, Sir, I may be asleep, he might run away," criedJohn.

"If he's not here in the morning, you'll get a bad whupping," warned the man, certainly not so gentlemanly as he had been on the journey.

John lay back down, telling the newcomer to lie close beside him so's he could watch him. He certainly didn't want to get a whipping. But the man from South Carolina returned with some ties and locks, and, explaining that he didn't trust "any of you sorry brats," tied the boy up to a metal post near the wall of the barn. John fell into a fitful sleep for the next few hours. Near dawn, he awakened to the sound of clanking chains, and jumped up right into the arms of the whiskered man that Miz Gertrude had chatted with on the journey. Mr. Heinz, along with another small skinny white man with long unkempt hair, grabbed him, and pulled him to a cart outside, which already contained the boy from last night.

John cried out loud, "Nossir, nossir, I have to wait for Miz Gertrude, she told me she'd be here to get me, she won't understand why I'm not here."

"Well, boy," answered Mr. Heinz. "Your Miz Gertrude has asked me to take you down to the waterfront. She'll meet us there. And we're to take this other boy with us too. We have our instructions, and she plans to sell you to us." He laughed quietly, while John continued to protest in vain that Miz Gertrude would never sell him, and he must stay there.

In great haste, they left the inn, and with the two boys locked in the mule drawn cart and the two men on the driver's seat, they proceeded down the street toward the boat landing where they had arrived the evening before. John began to realize that this was a bold heist, a predawn robbery. He became terrified, shouting out into the darkness for help, yelling repeatedly until the whiskered man reached back with a stick and clobbered him on the side of the face. He fell back into the cart bed, stunned and terrified. His companion uttered not a word but sat and stared at him until the cart suddenly stopped. Both boys sat up and watched.

Through the shafts of early dawn light, they witnessed an exchange of coins and notes from the skinny white man to Mr. Heinz, who swiftly pocketed the money, walked fast away, and disappeared down a side street. They stayed parked on the sidewalk overlooking the harbor while the skinny man counted his money. Soon the sun was rising above the horizon, flooding the water, the streets, and the pretty houses with a rose-colored glow. The streets and dockside were dead quiet. John kept his eyes on this strange man, who reminded him in some small way of Massa Archie, a fearful thought. He was reminded of the stories told by slaves newly arrived at the Inveraray—no, Dogwood Plantation—stories of beatings, of sale, of all kinds of torture, much worse than Massa Archie ever doled out. Would that now be his fate, wrenched away from his family and friends, and, indeed, from the kindness of Miz Gertrude. He sat up and shouted her name over and over, as loud as possible, into the chill of early morning, until the skinny man raised his whip and told him to shut up.

Finally, John recognized, from far away, a familiar voice shrieking out, "John, John, John." He looked over the side of the cart and a comical sight met his eyes—a woman who appeared to be Miz Gertrude, running full tilt, holding up her skirt and hugging her traveling bag with one hand while clutching her hat on her head with the other. She was shouting his name repeatedly, and John waved to slow her down, fearing above all that she would trip on this cobble stone street and crash to the ground. He heard windows opening above and knew that he was saved from a fate like his father's. The sight of Miz Gertrude running to the rescue would have been funny if he hadn't been so afraid. He thought of Robert uttering a wisecrack about his mother and their laughing together; in fact, he wished sincerely that his friend were here beside him instead if this strange, silent, quivering person, whose only utterance during the past hour had been his name—Alfonso.

Miz Gertrude arrived, dropped her bag, grabbed the whip from the man's hand, and began beating his head and back with it. John smelled breakfast cooking in the houses. He relaxed, even felt hungry, for the first time on this terrifying morning. She shouted at the man, "You stole my John, how dare you, you wicked thief."

"Miz Gertrude he's not the one who took us from the inn, it was the big man with big clumps of hair on his face who you was talkin' to on the trip. But first, in the night, this boy here was brought in by the South Carolina man whose nose was stuck up in the air." At this point though, John could see, Miz Gertrude was in such an outraged state that she was only half listening.

A crowd was gathering, folks abandoning their breakfasts to witness the commotion. Gertrude quit hitting the man, looked at his face and announced with some surprise that this was Tim Blakesley, the slave trader for whom she had been searching. "Please, man, unlock these chains immediately, or I will either kill you or call in the sheriff. This is John, my servant. And you are not only a trader, but I see now you are a thief too." She was in great shock and rage.

Rubbing the back of his neck, the man obeyed her, unlocked and untied the boys, while insisting on his innocence. He shouted that he had bought these two boys from a man named Ebenezer Wilson, who was well known in slave markets around here, and he, Tim, certainly never knew they were stolen. "But, Ma'am, I paid good money for these two, so you need to find Wilson to git my money before you take them from me." John was wishing that Alfonso would jump out and run away, but the boy seemed unable to think or react for himself. He sat in silence watching and waiting.

Gertrude lowered her voice and spoke to Blakesley, "All right, Mr. Blakesley, I will make a deal with you, an unusual deal, but it will at least partly pay you back for your loss. You are indeed partly responsible for this crime. You bought these boys without question from a known thief, and so you are involved. We will just go down here to the ferry landing and have a conversation, and if you refuse my offer, we will turn you in to the law." She turned to John and asked him to repeat the part about the whiskered man and the nose-in-the-air man, which he did, all of which renewed her shock and horror at the untrustworthy nature of mankind. She put her hand to her head in incredulity, "John, I am astonished, ashamed, too, at being so gullible. Shame on this town and on this whole seacoast region of our state, to think of what goes on, apparently daily, with this wicked slave business." While she climbed up beside Tim Blakesley, the placid mule began to slowly pull his load downhill. They could see the ferry, far out on the sound becalmed with sails hanging. John wondered where they would be headed next, surely not across the water again? He looked carefully at the slave trader, at the gray color of his skin and the worn texture of it. He bore resemblance to a starving rat. His head was shaking too.

"What's wrong with him, Miz Gertrude?"

She leaned back, whispered that he was a whiskey drinker, then turned to the man, "Mr. Blakesley, one or two months ago, you bought from my husband, from the Inveraray Plantation in Culbreth County, a slave man in prime of life named Adam, a man you might remember for he was hard to handle, I was told. We have traveled all this way to find him and buy him back. So please tell me where you sold him and where I might find him now." Tim made no answer.

Gertrude looked at the boy and asked him his name. "Alfonso, but they sometimes call me Alfie."

"So, you can talk," said John. Alfonso looked away, clasped his legs and dropped his head down on his knees. Watching Gertrude again, and remembering how she used to deal with her husband, John predicted silently that Mr. Blakesley didn't have a chance. He looked at her face, the face, and the voice, that would find his papa. He knew it now, had complete confidence that if his papa still lived, they would bring him home. No one else could or would overcome the obstacles, no one except Miz Gertrude. He felt a lump rising in his throat, remembering his own mother.

"Mr. Blakesley, please tell me where you sold Adam." She continued, "then, please take us there so we can buy him back. If you do as I ask, I'll be willing to pay you for this boy Alfonso and for use of your cart and mule to take us home. I'll not pay you for John because he was stolen from right under my nose, and he's like my own child. I will give you bank notes on my bank at home. If you refuse to help me, I'll turn you in to the sheriff here in Edenton. So, before we embark on yet another journey on the ferry, please tell me your decision." Gertrude folded her hands and waited.

John looked again out across the water and saw the ferry almost at the dock, powered by the strong arms and oars of the boatmen. He then heard the gloomy voice of the slave trader, "Miz McLachlan, I'll do what you say. I gotta git outta here." Gertrude turned back to John with a conspiratorial smile and whispered that she certainly understood why.

Chapter 17

Robert had chosen to stay in Soola's cabin with Lucas and Mary Alice, shunning the big house where he believed his father's spirit still hovered in the corners and the ceilings. However, on a night at least two weeks since his mother and John departed, he ventured there to sleep on the couch, which he pulled as close to the front door as possible. Mary Alice failed to understand this move, but he hesitated to explain that her loud snoring interfered with his thoughts and his sleep, so he said it was only for one night.

Around midnight, as a quieter noise disturbed his sleep, he saw the door open a crack. In another moment, he was flinging his arms around his mother's neck, in tears of happiness, crying out the big question, did you find him? And her answer whispered was yes, my darling, we have him with us, he is alive.

All was hushed in the chilly midnight air. Gertrude woke John who lay beside his father in the wagon. "Robert, go rouse George to help us with this exhausted mule. He ain't different from a horse except he's slow, dull-witted too. Alfonso, help me carry Adam into his cabin. You will stay in here with John too until we figure out where to place you." So quiet were they that, until morning, only George and Robert knew of their arrival. Mary Alice was snoring so loud that the sounds of their movements were drowned out as they gently placed Adam on his mattress behind the curtain, while Lucas continued to sleep.

In the morning, Tabitha and Judith were so overjoyed to see them returned safely that they personally helped Gertrude wash all the clothes and heat water for bathtubs for all. This cleanup stretched over two days while Robert and all hands toiled on with finishing one harvest and starting the next. The workers, especially the women, came in to see Adam. Bejida and Sally spent hours with him in the cabin, doctoring with every plant from the forest they could think of.

"John, your daddy is suffering from the yellow fever, it's in his eyes," Bejida said, "but we hope he's over the crisis and maybe he'll soon be well. You saved your papa."

"Miz Gertrude too," John replied. "She did this for me and Lucas, and for Robert, and for Mama's memory."

And on that first morning home, Gertrude explained to Robert about the boy Alfonso, adding a reminder to John as she cleaned up from eating breakfast, her first good meal in two weeks. "You must introduce your new friend to all the people on this plantation, make him feel at home, then take him to the fields with Robert. You can both put in a couple of hours of work, then come back and get cleaned up. We all look like traveling ragamuffins."

"He ain't truly my friend, Miz Gertrude, but I'll do what you say." Robert was concerned about his mother's response to that ever-so-slight rebellion, but she smiled and left.

But Robert was more worried that Alfonso angled around the work, kept sitting down, uninclined to exert himself. "Well, John, it has been so hard getting the people to work without father cracking the whip, not that I would ever crack the whip, but there must be some other way to encourage them. Thank God you and Mother are here now in time to finish up. We are almost a month behind where we should be in this work, but then many other farmers will be late getting their tobacco to market too because of the storm. But that Alfonso, what in hell's wrong with him?"

"Yeah, sure," John answered slowly. "We'll figure it out, but he's been like this from when we first got him but, Robert, Alfonso is part of the terrifying story that truly happened to us. In fact, you cain't imagine what all we've done, and where all we've been," said John as they took a break from work. "Almost as if we'd been traveling in foreign lands, like in the books. We gotta tell this story to everyone. We gotta have a big campfire next Sunday. Me and Alfonso and your mama will tell of adventures that they won't even believe. The world is crazy, and I'm sure happy to be home." Then he couldn't help but give Robert a short preview of the story, telling of the journey north, the bears, the sailing ferry across the Albemarle, the slave trader Mr. Blakesley and his whiskey drinking, his gray face and hair, the forest paths so narrow and muddy, way back into the trees. "You see, Robert, that drunken Mr. Blakesley had sold my Papa to this place to work on the canals, and some men there carried him to us wrapped in a sail cloth, he so sick we thought he was dead."

"But wait, John, I don't understand how any of all this happened, and, were you sleeping on the ground? And what did you eat?"

"Yes, we slept, cold and damp on the forest floor, your mama right with us, and we had stopped at a store when we got off the ferry to buy food. And that man Tim Blakesley got some whiskey which he soon loaded up on til he about fell out of the wagon. Your mama searched his pockets for flint to light a fire, but even then, it was too wet. Poor mule too. We were lucky we had him; a horse wouldn't have borne them rubbishy places. I tell you, Robert, the forest that we went through was deep and dark, seemingly full of cruelty and misery, it smelled bad, and we felt it when they brought Papa." Then the boys had to get back to work. Jake was looking over at them.

"That's fine John, but I'm confessing to be still a little jealous that you had such exciting times without me. But then, my mother wanted to go alone, so I'm happy she had you with her at least. So yes, we must have the big bonfire Sunday. And you'll have to start again and tell everything that happened in the right order. I don't understand half of what you just said, especially that most shocking part. So, you'll have to wait and tell everyone on Sunday.

"But, John," said Robert, "speaking of rubbishy, I need for you to know about a threesome of wretched white men on hungry-looking horses. They came here while you were gone. One was called Billy. The other two were his brother and perhaps his father. They said the sheriff had sent them to check on us, but all they wanted was information about my father's death. I said I would talk only to the sheriff about that, so they left. I'm glad this happened before our three men ran off because they asked about runaways too. I didn't trust them."

"Thank you for telling me, but I guarantee your mama will take care of them if they show up again." They both laughed at the likelihood of Gertrude's raising a whip again.

Over the next few days, their worries about Alfonso disappeared, as Judith and her daughter Ida, now grown, took him in, under their combined wings, fed him good food, and made him a mattress. What about his laziness, asked John of Judith while munching a fresh corncake, to which Ida answered, "He's a special boy."

"Yeah, specially spoiled and lazy," replied John and Robert in unison.

At the gathering on the following Sunday, Gertrude was the first to stand up. "I want to thank all of you here for staying with Robert, for not leaving the place while we were gone, for helping to finish the tobacco, for sorting out all those leaves." She had told John already that three men were absent but did not mention them now. "When I figure out my new system for running this farm, all of you who stayed will be rewarded for your work during my absence. Thank you." She was somewhat uncertain of what she would do. Bonuses were somewhere in her mind. Perhaps the folks would prefer more time off, or perhaps they would have the choice, money or time, one or the other. She smiled at her people and clapped her hands.

Then she told of the journey, of the ferries, of the mama bear threatening, of John's fearless treatment of them, and of John's skill with the frightened horses. She then told of running down the street to find John, of the wind driven ferry back across Albemarle Sound, of carrying Adam almost dead in the canvas, and of the road home.

. Then the slave stealing. "Oh, my goodness, you wouldn't believe it. But John, you must take it from here and tell the rest of our story because this part happened to you."

John stood up and told what happened at Edenton. He told of spending the night in the slave quarter and later that night there came the thin, snobbish man from Charleston who had ridden all the way with them on the stagecoach. "He brought with him a boy that he'd just bought from a slave trader in the street, and he asked me to watch out for him, and that boy is here with us today, his name's Alfonso, or Alfie." Everyone turned, craning their necks to find the boy, who was sitting under a tree with head in hands, a beat up geetar beside him. John was eager to continue, enjoying this unusual moment of glory. "Well, y'all won't believe this. Well, there was another man on the stagecoach the whole way who was sitting on the back bench of the coach beside Miz Gertrude, and they were talking, and he was acting all nicey nicey, and he said he had no interest in the slavery business and he didn't approve of it at all and he told Miz Gertrude that the best place to find my papa would be up in Suffolk, Virginie, because they needed slaves on the canal building up there and all that, but every little thing he said was big fat lies." John went on to explain how this lyin' white man had stolen him and Alfonso from their sleeping quarter, paid money to the trader for them, who then had taken them down to the harbor and how Miz Gertrude had come running down the street to save them. "And this cart driver was drunk, smelled bad of whiskey and no tellin' where he was taking us, back across the water I reckoned, but we soon realized that he was Mr. Blakesley who Massa Archie had sold Papa to." John stopped to catch his breath; he'd been talking fast so he could tell all the details of his story. He bent over to stretch his back, and the folks all clapped and yelled out encouragement to "Johnny." When he told how Miz Gertrude grabbed the whip and commenced beating the drunken man over the head, many in the crowd stood up cheering, laughing, and bellowing. They had seen her do some of that with a stick on Massa Archie.

"Anyway, to make this shorter," he continued with more confidence, "this slave trader, as I just said, turned out to be the same man who had bought Papa from Massa Archie, so he knew where we could find my Papa because he had sold him to a forest plantation across the other side of the Albemarle Sound. So Miz Gertrude made a deal with this Mr. Blakesley to take us there and she wouldn't press charges, although I can tell you, he was telling her and telling her that he had committed no crime, he had bought us for a high price from the whiskers man. But Miz Gertrude was in a rage, and Mr. Tim had a look of fear on his face, and as I said he was drunk. Anyway, we got on the ferry again; I helped the man with the rowing when the wind died down, and we found Papa almost dead at the deep forest farm. The place was dark and fierce, and the men not caring, and the track so full of holes but the mule pulled us through. Alfonso found his broken geetar by the gate there, and look see, he's still holding it. Then Mr. Tim abandoned us, said he couldn't wait at that gate no longer, cause we were waiting a long time there til they brought Papa out. He took off through the mud whipping that poor dumb mule. He was so drunk and fell on the ground up there somewhere where he had stopped before we had ever caught up with him. I was very scared that they would never find my papa. But they brought him out and we had to carry Papa almost dead in the canvas, me and Miz Gertrude, then slept on the ground, then we got up with Mr. Tim and found him to be dead where he fell. We took the body to the next town, what was that town, Miz Gertrude?"

"That was Plymouth, John, you're a fine storyteller."

"Thank you, ma'am, but you see, folks, we kept the mule and cart, cause there was no family to claim it, and the sheriff said take it, he'd come find us if a family shows up. You see, Miz Gertrude laid it on thick about the slave stealers who had stolen us. So, we came home real slow, holding Papa, making him eat some sweet tater, and the four of us huddling together to keep warm in those nights beside the road or in the wagon. Yes, Miz Gertrude, she put her arms around us all, but mainly to keep Papa warm. And I wished Mama had been alive so she could see us there, all in a tight pack. It's been a cold October here too, right? And we arrived home with Papa alive. And already he's better. We had told Papa that Mama was back home, and that was no lie because she is here with us, specially in our hearts, right?" John bowed and smiled wide.

The crowd stood, cheering and clapping, including Robert who had recovered from his jealousy. Robert said to John, "It seems that everyone who tells about your journey, tells it somewhat different, and each time, I hear more details." John laughed. "And, John, my mother amazes me. I am seeing her now to combine all the people, and no longer distinguish between slave and free, not even between dark and light." John grabbed his friend's hand and shook it with delight.

Alfonso never said a word, until the end, at which time he surprised everyone by standing up and saying that Mr. Blakesley had got him from that forest place and that's why they found his geetar there. He then, without prompting, sang a song called My Poor Nelly Gray in a fine boy's soprano voice, while he still held tight to the broken geetar.

There's a low green valley on the old Caroliny shore,
There I've while many happy hours away.
A-sitting and a-singing by the little cottage door,
Where lived my darling Nelly Gray.

Chorus:
Oh! My poor Nelly Gray, have they taken you away,
And I'll never see my darling anymore.
I'm a sitting by the river and I'm weeping all the day,
For you've gone from the old Caroliny shore.

One night I went to see her but "she's gone," the neighbors say,
The white man bound her with his chain,
They have taken her to Georgia for to wear her life away,
As she toils in the cotton and the cane. *Chorus again*

    The sound of this voice, so high, so clear, touched the hearts of the slaves of the Dogwood Plantation. And, despite the sad words, the rhythmical swing of the tune thrust a glimmer of hope into this crowd of habitually distrustful humanity.
    Adam then spoke, sitting in a chair and hollering loud. "You're all my folks, the only family I know. My son John is the pride of my life and his little brother Lucas too, and Soola's girls, Paddy and Mary Alice. Now that Soola is lost to us, I must take her place and act as mother as well as father. The honor of my rescue goes to John and our mistress Gertrude. She put her own life in danger, she traveled far, she slept on the ground, she fed me, she never quit til she and John found me almost dead. She's larger than life, she lives the message of God and his son Jesus. Thank you Miz Gertrude. And I need tell y'all it is a wicked world out there, even more wicked than Invary when Massa Archie was with us, pardon me Miz Gertrude, the canal work, the beatings, the dogs, the laying out in the open air in the mud in cold and wet with no food, even cages, yessir, even cages for the slaves, so they won't run, the sickness and death, the dead bodies layin' around; law, y'all don't know." He paused, while some in the audience laid their hands over their faces. "Yes," continued Adam, "I see that some of you do know."
    "Yessir, tell us Adam, we listen." And people clapped their hands.
    "And what I want to say too is this: we now feel protected here, we got good leaders now, we got Miz Gertrude and young Massa Robert, and yes, I believe John, my Johnnie, he'll be the leader of us people, he is our future. But that wicked world is only

one inch outside this place. We need to be with our leaders and each other so this place will stay safe, we gotta be together to keep that dark, sinful world outside. We just want it to stay out there, cause if it starts creepin' in, then we'll be done for," and the people answered, "Yessir, please Jesus, let it stay out there."

Finally, Gertrude stood up, and in her loudest possible voice, promised again that Dogwood would be a new kind of plantation, where beatings would be only a memory, where the work would be scheduled and rewarded with a bonus at the end of each week, if we can see you have cooperated. There, she had said it. "We will raise our children together and feed them, we will work hard, and we will rest merrily on Saturday afternoons and Sundays. We will have music and dancing, trying to remember Africa, the home of your ancestors. Fear will be replaced by love in our lives. The wicked laws that support slavery still rule our state, but we will hope for change and pray that God will help us."

A breeze came up bringing the fresh smell of water from the river as if to support these promises of a better life. The dogwood trees, too, tossed their newly crimson leaves in preparation for the winter season.

Gertrude sat down. She suspected that, with such a varied crowd, the road ahead would be jagged and bumpy. Could she manage? She assured herself yes, despite a few trouble- makers who might agitate now that the fear-inducing master was gone. With the two boys and Adam, Bejida and Sally, with Jake, if he minds his health, Tabitha and their children, and of course with Judith and Ida, and the steadfast support of many others at this farm, they could maintain a disciplined schedule and profit without the cruelty common at many farms in the region.

One mystery remained unsolved, but no one wasted even a whisper on the question. Without doubt, it was in the minds of many that Miz Gertrude probably knew who had fired the shot at her husband's face. But when the sheriff handed her his report, Gertrude had been seen to raise her shoulders in a shrug with palms up. Such a gesture was her only public response to the mystery; therefore, it was not mentioned again.

And as for Gertrude McLachlan's forecast for the future, she would rely on the springtime dogwood blossoms to remind her of the promise made to her people upon this autumn day.

Acknowledgements

I would like first to thank my three editors, Katrina Denza, Nancy Ellis, and Rosemary Peele. They each, in different sections of the book, guided me in forming its structure. In the end, the story became a series. They suggested some major changes and omissions, as well as small line by line corrections, and I diligently followed most of those recommendations. I am also grateful to Tess Gillespie, who gave me comments from a reader's point of view in the early years of this work.

I discovered many contributors to my research into 18th and 19th century life in eastern North Carolina. The librarian in Edenton discovered for me details of the Albemarle Sound ferry service, and the author who had researched the old roads shared with me details of the difficulties of travel in the early days. Libraries at UNC Chapel Hill, Eastern Carolina University, Greenville, and the "little" town of Washington, revealed treasures of primary source materials—maps, newspapers, and letters, especially from the Civil War years. And I must add my husband, who helped me drive around on the old roads of eastern North Carolina trying to figure out the old King's Highway.

And let me not forget to mention the wonderful museums in the eastern part of our state, where the staff members were always eager to help me find photographs and many artifacts of the past—at Harkers Island, Elizabeth City, and Plymouth. Primary source materials are also to be found in books like The Children of Pride, letters from Civil War days among members of a plantation family in Georgia, gathered together and edited by Robert Manson Myers.

Also, the Slave Narratives, stories told by African Americans born in slavery. These are today in the Library of Congress. Many have been gathered into bound books, painting fascinating historical pictures of the lives of the African people who arrived here in misery but did the work and helped to build this nation. The interviewers and writers were part of the Federal

Writers Project under the Works Progress Administration (WPA) in President Roosevelt's New Deal.

Thus, the author's research into historical events and details of daily life has, I hope, brought authenticity in guiding the story. Many of the events have been inspired by reading both the primary sources mentioned above and secondary sources by many current authors. Especially important have been books by North Carolina historians: David Cecelski, John Hope Franklin, Judson Browning, Juanita Patience Moss, Joe A. Mobley, and more.

If I have omitted an important name, please forgive me. The omission is unintentional. I am deeply grateful to the authors of all the many books I have read and to those I have met and talked to. My thanks go out to all.

This book is a work of fiction, set in both real and fictional places, inhabited by mostly fictional people. A few politicians, governors, presidents, and military officers are historical.

About the Author

Clare Dundas has taught American History for much of her adult life and has lived in many states, as well as other countries. North Carolina has been her home off and on for more than forty years.

Her love of history has often led to a spirit of questioning: Why? How? And What If? These words have led her to embark on a long investigation into a plantation that could have been, might have been, historic reality.

She lives with her husband in North Carolina.